I know every damn inch of you, in fact.

"For the past two nights, I've been doing nothing but studying your lovely expressions, learning the curves of your gorgeous body, and figuring out all of your wants, needs, and desires. And trust me when I say that I *do* pay attention."

Max backed away and gazed into her eyes, making sure she understood him completely. "But most of all, Jess, I know your heart." He punctuated his words by flattening a hand on her chest, feeling the thudding organ beating beneath his palm. "And this is what matters the most."

PRAISE FOR ALISON BLISS'S PERFECT FIT SERIES

"Fresh, fun, adorable!"
 —Lori Wilde, *New York Times* bestselling author

"Romance novels with heroines who are not model thin are hard to find and valuable. Fans of Jennifer Weiner will enjoy Alison Bliss."
 —*Booklist*

"4 Stars! Bliss's second installment to this fun series will convince readers that sexy comes in all shapes and sizes. Valerie is a confident heroine and the kind of cheeky role model women of all ages need in their life. Fun, sexy, and calorie-free!"
 —RTBookReviews.com on *On the Plus Side*

"*Size Matters* pulls at your heartstrings and your belly will be hurting from the amount of laughs you'll have while reading."
 —Heroes and Heartbreakers.com on *Size Matters*

"This book was so entertaining that, once I started, I couldn't put it down. I loved everything about it. Ms. Bliss gave us a story that was full of life, laughter, and felt so real."
 —Romancing-the-Book.com on *Size Matters*

ALSO BY ALISON BLISS

MORE TO LOVE

ALISON BLISS

FOREVER

NEW YORK   BOSTON

Copyright © 2018 by Alison Bliss
Excerpt from *On the Plus Side* copyright © 2017 by Alison Bliss
Cover photography by Claudio Marinesco.
Cover design by Elizabeth Turner.
Cover copyright © 2018 by Hachette Book Group, Inc.

Forever
Hachette Book Group
1290 Avenue of the Americas, New York, NY 10104
forever-romance.com
twitter.com/foreverromance

First Edition: January 2018

Forever is an imprint of Grand Central Publishing. The Forever name and logo are trademarks of Hachette Book Group, Inc.

The publisher is not responsible for websites (or their content) that are not owned by the publisher.

The Hachette Speakers Bureau provides a wide range of authors for speaking events. To find out more, go to www.hachettespeakersbureau.com or call (866) 376-6591.

ISBNs: 978-1-4555-6810-9 (mass market), 978-1-4555-6808-6 (ebook)

Printed in the United States of America

OPM

10 9 8 7 6 5 4 3 2 1

For my mother-in-law, Terry.

Thank you for your love and support…and for single-handedly raising a hero I could call my own.

Acknowledgments

I always have many people to thank and very little space to do it in, so I apologize if I leave anyone out. Thank you to my husband, Denny, for always having my back and supporting me in ways I never even imagined. I'm grateful for all that you do for me. Big kisses and hugs go out to my boys, who I sincerely believe are the best kids in the whole world. You guys make me proud!

Thank you to my family and friends for always supporting me in everything I do. It means a lot. Thanks also to my awesome PA and good friend, Crystal Wegrzynowicz. One day I will learn to pronounce your name correctly. Thanks as well to the other members of my Pure Bliss Street Team. I can't tell you all how much you mean to me.

Thanks to my wonderful agent, Andrea Somberg, whose support and guidance have been invaluable. To Alex Logan, my genius editor, thank you for being such a pleasure to work with. Those late night e-mails where you ask me why I'm still awake always make me smile. Also, thank you to the other members of the Grand Central gang for all of your never-ending support.

And last but never least, thank you to my readers. I hope you all keep enjoying my stories of love, laughter, and friendship.

MORE TO LOVE

Chapter One

Max Hager was starving to death.

Okay, maybe not *to death*. That was a little dramatic, even for him. But as he pulled his truck into the parking lot of the Empty Plate Café in Granite, Texas, his stomach growled so loudly that he considered checking the backseat for a rabid dog.

He might've done so if he hadn't already known what was back there. He'd tossed a small black suitcase behind his seat this morning after saying farewell to his family, and it had rattled against the door for the entire four-hour trip back home from Galveston. About drove him half-nuts. And since his overbearing parents had taken care of the other half during the past two weeks, that meant he was almost at his limit.

Sure, he could've stopped somewhere along the way and adjusted the suitcase to give his ears and jumbled nerves some much needed relief. But every time he'd considered the idea, the only places he found to pull over were fast food joints with drive-thru windows. As hungry as he was, he didn't trust himself not to pull through one rather than waiting until he got back into town to eat.

If he had wanted something unhealthy, he would've eaten the calorie-laden breakfast his mother had offered him before he'd left. Fried eggs, grits slathered in butter, and bacon biscuits...with cheese. Because apparently consuming eight hundred calories at one meal wasn't enough. Why not go for an even thousand?

Dear God. Just thinking about it had his arteries cringing.

He couldn't believe he'd grown up eating that kind of stuff and actually lived to tell about it. It was like consuming an entire day's worth of fat in one sitting. Which was exactly why he weighed over two hundred pounds by the time he'd entered junior high. And his weight had only ballooned upward from there.

Being an only child had been lonely enough without the added complication of being the heaviest kid in school. The constant harassment from his peers in the halls after class or in the boys' locker room had been enough to make him want to quit school altogether. Thankfully, it had never come to that.

As an army brat, he had always hated being the new kid on the block and regretted not ever having that one special place to call home, but being the son of a brigadier general did occasionally have its perks. All he had to do back then was ignore the bullies long enough and his father would eventually end up receiving orders to some new faraway location. It was inevitable.

They moved from one military installation to another

so often that Max had never really seen much of a point in unpacking... or making friends. Not that anyone had wanted to be his friend back then. When he was younger, his parents had been the only constants in his life. But after graduating high school, Max had decided he needed to grow the hell up and make some actual career plans.

So he'd entered trade school and signed on to an electrician's training program, much to his father's chagrin. Then, to make sure his mother was equally disappointed in him, Max had stayed behind in Texas as his parents moved on to his father's next duty assignment without him.

Between working outdoors in the heat and not having his mom there to cook mostly unhealthy meals for him, Max had lost an entire pant size in just the first month of being on his own. Without even trying. That had only motivated him to make more changes in his life. Bigger ones.

He'd joined a local gym, hired a personal trainer, and started following a strict diet and exercise regimen that had him shedding pounds as quickly as sloughing off dead skin cells in the shower. As strange as it was, losing weight was the easy part for him. Of course that probably had something to do with being so young at the time.

Too bad that was no longer the case.

Max wasn't eighteen anymore, and his thirty-two-year-old body didn't work in quite the same way. Over the years, he'd built a muscular physique, one he was damn proud of. Every cut and bulge was worth the hours he'd spent in the gym perfecting them. But the hard part now was keeping the excess weight off. Unfortunately, it was a daily challenge.

Each time he veered from his diet plan, even just the slightest, he gained weight back and had to work extra hard to take it off again. Especially whenever he'd go to his parents' house for a visit. Maybe most grown men couldn't wait to get one of their mom's home-cooked meals—the ones they had been accustomed to while growing up—but not Max. He couldn't eat like that anymore without suffering the consequences.

His parents, however, hadn't adopted his healthier eating habits. They just didn't get it. Unlike him, they ate red meat at nearly every meal, loaded up on unhealthy carbs, fried everything in oil, and added gobs of cheese or butter to whatever was on their plates. Basically, they ate the same way they always had.

Which meant Max didn't visit them often. Only once or twice a year. The last thing he'd wanted to do was be an inconvenience. He didn't want to put his mother out by asking her to prepare two separate meals. And he couldn't cook to save his own life. So he'd spent the last two weeks living off of bagged salads, fresh fruits, raw vegetables, and protein shakes... all the while feeling like he was slowly starving to death. It had been miserable.

That was exactly why he couldn't wait to get back into town. Max needed a hot meal or he was going to crack up at any moment. Unrelenting hunger did that to a guy. He'd been longing for some real food—something satisfying that would fill his belly and warm him from the inside out—and couldn't wait to sink his teeth into today's special over at the Empty Plate Café. Now that he was finally home, he could. *Thank God.*

As usual the parking lot was packed with vehicles,

so Max found an available spot around the back. The sizable, bluish-gray building was in desperate need of repairs and a fresh coat of paint, but this place had been the local hangout for the past forty years. Not that Max had witnessed that personally or anything. He hadn't even been born when the restaurant first opened, much less lived in Granite. Hell, back then, he'd still been a twinkle in his dad's eye.

But that didn't stop him from enjoying it to the fullest now.

Max headed inside the restaurant, barely noticing the familiar ding of the door chime as he entered. As usual, he expected to see patrons milling about the room with the dull roar of conversation in the background. But instead, only silence greeted him, which had him coming to a dead stop just inside the doorway.

He'd been eating at this place for the past ten years straight, and not once had he ever seen it so desolate. Instead of calling it the Empty Plate Café, maybe the name should be changed to the Empty Café. Because at the moment, other than him, there was no one else there.

"Hey, anyone around?"

The restaurant owner, an elderly gentleman with a full head of white hair, stuck his head out of the kitchen door. "Hey, Max. Good to see you back. Did you have a nice visit with your parents?"

Max smiled at the kind, old man everyone in town lovingly referred to as Pops. "Yeah, Pops, I did. But I'm ready to get back to my regularly scheduled programs." Max glanced around the empty room once more before letting his gaze shift back to the man in front of him. "Um, so what's up?"

Pops shrugged. "Not much. What's up with you?"

Max shook his head. "No, I mean, where is everyone?"

"You mean what happened to all the customers?" When Max nodded, Pops gestured to the room around him, "Well, as you can see, business has been a little slow lately."

"A little? This place is dead. There's no one here."

Pops grinned. "You are."

"Yeah, but your place has always been busy as hell. Where did everyone go?"

"Gone."

"What do you mean 'gone'? You have a shit load of cars outside. What did they do—park here and run for the hills?"

"Not really. More like they left their vehicle here and sprinted over to the park across the street."

Confusion swept through Max. "I don't get it. Why would they do that? Is there a marathon or something going on today?"

"You haven't heard?" Pops waited until Max shook his head before continuing. "Hmm, I guess you must've already left on your vacation before it happened."

"Before *what* happened?"

Pops sighed heavily. "A new food truck pulled into town last week."

"So?"

"So it's been parking across the street in that small lot next to Windsor Park. Ever since it showed up, business over here has been slow. It's been this way all week and only gets worse every day."

"Well, go over there and tell that idiot to move the truck."

"I can't. It's not like they're parked at my restaurant. And I don't own the street or the park. That's all public property."

"But those customers are using *your* lot. You could have their cars towed, ya know?"

"And alienate everyone in town? Come on, Max. You know I can't do that. A lot of these people are my long-time friends and neighbors. Besides, they would never come back here to eat if I had their vehicles towed away."

"Some friends and neighbors," Max said, gritting his teeth. "Sounds more like a bunch of traitors."

"Yeah, maybe. But it's not like I can tell them where to spend their hard-earned money."

"Well, you have to do something. You can't possibly take this lying down. That jerk across the street is stealing your customers."

Pops shrugged. "Doesn't matter. It would be no different if a new restaurant opened across the street and took some of my business."

"But they aren't taking some of your business. They're taking *all* of it. Pops, there's no way you can make a living this way."

"I know," Pops said, expelling a hard breath. "And as unfortunate as the timing is, I recently made some bad financial decisions that are making this even rougher on me. I have no savings to count on during rainy days, and from the looks of things, it's going to be one hell of a storm. I hate to say it, but I won't be able to ride it out. If something doesn't happen soon, I'm going to have to close down."

The bottom fell out of Max's stomach. "What? You can't do that."

"Sorry, Max. But I'm already losing hundreds of dollars a day, and I can't afford to keep this place going if I'm not making money. I won't be able to pay my vendors, and the last thing I need at my age is to take on a huge amount of debt. I've got just enough to keep me in business until the end of the month, but after that...well, I just won't be able to do it anymore. I'll have to shut down for good."

Max ran a hand through his hair. "God, Pops. I'm sorry. If there's anything I can do..."

"Thanks. I appreciate it." Pops shook his head. "But there's nothing anyone can really do about it. This is just how life works. You win some, you lose some." The old guy straightened his shoulders and proudly held his head up high. "Now tell me what I can get for you. I have to take care of my loyal customers while I still have them."

Though it wasn't heartfelt, Max tried to smile. "I'll have the special."

"You got it. One special coming up," Pops said, nodding and heading for the kitchen.

Max leaned back in his chair and stared out the window, glaring at the park across the street. There were too many trees blocking the view for him to see the food truck itself, but he noticed the long line of customers standing in formation along the sidewalk, the scattered crowd sitting around picnic tables eating, and the people traveling to and from the park via Pops' parking lot. And every bit of it burned his ass.

When Max had first moved to Granite ten years ago, he'd been determined to find a restaurant in town where he could eat a quick, healthy lunch without having to make it himself. So he'd stopped into this very café to look over the menu. After one glance, he'd frowned and headed for the door. Pops had been a stranger to him at the time, but he'd met him there with a frown of his own and asked why Max hadn't ordered lunch. Max hesitated to tell him the truth since his move to this town had been all about giving him a fresh new start in a place where no one knew about his past and his issues with food. But something about this man had assured Max that Pops was someone he could trust.

So Max took a chance and had whispered to Pops about the strict diet he was on and how it wouldn't allow him to eat anything listed on the menu. Rubbing at his chin, Pops had rocked back on his heels, taking a moment to think about what Max had just said. Then, with a sly wink, he'd suggested Max order "the special" whenever he came in and promised to make sure it would be diet-friendly…and kept strictly between them.

From that day forward, the kind old man had lived up to his word.

Not only that, but when Sam had moved to town and started up his construction business, Pops had been the one to put a good word in for Max. Now Max handled all of Sam's electrical work, which had tripled his income and given him steady work, and they had become best friends.

Max owed Pops a lot.

But that was just the kind of guy Pops was. He was a great friend to everyone in town and a decent person who worked hard to make a good living. What kind of insensitive asshole would take business away from an old man? A real jackass, that's who.

"Hey," someone said from the door.

Max twisted his neck to see his best friend weaving around a table and crossing the room to join him. "About damn time you showed up. You're late. I told you to meet me here at noon."

Sam slid into the seat across from Max, pulled up his right sleeve, and glanced at the gold watch on his wrist. "It's only fifteen after. Couldn't be helped. I got hung up on the job site."

"By who—your wife?"

Sam grinned. "Just because I let Leah seduce me in the construction trailer one time doesn't mean that every time I'm late I'm off with her having sex somewhere."

"Maybe I should remind you that you bailed on me for lunch three times last month because you went home for a nooner."

"That wasn't my fault. Leah lured me there with the promise of two things: a chocolate dessert and her being naked by the time I got there."

Max chuckled. "The woman sure knows your weaknesses."

"No doubt," Sam agreed. "But she's not the reason I'm late. At least not this time. She's busy over at the bakery today. She's been training a new girl ever since Valerie started working full-time at the bar with Logan. This time my holdup was actually work-related."

"What's the problem?"

"That dumbass plumber I hired broke another pipe, and we had to shut off the main water supply before I left the construction site. It's the third time this week he's done that."

"Jesus, man. You were having problems with him before I left for vacation. Why don't you just fire the guy already?"

Sam sighed. "Because I'm a sucker, that's why. One more incident and I'm going to find another plumber to bid this damn job and finish it for me."

"Yeah, sure. You said that two weeks ago."

Pops came out of the back with a glass of water in one hand and a plate of food in the other. "Hey, Sam. Good to see ya."

"How are you, Pops?"

"I can't complain." Pops set the glass of water down on the table and slid the plate in front of Max. Then he looked at Sam. "What can I get for you today?"

Sam glanced over and eyeballed Max's plate, which held a grilled chicken breast, a baked sweet potato, whole green beans, and a side of fruit salad. "What are you having?"

"What I always order. The special," Max replied, grinning.

"I'll have one of those too with a glass of sweet tea."

Pops shook his head. "Sorry, Sam. I'm all out of the special today. You'll have to order something else."

Sam glanced around the empty restaurant, and his brows drew together in confusion. "Okay, well then I guess I'll have a cheeseburger and fries."

"Coming right up," Pops said with a nod before heading back to the kitchen.

Sam's brow rose as he turned his attention onto Max. "You know, in the past whenever I've tried to order the special and there's none left, the restaurant has always been packed. This time, there's no one here and there's still none left. I'm starting to wonder if Pops just doesn't like me."

"Maybe." Max shrugged. "Or maybe I'm just special."

Sam groaned. "I think I'll stick with the theory that Pops doesn't like me. Seems more logical somehow."

Max laughed. "Whatever helps you sleep at night, buddy."

A few minutes later, Pops delivered Sam's cheeseburger along with the side of greasy fries and glass of iced sweet tea that Sam had ordered. "You want dessert today, Sam?"

"No thanks," he replied, digging into his lunch.

Unfazed, Pops nodded and went on his way, but Max sat there staring at his friend in surprise. "You've got to be kidding me, right? Since when do you ever turn down dessert?"

Sam finished chewing a bite of his burger and swallowed. "I don't. But I'm saving up a little room for tonight. Leah promised to make me a chocolate truffle cheesecake, and I plan on eating the whole damn thing in one sitting... after she gets herself a slice, of course. I'm a gentleman like that."

Max shook his head but didn't even bother to ask Sam if he was kidding. The guy rarely joked when it came to his wife's desserts. After all, she was the owner of Sweets n' Treats, a popular local bakery. And judging by the way Leah's cheeks pinked up every time Sam walked into the same room, the baked goods she created weren't the only thing Sam was insatiable about.

For a few moments, they ate in silence. Sam practically inhaled his food like a starving lion while Max picked at his like a baby bird learning how to eat. He had been hungry when he'd first arrived, but after hearing the news about Pops possibly having to close down, he didn't really have much of an appetite anymore.

The moment Sam finished, he wiped his mouth and rose from his chair. He pulled his wallet from his back pocket and tossed a few bills on the table to cover his meal. "All right, buddy. Sorry to run off, but I have to get back to work. I need to see if that idiot fixed that busted pipe yet. See you here tomorrow?"

Max nodded. They always ate lunch at the Empty Plate. "Yeah. Do you need me to come back early? I wasn't supposed to start back until tomorrow, but I can go in today if you need a hand with something."

"Nah. Take the day off. You can start doing all the wiring on the house tomorrow afternoon like we'd planned. The last thing I need is for you to be playing with electricity while that good-for-nothing plumber is busting waterlines all over the place. Someone could get electrocuted."

"Well, it wouldn't be me. I'm a master electrician for a reason. I know what the hell I'm doing."

"True, but chances are good that it would end up being *me* who gets electrocuted. I already scared the hell out of Leah once by getting shocked. I don't need to do it again." Sam grinned and headed for the door. "Thanks, Pops," he called out.

"No problem, Sam. See ya tomorrow," Pops yelled from the back room.

Max painstakingly finished the rest of his meal and then pushed his empty plate away. He rubbed at his content belly and sighed. The entire time he'd spent with his parents, he couldn't wait to get back to eat at the café.

Now, there was a good chance that Pops would be closing down for good.

Max didn't know what he would do if that happened. It was bad enough that whenever he shopped for groceries and made himself a basic meal, he struggled with cravings and portion control. If it wasn't for Pops cooking him a healthy lunch every day, he would be back to eating bagged salads. Jesus. He couldn't live on that rabbit food for the rest of his life. If it hadn't been for Pops feeding him every day, Max had no doubt that he would've eventually gained some, if not all, of his weight back. Damn it, he needed him.

Ten minutes went by before Pops came back out to grab the two empty plates left on the table. But Max barely noticed because he was still staring out the window and stewing over the newcomer across the street who was screwing his good friend out of business. The whole thing just pissed him off.

He wished like hell that the old city health inspector hadn't resigned and moved away. The guy still owed him a favor, and Max would've definitely called it in to get the food truck removed from the area. Surely the guy running the food truck had made some small infraction that the health inspector could've called him out on.

But it didn't matter. The old health inspector was gone, and the new one hadn't started yet. That guy wasn't going to be of any help though since Pops had already said he couldn't hold out much longer. Too bad there wasn't a temporary health inspector that Max could sic on the imbecile across the...

Max's train of thought came to a crashing halt as a crazy, half-baked scheme took over his brain. No. He couldn't do that, could he? The whole idea was stupid. Yet, he couldn't help but feel the plan might actually work. Even if it didn't, he couldn't just sit by and let someone take advantage of Pops like this. The man had gone out of his way to help Max out lots of times during the past ten years, and it was about damn time he returned the favor.

Over the years he had pulled some stupid-ass stunts, but this one would really take the cake. "Okay, that's it. I'm going over there."

Pops had already stacked the two plates onto a tray and was wiping the table down, but he paused mid-swipe to peer at Max. "Where? To the park? For what?"

"To get rid of that damn food truck once and for all."

"Son, it's a public road. You can't force them to leave."

"You're right. *I* can't." He grinned. "But the city health inspector can."

"But the new health inspector hasn't started working for the city yet."

"*I* know that and *you* know that," Max replied, still smiling. "But that doesn't mean the owner of the food truck knows it. You said they were new to town, right? Then they won't know who I am. I'll just pretend to be the health inspector and run them off."

Pops sighed and wiped his brow with the back of his hand. "While I appreciate what you're trying to do, I can't let you go over there and harass that—"

"Oh, come on. It'll be fine." Max chuckled as the grateful look on Pops' face changed to one of concern. "Seriously, Pops. I'm not going to bully him...much. I'm just going to go over there and give this guy a bit of a hard time. Maybe that'll be enough to have him wanting to move on and find a new town to park his truck in."

"No, Max. That's not a good idea. There's something you don't know about—"

"Pops, it's okay," Max said, rising from his chair. "Don't you worry about a thing. I've got this." He headed for the door before the old man tried to talk some sense into him. "I'll have this food truck pulling out of here by the end of the day."

* * *

Jessa Gibson scraped the pieces of prime beef, sliced scallions, and strips of red peppers into a pile with her metal spatula and gave them a quick toss. The medium-rare meat sizzled as it hit the searing-hot grill, and an aromatic puff of steam lifted into the air. She loved that mouth-watering scent almost as much as she loved the taste.

And apparently she wasn't the only one. Her gourmet steak tacos were one of the bestselling items on the menu, and customers constantly praised her for the delicious aroma hovering around the Gypsy Cantina.

That was the great thing about owning a food truck.

In most restaurants, the chefs were way back in the kitchen, hidden from view, unable to see or speak with anyone other than the staff members. Most of those poor souls never got the chance to communicate directly with their diners, much less receive any feedback on their edible creations.

But that wasn't the case for Jessa. No matter how busy she was, she always managed to prepare the customers' meals while chatting with them. And not only had getting to know her customers been great for business, but it had been a huge help to her as well.

When she'd casually mentioned to a few of the local folks that she needed to hire some extra hands to keep up with the growing demand, her customers had jumped to the rescue. Through their reliable recommendations, Jessa had quickly found two dependable employees who had experience in the food industry.

Lisa, a middle-aged mother of twin girls, had once been a line cook but had decided to quit her job and become a stay-at-home mom. Now that her daughters were in kindergarten, she had been looking for a part-time job to help supplement her husband's income yet still enable her to make it home in time to greet her kids at the school bus. Which meant the truck's flexible working hours had been perfect for her.

The other worker, Mary, had once owned a restaurant in Midland but sold it five years ago when she and her husband had moved to Granite to retire. Unfortunately, her husband had passed away last year, and Mary had grown tired of sitting around the house by herself. Working on the truck had been keeping her busy, and Mary loved seeing all the familiar faces.

In a week's time, both women had proven themselves to be dedicated employees of the Gypsy Cantina. They were great at multitasking, always on time, and both women seemed to really enjoy their jobs. Jessa couldn't ask for more than that. Besides, she'd made two new friends in a town where she had none. That was a huge bonus.

Working fast, Jessa lifted the two homemade corn

tortillas from the back of the flat-top grill, where she'd left them warming. She folded each in half, placing them side by side in a paper boat, and then filled the empty shells with a good-sized portion of meat, onions, and peppers. She added some pico de gallo, crumbled queso fresco, cilantro for garnish, and then finished each off with a drizzle of her signature sweet lime sauce.

Then she slid the completed dish down the counter to where Mary stood at the pick-up window. "Order up."

"Thanks, Jess," Mary said, glancing down at the ticket before calling out the customer's name through the window.

An older gentleman in brown corduroy pants and a checkered knit sweater stepped forward with a pleasant smile. "Thank you, ladies. I'll see you three beauties tomorrow," he said with a wink. "Same time, same place?"

Mary nodded over to Jessa. "That's up to the boss lady."

She laughed and gave him a wave. "We'll be here, Tom. Have a great day."

Lisa had just finished helping someone at the order window when the next woman in line stepped up, sniffed appreciatively, and said, "Goodness, that looked and smelled great. What did that gentleman order?"

"Those were the steak tacos," Lisa told her with a smile. "You should give them a try. They're terrific."

The woman nodded. "That sounds good. I think I will."

"Two steak tacos coming right up," Jessa chimed in, tossing more meat on the grill.

Lisa came closer. "Jess, why don't you let me get this one. You probably could use a break."

"I'm okay," Jessa said with a shrug. "I'm used to being behind a hot grill all day."

But Mary shook her head firmly and used her motherly tone on Jessa. "Lisa's right. You've been on your feet for hours. Step outside and get some fresh air. We've got this handled for now."

Jessa couldn't help but smile. These two had only been working with her for a week, but they were constantly telling her to slow down and take it easy. "Okay, then I'll take these squeeze bottles that Mary filled out to the condiment station and check the trash while I'm out there. How about that?"

· Lisa laughed. "God. Can't you sit still for even a minute? You always have to be doing something."

Jessa grinned. "I guess I'm just used to working by myself and having everything fall on my shoulders. But it's been nice having you two helping me out. Definitely makes my life a whole lot easier."

"We're not going anywhere," Mary said, moving to take over Lisa's vacated window. "I think I can speak for both of us when I say that we're with you until the end."

Lisa nodded. "Or until you fire us for bossing you around."

Jessa smiled, and her heart swelled inside her chest. "I wouldn't dream of it. I'm so glad I found the two of you. I really needed the extra hands, and I couldn't ask for better employees...or friends."

Both women smiled, and then Mary handed her the squeeze bottles and shooed her toward the door. "Go on already, Jess. And do us a favor. Take an actual break. Don't just work while you're out there."

Laughing, she nodded. "Yes, ma'am," she said in a childlike tone.

The moment Jessa stepped out, she realized that she was still wearing her disposable pink gloves and white plastic apron. Crap. *Oh, well.* It was probably best to keep them on until she finished with the trash anyway.

She continued on her way to the condiment station, which was sitting around the front side of the truck near the pick-up window. Jessa left the squeeze bottles on the table, grabbed a bottle of water from the drink bin on the outside of the truck, and moved to stand in the shade of a nearby tree. She sipped the water slowly, letting the cold liquid trickle down her dry throat.

After standing in front of a searing hot grill for the past few hours, the cool breeze wafting over the perspiration on her skin felt like heaven. But it did make her wonder if a storm was coming in. Even though it was the start of the fall season, South Texas had never been well known for its cool air.

At least not according to her deceased mother. Mariah Gibson had been quite the free spirit back in the day. Before Jessa had been born, her mother had rolled through this town faster than a rampant tumbleweed, letting the wind sweep her in whatever direction it had been blowing. Maybe it was the gypsy heritage in her bloodline or the thrill of adventure, but Jessa's mom had never stayed in one place for very long.

But one thing was for certain. The woman had loved every minute of the short time she'd spent in Granite, Texas. She had always spoken so fondly of the people in this town and their overall sense of community. In fact, her mother had loved it so much that she'd even planned for the two of them to return together someday.

Unfortunately, that day never came. Her mom had always been the picture of health and a woman of vitality. She took chances, made daring moves, and lived her life in a way that most people could only dream to live theirs. But the cancer had seemingly come out of nowhere and swept through her body so fast that her mom's desire to do anything had quickly faded out, along with her spirit and the light in her eyes.

After her mother passed away, Jessa had tried her best to live her life in a way that her mother would've been proud of. She spent a few years traveling from town to town, working as an assistant to a well-known chef who specialized in pop-up venues. At first, the traveling had been fun and inspiring, exposing her to lots of different cultures and new people. It had been just what she needed at the time.

But since the pop-up dining events were never in the same location twice, Jessa had quickly grown tired of never seeing a familiar face. And she hated that.

Unlike her mother, Jessa had the strong urge to plant her feet and put down roots, which is why she'd chosen to move to Granite in the first place. Maybe it was strange for someone who longed for something familiar to move to a new place where she'd never been and knew no one, but Jessa had a desperate need to fulfill her mother's dreams as well as her own.

Now she wanted to pursue the rest of her mother's dream by coming back to the one place her mother had loved so much. Besides, being in this quaint, little town that her mom had visited, even for a short time, somehow made her feel closer to her.

Jessa's eyes flitted over to the colorful mural decorating the side of her food truck. A redheaded gypsy woman—painted in her mother's likeness—stared back at her with a bright crimson-colored head wrap, dangling gold earrings, and a slight smile on her calm face. As much as her mother had loved to travel, it seemed only fitting to take her along on a new adventure.

"Miss you, Mom," Jessa whispered under her breath. She swallowed hard and exhaled slowly to keep the sadness from welling up in her eyes. Then she added, "But I'm here in Granite just like we planned. I made it."

Jessa took a moment to compose herself while finishing off her water, and then she tossed the empty bottle into the recycle bin before checking the trash can next to it. She noted that it was only half-full. No point in changing it out yet. But there was some garbage littering the ground nearby, so she stopped long enough to pick it up and throw it away.

A voice cleared behind her. "Excuse me, ma'am."

Startled, she whirled around, almost bumping into a man with light brown hair and deep set eyes. He stood so close to her that he towered over her short frame. At five feet four inches, she was usually shorter than most people. But this guy? He had to be at least a foot taller than her, which was a bit more intimidating than men of average height. Staring up at him was like trying to see the top of a skyscraper while you're standing on ground level.

Jessa took a wary step back but smiled politely. "Yes?"

The handsome gentleman had a lean, muscular build, broad shoulders, and intense hazel eyes that seemed to bore holes straight through her. He was great to stare at, but he wasn't smiling back, which unnerved her even more.

"Do you work on this food truck?" he asked, taking another step toward her. His words were neither friendly nor unfriendly, but his underlying tone sounded a bit hostile.

She nodded shakily. "Yes, I do. Is there something I can help you with?"

She'd never had anyone complain about her food before and hoped that wasn't what this stranger was about to do. But if he did have a problem with something on her menu, then she definitely wanted to know about it.

"Yeah," he said, shifting his position even closer. "You can get the owner of this food truck out here so I can have a word with him."

One eyebrow rose as she took another step back, as if they were somehow unknowingly dancing with one another. "Um...him?"

"Yeah, the moron who owns this rig."

For a moment, words failed her. She stood there blinking up at him while acid bubbled up into her throat. Did he really just call her a moron? And why the hell would he assume the business was owned by a man—because it happened to be on a truck? What kind of sexist bullshit was that?

Then again, judging by the guy's lack of consideration for a woman's personal space, she shouldn't be surprised. He was obviously a jerk. *A tall, handsome one, but still a jerk nonetheless.*

As strange as it was, she almost couldn't wait to see the look on his face when he realized he had just insulted the actual owner...who also happened to be a woman. *Now who's the moron, you chauvinistic pig?*

Lifting her chin, Jessa tossed her head back and looked at him directly. "What can I do for you, sir?"

Confusion flickered in his eyes. "I already told you what you can do for me. I'd like you to get the owner out here so I can talk to him."

She smirked. God, he was really cute but a little dumb. "Like I said, what can I do for you?"

His eyes narrowed. "Do you have a problem with your short-term memory or something? How many times do I need to repeat myself?"

Jessa gasped at his rudeness, and her blood boiled in her veins. "Look, I don't know who you think you are, but—"

"Max Hager, the new city health inspector, that's who."

Oh, crap. Jessa froze in place as panic swamped her system. She'd just come close to telling off the one man who could shut down her food truck business with a click of a pen. Jesus. Thank goodness he cut her off and hadn't allowed her to finish what she had been about to say. It definitely wouldn't have been nice.

Whew! Dodged that bullet.

She sighed.

Weeks ago, when she'd applied for the permits at city hall, the previous inspector had passed her new food truck with flying colors. But that had been before she hit the road with it. She should've figured it was only a matter of time before the new health inspector showed up here to make sure everything was still up to code.

But God. Did he have to be so arrogant?

And really, why the hell was he so young and good looking? Every health inspector she'd ever crossed paths with in the past had been at least twenty or thirty years older than her and usually had something unattractive about them...like unruly nose hairs. But this man looked to be around his early thirties at most and didn't seem to have an imperfect bone in his drool-worthy body.

Although Jessa was almost certain this guy couldn't read her thoughts, he smirked as if he had done just that. And it sent something hot spiraling through her. God. What was wrong with her? She was getting hot and bothered by the hunky dimwit who happened to be the health inspector. As if that was a smart move.

Mr. Hager shifted his weight and crossed his arms. "Now, as I was saying...If you can get the owner out here so I can speak with him about a few infractions, I'd appreciate it."

Oh no. Dread filled her. "Infractions?"

"Yeah." He motioned to her truck and grimaced. "Apparently, this guy doesn't know how to stay within the city ordinances," he said, his tone full of arrogance. "So I'm here to educate him on the matter."

Shit. Shit. Shit. Jessa didn't know what she did wrong, but whatever it was, she would fix it immediately. She just hoped he wouldn't suspend or revoke her permits in the meantime. "Um, okay. Give me just a second," she said, heading toward the truck to tell the girls that she would be a little longer than they'd expected.

She barely made it halfway to the truck when the man behind her said, "By the way, what's this idiot's name?"

Jessa stopped dead in her tracks, and her stomach

burned with irritation. *Did this cocky bastard really just call me an idiot?* Then she counted to ten slowly before turning around to face him. Being that he was the health inspector, he clearly had an advantage over her, so she thought it was best to keep her control—and her mouth—in check. But the mental restraint required to do so had her head throbbing with pent-up frustration.

This dickhead was really starting to get on her nerves, but she managed to answer him anyway. "It's Jess."

"Jess, huh? Does he have a last name?"

"Gibson."

He nodded. "Okay. Well, tell this Jess Gibson fella that I don't like to be kept waiting long, will ya?"

She nodded while gritting her teeth. "Sure. No problem." *Imbecile.*

Jessa headed through the door to let Mary and Lisa know that she would be outside for a little while longer and to make sure they were handling things on their own. The last thing she wanted to do was leave them in a bind. But as she suspected, things were running just as smoothly as ever.

She didn't bother telling them that the health inspector was waiting for her outside the truck. They didn't ask anyway, so she figured she would just explain her whereabouts later. It wasn't like they had anything to hide. She just didn't want one of the customers to overhear and get the impression that something was wrong with her food. Because there definitely wasn't. And if at any point the inspector asked to see inside the kitchen, she would be happy to prove it.

By the time she made it back outside, Mr. Hager had moved closer to the backside of the truck and was glaring at it as if he were looking for more problems. Figures. It was a little strange that he'd chosen to look at the back of the truck first since there wasn't much of anything back there to actually look at. But at least he was away from the crowd, and the customers wouldn't be able to hear whatever it was that he was about to tell her. She still wasn't sure what it was, but judging by the scowl on his face, it didn't look good.

She headed straight for him. "Mr. Hager?"

He glared down at her, making her feel even shorter than she already was. Then his hazel eyes narrowed. "Don't tell me the owner wouldn't come out of there to meet me."

"Um, no. Nothing like that."

Now he just looked confused as ever. "Then where the hell is the guy?"

Sighing, she peeled off her pink disposable gloves and thrust out her hand. "You're looking at her. I'm Jessa Gibson, but my friends call me Jess."

Chapter Two

Max's mouth fell open and then snapped shut.

He couldn't have heard her right. Rarely was he thrown for a loop, but he'd been temporarily distracted by the insanely delicious aroma billowing out of the food truck. "Uh, did you just say that *you* were the owner of this business?"

She nodded. "I did."

Well, shit. He hadn't at all expected the owner to be female. Mostly because he figured that anyone who was callous enough to steal business ofrom an old man would have to be a real dickhead. This lovely, angel-faced redhead didn't fit that description at all. But then he glanced up at the truck and sighed. Yeah, he looked like an idiot all right. The truck was called the Gypsy Cantina, and a woman's face was plastered all over the side of it.

Her face, perhaps?

He stared at her in silence, letting his curious gaze

roam over her. Yeah, it looked like her all right. Except the pretty, petite redhead standing in front of him was much more appealing than the picture on the truck.

She was curvaceous and feminine without being too girly. A deep amount of cleavage separated her full round breasts and was probably only visible to him because of their height difference and how closely he stood to her. But that rear end and those hips. Heaven help him, he'd gotten a good look at both earlier when she'd sashayed away from him.

"What can I do for you, Mr. Hager?"

With a gorgeous body like hers and a question like that, he could think of lots of delicious things she could do for him. Unfortunately, none of them had anything to do with her moving her fucking truck.

"Mr. Hager?"

Momentarily stunned by the pretty blue eyes that had lifted to his, Max blurted out, "Mr. Hager is my father. Please, call me Max."

The second the words fell from his lips, he instantly regretted them. How the hell was he supposed to have any credibility as a health inspector when he was talking to her as if they'd just met in a bar? Lord, had he lost his damn mind?

But she smiled meekly at him and said, "Um, okay... Max."

As strange as it was, he liked the sound of his name rolling off her tongue. That one little word said in that low, husky voice of hers had ignited a flame somewhere deep inside of him that sent sparks shooting straight to his groin.

It wasn't like she was wearing anything too low-cut

or provocative. Just a white V-neck top paired with khaki shorts and leather sandals. But the plastic apron cinching her waist made it easier to see the rounded curves of her voluptuous body. And her womanly figure held an underlying sexuality that stimulated much more than his brain.

Max swallowed hard, removing the lump from his throat.

He would do good to remember that she was nothing more than a customer-stealing vendor who just happened to look good enough to eat. He could ignore that last part of her though, couldn't he? Yeah. Sure he could. Yet when she gave him another slight smile that sent shivers traveling down his spine, he knew his problems had only just begun.

"I guess it's only fair that you call me Jessa then."

Max frowned and blurted out, "Why not Jess?"

"Huh?"

"You said that your friends call you Jess."

"Oh, they do. I'm sorry. I guess I was just thinking this was more official or something. But I wasn't trying to imply that we couldn't be friends."

"Good. I'm glad to hear it." He smiled at her, while punching himself in the gut with a hard mental fist. *Quit worrying about whether or not she wants to be friends with you, dipshit. She's not your friend. She's the enemy. Fuck.*

She stood there fidgeting with her fingers, looking every bit as confused as he felt. Her full lips retained an almost childlike pink hue though she seemed to be pursing them together. God, she was beautiful.

"Well?" she asked. "You said you needed to speak with me."

"I, ah..."

Nope. He couldn't do it. He couldn't possibly dupe a woman. Especially one as sweet and innocent looking as her. Maybe it was the smooth, flawless, pale skin with a smattering of light-colored freckles running across the bridge of her nose, but she came across as young and vulnerable. And that only made him want to protect her from anyone who would dare think about upsetting her.

Unfortunately, at the moment, that person was *him*.

When he'd first come over there, he had been looking forward to doling out a little retribution on Pops' behalf. Now he couldn't stand the thought of saying anything negative to her that might hurt her feelings. Max was a lot of things, but he wasn't a man who would mistreat a woman.

Yet it wasn't like he could really back down now. It was too late. He'd already stuck his foot in his mouth by telling her that he was the damn health inspector. And she was standing there waiting nervously for him to elaborate on the infractions he'd mentioned. Shit.

Say something to her already, moron. "I, uh...uh..."

Oh yeah. That was worth hearing.

God. What the hell had he gotten himself into? This whole charade was about to blow up in his face, and he couldn't seem to stop it from happening.

Apparently, this Jessa woman had the patience of a saint because, after a full minute of awkward silence, she finally said, "Max, do you have a problem with me being a woman?"

Huh. Direct. Okay. He hadn't really expected that out of her, but he liked it. Actually, he liked a lot of things about her. Although he didn't mean to do it, his roving eyes raked over her shapely figure once more, and his pulse began to race. Damn it.

Maybe he wasn't looking forward to this any longer, but he didn't have a choice. Whether he liked it or not, he had to go through with it. "No, Jess. Not with that, specifically. But there are a few issues with your truck that we need to address."

"Such as?"

Sonofabitch. I probably should've figured that out instead of watching her backside when she'd walked away earlier.

Glancing around, Max's gaze fell on the food truck's large back tires, hoping to think of something brilliant to say. "Well," he said, giving himself a second to come up with something, anything. "I hate to inform you of this, but you're parked too close to the curb."

Yeah, that definitely wasn't it.

She leaned around him and craned her neck to check the distance for herself. "Really?"

"Yep." Max straightened his posture, hoping it would give him a more authoritative appearance. "Unfortunately, the city ordinance requires the tires of a food truck to be exactly ten and three-quarter inches away from the curb at all times. Your back wheel looks to be only about six inches from where I'm standing."

"You're serious?"

He forced himself to grin. "As a heart attack."

"Okay, then. But why does the tire have to be that far away from the curb?"

Max felt his smile collapse. Jeez. Did she have to ask him a question he didn't know the answer to? "Look,

Jess, I don't make the ordinances. I just enforce them."
Or make them up on the spot.

She stared blankly at him for a moment. "I—I'm sorry. I was just curious, that's all." She glanced at the tire once more. "It's fine. If you say it's too close, I'll take your word for it and will avoid that problem in the future."

He nodded and added some firmness to his tone. "By parking somewhere else, you mean?"

"What? No way!" She blinked at him and then shook her head adamantly. "Business is great here. There's a nice breeze in the park, and my customers can sit at the picnic tables under the shade trees to relax and enjoy their lunch. It would be stupid of me to leave such a great location. But I promise next time I'll be sure to check the distance to the curb to make sure I'm not violating any codes."

Max ground his teeth together. "Might be easier to just move your truck somewhere else since..." He glanced around to find another issue and spotted a silver electrical box coming out of the ground. "You also need to be at least thirty feet away from the electrical box over there as well."

She gazed past him at the large box sitting on top of the soil and then glanced at the backend of her truck. The distance couldn't have even been half of what he said the made-up code required. "Hmm. Okay, well, I'll check that next time too. Trust me, it won't happen again. I don't want to lose such a great spot."

Damn. He sighed. "See that it doesn't."

Her voice turned bright and cheery. "So are we all done here?"

Nope. Not even close. Apparently, we're just getting warmed up. "Not quite," Max told her. "We still need to go over a few other issues."

"Um, other issues?"

God, he hated this. But he needed to quit beating around the bush and put some real pressure on her if he was going to get her to actually leave, because she wasn't budging as easily as he'd hoped.

"Yeah," he said, his voice gruff. His throat tightened, but he shoved the rest of the words through his teeth anyway. "I don't want to close you down, but I will have to if these problems aren't immediately resolved. As the health inspector, I take my job very seriously."

Christ. Even he thought he sounded like a prick. He could only imagine what she thought of him. He hated to think that he might be frightening her with his fake power of authority, but he had to play that card in hopes it would be enough to motivate her. If he was going to help Pops, then this gal needed to pack up and leave town. The faster, the better.

But unfortunately, she didn't look worried at all. And when she spoke, her voice held a calm, soothing quality. "That won't be necessary, I assure you. Just let me know what problems I need to correct, and they'll be taken care of as soon as possible. I take my job very seriously too."

Max's stomach tightened into a knot. The lovely Jessa was proving herself to be cooperative, responsive, and eager to please, which only had him wondering if that open-mindedness extended to the bedroom. Not that he would ever find out. "Okay," he said in a strangled voice, mentally rearranging the bulge in his pants, "so why don't we go over a few more things then."

She nodded in agreement. "Sure. I'm guessing you want to know all about my operation. For starters, my truck abides by the strictest sanitizing procedures. In fact, if you'd like to take a look inside the kitchen, I'd be happy to show you around."

Max shook his head furiously. "Maybe later," he said, worrying that one of the customers might recognize him and out him before he could finish what he started. "Right now, I'm more concerned with the other things I'm seeing out here."

She shifted nervously. "Like?"

He gazed around quickly and then motioned toward the entire park with one arm. "Like how you don't have tablecloths on all the surrounding picnic tables. That's unsafe and unsanitary."

"Oh no," she said with a jubilant giggle and a shake of her head. "Those aren't my picnic tables. They belong to the city."

"Doesn't matter. *Your* customers are the ones using them. That is what you just said, after all. And that makes you responsible for their condition."

She squinted at him with uncertainty. "I've never heard of such a thing before. Are you sure?"

It pissed him off that she was questioning his authority...even if it was as fake as the stupid violation that he'd just come up with. "Are you insinuating that I don't know how to do my job?"

Her eyes widened at his harsh tone. "Oh, definitely not. I was just...um, asking a question, that's all. Seems a little strange that I'd be responsible for structures in the park that I didn't even put here."

"I don't know why you think it's strange. Your customers eat their food on them, don't they?"

She gazed up at him with a weird expression on her face. "Well, yeah. But my food comes in either a container or wrapped in parchment paper. Besides, it's not like I tell my customers where to eat."

Damn good point. He sighed inwardly. "Yeah, maybe. But your truck is in Windsor Park. Where else are they supposed to sit—on the ground? You want them to get ants in their food?"

Ants? Christ. Where the hell did that come from?

She blinked at him incredulously, probably thinking he was as crazy as he sounded. "Um, no. Of course I don't. Okay, I'll make sure I get some tablecloths or something to cover the picnic tables with."

"You do that."

"Anything else?" she asked softly.

He nodded. "There's also not enough trash cans. You'll need a couple more big ones out there in front."

"But the trash cans belong to the..." Her words trailed off and she waved her hand through the air, dismissing whatever thought she had. "Never mind. I'll buy a couple more to put out for my customers. What else?"

A faint scent wafted toward his direction, and he inhaled deeply. Damn. That scent was too much. "The...uh, bug spray you're wearing."

"Bug spray?" She chewed on her bottom lip in total confusion.

Man, it was adorable. "Yeah, you really shouldn't

wear it while you're cooking. It could contaminate the food."

He struggled to keep his face neutral and stop his lips from curving. The lovely fragrance she wore wasn't even close to being a pungent odor. It was more like the scent of ripe strawberries on a warm summer day. Bright. Heavenly. Distracting as hell. How was he supposed to stay focused on the task at hand with something like that pumping all of his blood to lower parts of his anatomy?

She blinked at him in rapid succession, as if he'd just told her that he was pregnant with a litter of puppies. "You mean my...perfume?"

Max faked his surprise and let his mouth fall open slightly. "Oh. Is that what that horrible odor is? Sorry. I hope I didn't offend you or anything. You might want to think about switching to a new brand."

He cringed inwardly at his insulting dig and waited for her to be outraged by his comment. But she stood there blinking at him as the seconds ticked by. Then, after a few moments, she did something he hadn't expected at all.

She burst out laughing.

And that only made Max feel like an even bigger jerk than he already was.

Wonderful.

One thing was perfectly clear though. He wouldn't be able to upset this woman by using her vanity against her. Apparently she didn't have a vain bone in that lush body of hers. And looking at her again, he should've realized that she wasn't the high-maintenance type from the beginning.

Her clothes weren't anything name-brand or expensive. There wasn't a lick of makeup on her dewy face. And her fiery red hair was held off her neck by a clip that resembled a brown tarantula. The lucky woman just had a natural beauty that most women would kill for, even if she didn't play it up to meet society's standards. Good for her.

But that didn't help him with his problem. The problem being *her*. She was too calm and cool for his liking. He needed to find something to throw her off kilter, and he needed to do it now.

Max cleared his throat, and she finally stopped giggling. "If you're done, we need to move on and talk about your...er, gloves."

She was still smiling as she wiped the tears from her eyes and held up the pair of disposable plastic gloves in her hand. "You mean these? What about them?"

Without thinking, Max took her hand into his much larger one. Her entire body jolted, and the smile melted from her face. *Hmm. Interesting.* "You need some new ones."

"I...ah...these are disposable. When I get back inside the truck, I'll grab a pair of fresh gloves from the carton."

"No. What I mean is that you need to purchase new ones."

Her chin lifted, and her eyes probed his. "Why? What's wrong with the ones I already have?"

"They're pink," he said, rubbing his thumb in a slow circle on her palm to see if he could get another reaction out of her.

Her hand trembled beneath his, along with her voice.

"If that's supposed to be some sort of chauvinistic re-mark—"

He raised his free hand to stop her, wondering if his touch had caused her unease or if it was indeed the fact that she thought he was being sexist. "It's not at all. Though if you have a male employee, he might think you're the one being sexist by making him wear pink gloves. Clear disposable gloves are the standard to use in this type of business. They're gender neutral too."

She cocked her head. "I don't have a male employee on the truck right now, and as long as I'm using gloves, what does it matter what color they are?"

"Well, for one, the customers can see through the clear ones better to make sure your hands and nails are clean."

"But if I'm wearing gloves, then what does it matter if they can see that my hands are clean or not?"

Max raised one arrogant brow. "So you're admitting that you serve food to your customers with dirty hands?"

"What? No, of course not. Don't be silly. I'm just trying to point out the obvious. I mean, if you think about it, the whole thing sounds really stup—" Her words cut off.

"Go on."

"Ah, I...uh, never mind," she said with a polite smile and an even softer tone.

Judging by the heated daggers shooting from her brilliant blue eyes, Max could've sworn he'd upset her and that she was about to tell him off. Not that he blamed her after the hard time he was giving her. Hell, he definitely deserved it. But now she was back to showing a painfully submissive side that seemed to override her irritation. Strange.

He didn't know why she had stopped herself from saying whatever was on her mind, but it frustrated the hell out of him. *What in the hell does it take to rile this sensible woman up?*

* * *

Jessa gave Max a cheeky smile.

She was more than happy to comply and correct any health code violations he had insisted she'd breached...if only they made any sense. Parking too close to the curb or an electrical box was one thing, but since when had it become such a crime to serve food in pink gloves rather than clear ones? Even though she knew ordinances varied widely in every town, this one seemed strange and...well, downright stupid.

But the last thing she wanted to do was to get on the new health inspector's bad side. She couldn't bring herself to question Max's authority, because arguing with the temperamental health inspector—even if he was a little finicky—could mean losing the chance to make her lifelong dreams of owning a restaurant come true.

The food truck, though it was a lot of fun, was only a temporary gig. Jessa planned to use the profits she earned from her gourmet kitchen on wheels to eventually open her own brick-and-mortar fancy dining establishment. That had always been the end goal, and there was no way she would give up on making it happen. Especially just so that she could tell Max where to shove his idiotic regulations.

The man was as frustrating as he was good looking, but arguing with him would only make things worse for her in the long run. So if that meant having to play nice with the annoying health inspector to keep him from shutting down her food truck business over something silly, then that was exactly what she would do. Put on her best smile, bite her tongue, and take care of business as usual.

Because Jessa damn sure wasn't going anywhere.

She smiled at that, knowing her mother would be thrilled. The carefree woman had always said that Granite would be the perfect place to live. It had all of the small-town charm that you didn't always find in the larger, bustling cities: a welcoming community, friendly neighbors who waved at each other in passing, seasonal festivals that weren't overly crowded due to the small town population, and best of all, very little crime.

Yet there were also still plenty of places to shop, eat, or even grab a drink after work. Actually, this town had almost everything a person would need. There was a small movie theater, a locally owned art gallery, a corner bookstore, a thrift store, a small park for children to play in, hiking trails, and even a concrete amphitheater for the occasional musical performance.

Jessa sighed though. She knew it had all been too good to be true. This town had been way too perfect. But who in their right mind would've guessed that the city officials in Granite had gone crazy and imposed dumb ordinances that made absolutely no sense? Go figure.

For the last few minutes, she'd feigned listening as Max went on and on about how there wasn't enough shade in the area around the truck and how she should move it to keep from killing her customers. Or some crazy bullshit like that. She let him ramble on, but all she kept thinking was how if he asked her to plant some trees, she was going to bury the aggravating man beneath one.

As he continued his rant, Jessa glanced over at the truck and noticed that the order line was getting a lot longer.

The health inspector cleared his throat, and with irritation coloring his tone, he asked, "Do you have somewhere you need to be, miss?"

Crap. She hadn't meant to upset him further. "Um, yeah. I hate to say it, but I actually do. I don't mean to be rude or disrespectful by rushing this, but I need to get back to work. I have two fairly new employees, and I can't leave them unattended for too long in case they need my help with something. Are we done here?"

His hazel eyes clouded over like a fogged-up mirror. "Nope," he said, letting the P sound pop off his tongue as if he were demonstrating his frustration with her. "Not even close."

Great, Jess. Piss the guy off some more. Smart. "Sorry. It's just that this is one of our busiest times of the day. Maybe we could continue this after the afternoon rush is over."

His tone turned even more sour than it was already. "Because I look like I have time to wait around on you?"

Shit. But well... if she was being honest, yeah. Technically, he did.

His lazy stance suggested a certain unhurried, casual demeanor, and his relaxed shoulders gave her a sense that he was fairly comfortable standing there. Besides, he was a young, healthy, virile-looking man who didn't seem in any danger of dying today. Unless, of course, she pushed him out into oncoming traffic...which was becoming a real possibility if he kept using that overbearing attitude and patronizing tone with her. The handsome prick.

Jessa blew out a slow, calming breath. She really needed to keep a cool head when dealing with the prickly health inspector or she was going to lose it. Her business, namely. She tried to keep in mind the old saying about how you can kill more flies with honey. Okay, so maybe it was "catch more flies with honey." But somehow this guy's death seemed a hell of a lot more imminent than a fly's short life cycle.

"Look, I'm terribly sorry. I'm not trying to brush you off, if that's what you're thinking," she said sweetly. "I know you are just doing your job, Max. But I have one to do too. So if we could schedule this at a more convenient time for both of us, that would be most helpful."

A muscle ticked in his jaw.

Yep, he's pissed.

But before he had a chance to respond, a voice rang out. "Hey, Max. How's it going?"

Jessa twisted her neck at the interruption and watched as a construction worker in paint-covered overalls waved to them from one of the picnic tables across the way. Then the uniformed man flipped Max off with a huge smile on his face. Clearly, the two of them were friends and knew each other well.

When she glanced back at Max, she could've sworn that she saw a flash of panic briefly cross his face, but he gained his composure so quickly that she wasn't entirely certain of it.

"Hi, Jim. Nice to see you," Max replied, although he

shifted sideways and transferred all of his weight from one foot to the other.

She didn't know why, but she got the distinct impression that Max didn't want to talk to the painter. Maybe there was some bad blood between them or something. Guess that made sense. After all, the guy did give Max the middle finger.

"You know what, Jess. I think you're absolutely right. Maybe coming back another time would be a good idea. You clearly have things to be doing right now, and I have my own stuff to take care of. So why don't we just reschedule this visit for another day?"

"That would be wonderful. Thank you."

Jessa started to offer a new time and date, but before she could, Max said, "Good. I'll see you around." Then he abruptly turned and walked away.

Only briefly did she wonder why he was in such a blatant hurry to get out of there. But honestly, she really didn't give a damn about *why* he'd left. Just that he'd left.

Thank God. I thought that annoying man would never leave.

Never had anyone looked so good walking in the opposite direction from her...and she wasn't saying that because of his tight jeans covering his muscled rear end. Though that was pretty nice too.

Still a little flustered with her run-in with the sexy new inspector, Jessa closed her eyes and blew out a long, slow breath. After being in that man's vicinity, she needed a minute to collect herself. Otherwise, she'd be going back to work with nipples so hard and pointy that she was liable to take someone's eye out with them.

But something Max had said stuck eerily in the corner

of her mind, and her eyes snapped open and she'd stared incredulously at the empty spot where Max had stood. At first, she hadn't noticed the slight undercurrent of his words that still hung in the air around her like an ominous warning or some kind of bad omen.

What the hell did he mean he'd see her around? And why did those few short words sound so much like a threat?

Chapter Three

The next day, Max strolled into the Empty Plate, noting all the vacant chairs though the parking lot was once again jam-packed with cars. He sighed and sat at his favorite table. "Pops, you here?"

Something clanged in the back before the old man came out of the kitchen, wiping his hands on a dishcloth. He draped it over his shoulder. "Hey, Max. Lunchtime already?"

"Close enough. Sam couldn't leave the plumber unattended, so I left for lunch a few minutes early. I told him I'd bring him something back."

"All right. What will the two of you be having today?"

"The special, but Sam will settle for another burger and fries." Max grinned.

The man shook his head. "Do you ever plan on telling Sam about our arrangement?"

"I don't know. Maybe someday. But I've had too much fun letting him think that you don't like him."

Pops chuckled and then nodded across the street. "So how did it go over there yesterday? Did you bully that rotten sonofabitch into leaving town?" His eyes filled with mirth, and a smirk tugged at the corner of his mouth.

"You knew the owner of that food truck was a woman the whole time, didn't you?"

Nodding, Pops let out another laugh. "Yeah, someone mentioned last week that it was a young woman running the truck. I tried to tell you."

"Well, you didn't try hard enough." Max gazed out the window and shook his head in disbelief. "You purposely let me go over there and make a complete fool of myself."

"Give me a break," Pops said, his eyes rolling. "Since when did you ever need any help in that department? You did what you always do. You went off half-cocked and didn't hear me out." He squeezed Max's shoulder. "You have a good heart, son. But that mouth of yours has always gotten you into an awful lot of trouble."

"Yeah, no kidding. But I don't normally go around picking on women. You know how I feel about that kind of stuff."

"So what happened over there? Did she believe that you were the new city health inspector?"

"Yeah, she bought it hook, line, and sinker. But judging by your lack of customers today, it didn't help any. Honestly though, I kind of wished she hadn't believed any of it. I don't like deceiving a woman. It just doesn't feel right."

"That's all right, Max. Like I told you yesterday, you win some and you lose some. Sometimes things are just meant to be."

Max shook his head furiously. "No, it's not all right. And I don't believe that. If you want something bad enough, you have to make it happen. Like I did with losing weight. I worked for that goal. I didn't wait around to see if the pounds would disappear on their own. Because otherwise they wouldn't have."

"True," Pops said, rubbing at his chin. "But when you moved here, do you remember what you said to me the first day I met you?"

Max nodded. "Yeah. I said that it was a good thing I met you when I did because I was really struggling with maintaining my weight loss."

"Exactly. Almost like us meeting in that exact moment was meant to be, right?"

Damn, he'd walked right into that one. "Okay, so I get what you're saying. But I don't think that applies to every situation. I refuse to believe that you're meant to lose your business all because some newcomer rolls into town and steals your customers. Where's the fairness in that?"

Pops shrugged. "Life isn't always fair."

"Yeah, you can say that again."

"It's fine, Max. It's just a restaurant. Not the end of the world. We'll take it one day at a time and hope that something good comes out of it all. In the meantime, I'll keep doing what I do best, which is feeding you guys lunch." Without another word, he headed for the kitchen.

While Max waited patiently for Pops to return, the

quietness of the surrounding room began to bother him. Truthfully, the whole situation weighed heavily on his mind. He'd barely slept a wink knowing Pops' business was in danger of closing the doors by the end of the month. That was only three weeks away.

His eyes surveyed the silent room, taking in all the open space. He'd never seen the Empty Plate Café so dead before—unless you counted yesterday, of course— and hated to think that he wouldn't be able to get another hot meal here once the month was over. Damn it. This wasn't just a restaurant to him. It was more like a second home. A place where he fit in with everyone else, which was something he hadn't always had in his life.

And Pops? God. Max hated the thought of the man he'd come to admire so much possibly losing his only source of income. Pops didn't have any kids or other family to help him out, and his wife had died several years before. The old man couldn't lose his business too. Without the restaurant, how would he be able to support himself?

Pops finally came back with a couple of to-go boxes in hand. "I'll put these on your tab, son."

Max rose from his chair, accepting the boxes from him. "Are you sure? If you need the extra cash on hand, I can pay up what I owe you now."

"Nah, that's okay. You always pay at the end of the month because I won't be writing any checks to my vendors until then anyway. You're good to go." He smiled at Max and tapped his finger on the to-go boxes. "By the way, your special today is a veggie burger and baked sweet potato fries. It's on the bottom, but I also wrote your name on the box in case you get them mixed up."

"Thanks, Pops. I appreciate you always looking out for me."

"It's been my pleasure, Max. You needed support, and I'm glad that I could've been the one to provide it. I'm proud of how far you have come and how determined you are to keep yourself there. I'll help you any way I can. You know that."

Max nodded. "I do. And I'll never forget it."

"You better get going so you can get that burger to Sam before it gets cold. Or he's going to think I did that on purpose."

They both grinned.

"See ya tomorrow, Pops." Max headed out the door and straight to his truck.

But after he climbed inside and set the to-go boxes on the seat next to him, he stared across the street at the long line of customers. He couldn't see the food truck past the flowering oleander bushes blocking his view, but he had no doubt it was there. And still ruining any chance Pops had at keeping his restaurant open. Poor guy.

He didn't deserve to be treated this way. The kind old man had always been willing to lend a friendly ear, share his wisdom, or help someone out. Hell, he'd even call someone out on their bullshit, if necessary. And over the years it *had* been necessary with Max plenty of times.

Truthfully, Pops had been practically like a second father to him. Max was not someone who liked being vulnerable in front of others. It only made him feel like that chubby kid getting picked on at school all over again. But with Pops, he could always talk openly about his insecurities and his fixation with food. He'd always been way too embarrassed to admit that to anyone else. Even his best friend Sam.

Max sighed in frustration. If the Empty Plate Café closed its doors, he was going to go right back to struggling with his weight again. He just knew it. And what would become of Pops?

Disgusted with the whole rotten situation, Max thought long and hard about it before finally coming to a conclusion. He didn't at all feel good about lying to Jessa, but maybe it was the lesser of two evils. Because no matter what, he couldn't stand by and watch an old man—especially one who had always taken care of him—lose his only source of income. Not when he knew there was something he could do to help.

If that meant Max had to keep pretending to be the health inspector to force Jessa to leave, then so be it. That was exactly what he was going to do. The moment he got off work today, he was going to have to pay the lovely Miss Gibson another visit.

Because like it or not, he owed it to Pops to see this through.

* * *

By returning to the scene of the crime, Max knew he was pushing his luck and could possibly be found out. He was impersonating a city official, for Christ's sake. Surely there had to be some kind of law that he was breaking. Probably several.

But he refused to turn back now.

Max chuckled as he remembered the look on her face yesterday when he'd told her that she couldn't wear her precious pink gloves anymore. Maybe it wasn't a nice thing to do at the time, but the bewildered expression she wore had kept him in a good mood and smiling the rest of the evening.

As he got closer to the park, he spotted her food truck parked in a different spot than before. Stupid him. Yesterday, he had thought it would be as simple as giving her a good old-fashioned ribbing in order to get her to leave. But he had apparently underestimated this woman's determination to keep her truck in Windsor Park. Didn't matter though. All of that would soon be changing, if he had anything to say about it.

It was unfortunate though. The frustratingly agreeable woman he'd met yesterday seemed to have a need to please. That wasn't the type of woman Max usually went for, but he hated the idea that he would never get the chance to get to know her better. As far as he was concerned, that was a tragic loss on his part.

As Max strolled down the sidewalk toward the food truck, an amused grin stretched his lips wider. He could only imagine her reaction when he showed up so soon to see if she'd corrected those fake violations he'd cited to her yesterday.

Of course he knew she hadn't. There hadn't been enough time. But watching such a charming, innocent-looking woman like Jessa lose her cool was going to be the highlight of his day. Or it should've been.

His feet stalled on the pavement, and he was suddenly seeing red. Lots of it. Every picnic bench in the vicinity of her truck had been draped with a red plastic tablecloth. And if that wasn't enough, there were two brand-new trash cans sitting off to one side.

Damn it. How in the hell had she accomplished that so fast?

The musical sound of laughter drifted through the air, and he turned his attention onto the food truck, noting a small line at the pick-up window that seemed to be moving fairly quickly. Well, if you could even consider two people a "line."

He had purposely waited to show up at her truck until the end of the day. Not only because he'd started back to work on the construction site today and had a lot to catch up on, but he also didn't want to have another run-in with one of his buddies from Sam's crew. If Jim had come over to talk to him yesterday in front of Jessa, things would've been a lot more awkward than they already were.

Max leaned against a nearby mesquite tree and crossed one booted ankle over the other. From his position she couldn't see him, but he had a damn good view of her. She flitted gracefully around the tiny kitchen on wheels, cooking and preparing her customers' meals to order under a bright fluorescent light. And though Max wasn't a great cook himself, he didn't at all mind watching her do it.

Maybe a little insight into the enemy was just what he needed to give him the edge and drive her out of there for good. Couldn't hurt, right? If only he could figure out what made this woman tick, he might have a better chance of getting her to leave.

Unlike yesterday, Jessa seemed to be the only one working, and it looked like she was about ready to call it a day. Good. He didn't want or need an audience for what he was about to do. He was already feeling guilty enough.

He waited patiently until the last person received their order and left with their food. Once it was all clear, he made his way over to the food truck and rapped on the entry door at the back of the truck with his knuckles. She opened it within seconds.

After their first unpleasant encounter, he was surprised to see her greet him with a smile. Granted, her curved lips did seem a little stiff and possibly a bit forced, but he couldn't really blame her for that. She hadn't been expecting him, and it probably wasn't fun to receive a spontaneous visit from a man who could shut down your livelihood without thinking twice about it. Well, if Max had actually been the inspector.

"Um, hi," she said, her voice just as sweet as ever.

"Hey, Jess. I hope you don't mind me stopping by unannounced." *Not that I gave you much of a choice since I'm already here.*

"No, of course not."

"Good. I thought I'd check and see if you made any progress on those corrections I mentioned to you yesterday."

Her words came out friendly, but they didn't match the scowl on her face. "Well, yeah. I mean I bought a couple of extra trash cans and purchased tablecloths for each of the picnic tables." She motioned to them. "I assume those are to your satisfaction."

He shrugged nonchalantly. "They seem to be."

"Great," she said, removing a pair of clear disposable gloves from her hands. "Well, as you can see, I bought new gloves too. And just for your peace of mind, I also left off the...bug spray. So you don't have to worry about that one either." One brow rose.

"Uh, yeah. Sorry about that," Max said, stifling a chuckle.

He probably should've felt worse than he did for saying that to her yesterday, but after the way his comment had made her laugh, he couldn't muster up the energy. He had liked hearing that surprised, rapid-fire laughter of hers. It was nice.

Jessa shook her head. "It's fine. I didn't like that perfume all that much anyway."

"Well, then I guess that leaves us with one last thing to check," Max said, whipping out the tape measure he'd clipped onto his hip before he'd gotten out of his truck.

Her mouth fell open, but she stood there quietly as he stepped over to her back tire and measured the distance from the tire to the curb. Sonofabitch. It was exactly ten and three-quarter inches. He glanced up long enough to judge the distance from the truck to the electrical box with his eyes. Yeah, without even measuring it, he knew she'd aced that one too. *What the hell?*

Not only had Jessa met all of the idiotic standards he'd given her yesterday, the frustrating woman had exceeded them. Damn it. He was impressed, but he didn't want to be. Now what the hell was he going to do to get rid of her?

"All good?" she asked, pride blooming on her face.

Max straightened and gave her a terse nod. "With this part of the inspection, yes." Then he wiped that smug little grin off her face by saying, "But I thought I'd do a walk-through of your truck while I'm here and make sure everything in the kitchen is in order."

Worry flashed in her eyes, and she picked at her fingernails. "Actually, I'm closed. I just served my last meal and was about to head out."

"I see," Max said, thinking fast. He couldn't let her get out of it. Not if he was going to get her to leave for good. "Then I guess I'll just come back tomorrow during the lunch rush and do it then. Have a great night." He turned to walk away while grinning to himself and doing a silent countdown in his head.

Three . . . two . . . one.

"Uh, Max?"

Yep. Called it. He stopped in place, wiped the smile off his face, and glanced back over his shoulder. "Yeah?"

She stood there with her arms crossed and her eyes narrowed at him. "It's fine. Why don't we just go ahead and do it now? I mean, you're already here so there's no point in you coming back tomorrow."

Max shrugged. "Sure. Totally up to you."

She sighed but then smiled lightly as she pushed the food truck door open wider to allow him entry. It was exactly what he wanted, but it irritated him that she hadn't looked more forlorn about being forced to invite him in. She clearly wasn't in the mood to deal with him again, but she was still biting her tongue. She'd done the same thing yesterday. *What the hell does it take to set this woman off? A fucking bomb?*

Then he remembered yesterday how her hand trembled in his and how flustered she was when he'd touched her. It was entirely possible that there was a legitimate reason for her reaction, but usually that kind of a response meant something.

Maybe he wasn't on the right track. But it was at least a theory. A damned good one, if you asked him.

One he wouldn't mind experimenting with. Not because he wanted to get her into bed...though the thought had crossed his mind. He definitely wouldn't mind seeing the sweet little Jessa come undone while lying beneath him. But right now what he needed more than that was to know if she was as attracted to him as he thought she might be. That way, he could possibly use it to his advantage.

Wait, what? *Fuck.*

Had he really just become one of those guys who thought shit like that? *Jesus. I should be publicly shamed and forced to turn in my man card.*

Max shook his head in utter disgust. When it came to women, he'd always thought of himself as more of the protector type. Heaven forbid some abusive idiot dare lay a hand on a woman in Max's presence. Because that dead-man-walking wouldn't be walking for much longer. Or breathing.

It wasn't just that though. Even the nonviolent mistreatment of women pissed Max off. Whether it was a man neglecting his woman, cheating on her, or just flat-out lying to her...which totally made Max feel like the hypocrite he apparently was.

Too late now. I'm already in too deep.

"Max?"

Jessa's words broke through his trancelike state, and he glanced over at her. "Yeah?"

"Don't you want to look around inside?"

Max hesitated. The last thing he wanted to do was sink to a new level of low, but he'd already lied to her about who he was anyway. Besides, if she was attracted to him, maybe flirting with her would fluster her enough to slip up and give him something he could actually use against her. Like a problem with the truck.

Even if she wasn't attracted to him though, the flirting would, at the very least, make things awkward and uncomfortable between them, which might still send her packing. She probably wouldn't want to stay in a town where she thinks the health inspector has it out for her because she turned down his advances.

God, he hated this. But he needed to do something to get her to leave. Unfortunately, nothing else had worked.

"Yeah. I'm coming." He stepped up into the doorway of the truck but paused and stared down at her before going farther inside. The narrow passageway inside the truck was the perfect opportunity for him to make his move. But could he really do it?

Hell, did he really have a choice?

Thank God I never claimed to be a saint. He put one firm hand on her shapely waist and said, "Excuse me." Then he brushed slowly past her, making sure every inch of his hard body slid firmly against her soft, lush curves.

Her spine stiffened immediately, and the quick intake of her breath sounded in his ears. But as he maneuvered past her into the middle of the small, narrow kitchen, it was his own body's reaction that alarmed him the most. An instant hard-on formed beneath his jeans while his blood pressure spiked so high that his ears rang.

She fumbled to close the door and turned to face him, her cheeks a bright shade of pink. She reached past him to toss her gloves into the trash behind him, but her eyes wouldn't meet his. "Sorry it's so…um, warm in here. I only turned the grill off a few minutes ago. It's going to be a while before I…I mean *it* cools down."

Max nodded and shifted uncomfortably from the bulge in his pants. "Not a problem." As an electrician, he often worked in the heat as well as tight spaces. He was used to it. But after rubbing himself against her like that, it was suddenly a hell of a lot warmer in the truck than he thought possible.

She reached for some utensils on the table. "Let me just put these away and we can get it on...I mean get on with it." She winced as she spun away from him with lightning speed.

It was cute how she was trying to appear unaffected by him and even more adorable that she was failing so miserably at it. So the short, sweet redhead with the amenable personality had the hots for him, huh? Well, this made his fake-ass job way more intriguing. And had his pants feeling even tighter in the groin area than they already were.

Too bad he couldn't act on it for real though.

Not that Jessa was his type or anything. Max wanted a woman who breathed fire and passion. One who would take an intimate walk on the wild side and had no problem letting down her hair. A partner with plenty of confidence who could hold her own, in *and* out of the bedroom.

He had no problem admitting that he was a handful in both of those areas, and he needed a woman who would be able to keep up. Possibly even one who could put him in his place on occasion. Unfortunately, Jessa hadn't done that at all. Which only made him wonder why she was so damn appealing to him. What was it about this woman that got his blood roaring like it did?

No question about it, she was beautiful. Those large, sparkling blue eyes had captured him almost instantly when he'd first seen her, along with her full, womanly figure and that fine heart-shaped ass of hers. And the perfume she'd been wearing? It was like some kind of an accelerant that had ignited flames inside of him and had left him feeling warm and fuzzy all over.

But none of that mattered. Max cautioned himself to curb his curiosity in Jessa and not get sidetracked. He couldn't afford to get distracted by anyone right now, because he had a very important job to do. And that job was getting her to move her damn truck. One way or another, it was going to happen.

Jessa cleared her throat. "So what would you like to look at first?"

Max's eyes fell on her breasts. *Stop that shit. You're making yourself look like a damn pervert.* This was never going to work if he couldn't get himself under control. Now.

He ran a hand over his face. It wasn't like he knew anything about food trucks. Hell, he didn't know anything about cooking at all. There was a reason why he ate lunch at the Empty Plate Café every day. Sometimes dinner too. "Why don't you tell me about your truck while I take a look around?"

"Okay, sure." She motioned to her surroundings. "As you can plainly see, the truck has a stainless steel construction on all food contact and prep surfaces, as well as the dry storage areas." She moved around him in the narrow kitchen, pointing out things as she kept talking. "The refrigeration is set below forty-one degrees at all times, and each of the gas-generated appliances and water pumps have their own shut-off valves, along with a fire suppression system."

Even though Max wasn't the actual health inspector, he was glad to hear that she had taken so many safety precautions within her truck. Chances were good that most of them had been actual requirements, but still, he was happy to hear it. He wanted her to move the truck, not die in it.

"Do you have hot and cold water in here?" he asked, then realized that he sounded like he didn't know the answer to that question. A real health inspector *would* know. "You do, right?"

Jessa nodded. "Of course. And it's pressurized. There's a thirty-gallon freshwater tank under the three-compartment sink as well as a forty-five gallon waste-water tank beneath the floor panel you're standing on. The hot water heater is in the front of the vehicle right above the driver's seat. It's one of those on-demand types and runs off of propane."

Max glanced around but didn't spot what he was looking for. "Where's your tank?"

"It's frame mounted," she said, pointing down toward the floor of the truck.

"Uh, what about fire extinguishers?"

"I've got several," she said, showing him which cabinet they were stored in. "I also have a generator in a locked panel on the back of the truck. The circuit breakers, transfer switch, and electrical receptacle are all toward the front."

Ah, now she's speaking my language. "What size breakers and wire are you using in the truck?"

She blinked rapidly and then stared at him with a

blank expression, as if he'd just asked her if she was a native inhabitant of another planet. "I...um, don't really know. The truck was already wired when I purchased it."

Max stilled. What if she had stripped wires or somehow overloaded the circuits by accident? Did she not understand how dangerous that could be? Especially for a food truck that housed a deep–fat fryer mere feet away from the breaker box. If something happened and sparks flew from it, she could end up with a grease fire on her hands that could burn down the entire truck.

Glancing around, he spotted the gray breaker box on the wall toward the front of the truck. He went for it and yanked it open.

After giving everything a good once-over, he checked the wattage on all of her appliances and did some quick math in his head. Although she watched him warily, Jessa never moved from her position and didn't say a word.

When he was done calculating the numbers, he finally turned back to her. "Okay, in case you need to know this information in the future, you're feeding a thirty-amp service and running on fifteen-amp breakers. The twelve-gauge wire they installed is a bit of overkill, but I think it's okay for the most part. I went ahead and counted up all the wattage on every appliance I could see in here, and as long as whoever wired your truck balanced out the loads correctly, then you should be fine."

Confusion still swamped her face, but she managed a soft, "Um, thanks." It sounded more like a question.

"You're welcome," Max said with an amused grin. Guess not everyone liked electrical stuff nearly as much as an electrician did.

But who cares? At least he knew her wiring system seemed fairly safe. The last thing this woman needed was a fire on board. And the last thing *he* needed was her leaving behind a trail of smoke when he finally ran her out of town.

Otherwise, he might be tempted to follow her.

Chapter Four

Jessa didn't know what to make of Max.

When he'd first showed up outside her door, she couldn't believe the arrogant jerk had come back so soon to check up on her. If she hadn't spent the better part of the morning making sure she'd corrected all the idiotic issues he'd mentioned to her the day before, he would've probably shut her down.

The meticulous man even had the nerve to break out a tape measure to make sure her tire was exactly ten and three-quarter inches away from the curb. She'd spent fifteen minutes getting that parking job exact, just in case, but she never really expected the health inspector to be *that* thorough. Seriously? Who does that?

He does, that's who.

Thank goodness she'd done the smart thing and taken him at his word yesterday. He had said he'd see her around, and apparently, he had meant it. She hadn't known that at the time, but if she hadn't corrected those issues he'd pointed out, she could very well have been packing it in for good right now.

Then again, that still might be a possibility.

Max was standing in her truck's little kitchen, looking for more code violations to point out. And knowing how picky he was yesterday, she would bet he was prepared to find something. Possibly anything. Keeping him from closing her business down over something stupid was proving to be a full-time job.

That was why she'd let Mary and Lisa both go home early. They'd covered Jessa's shift while she spent several hours running around town looking for two new trash cans, clear disposable gloves, and enough red plastic cloths to cover the picnic tables with. Once she'd found what she needed, she had raced back and got to work putting them all to good use.

Jessa thought she'd been paranoid for nothing since Max hadn't showed up all day. But then she'd heard the knock at the door and had a feeling his pile of muscle would be standing on the other side. She'd been right.

He wasn't fancily dressed or anything. Just dark jeans, a gray button-down top with a white undershirt peeking out from beneath his collar, and a pair of semi-clean work boots. But, have mercy, he looked good enough to eat.

He hadn't flirted with her though. Not really. She was pretty sure it was just her sex-filled imagination playing tricks on her. Though technically when he entered the truck, he'd practically dry-humped her in passing. With one strong hand on her waist, he'd slid by her, rubbing every hard inch of him across her body as he went.

Whether it had been intentional or not, she didn't know, but something hot and intense had moved through her at the speed of lightning.

Now every time he even looked like he was going to move in any direction, she had to keep from throwing herself into his path for a repeat performance.

"Jessa?"

Her eyes lifted to his. "Yeah?"

"I asked you a question."

"Oh. I'm sorry. I didn't hear you. Can you repeat it, please?"

The corner of his mouth lifted, causing her blood pressure to spike. God, that wickedly sexy smirk of his was all kinds of catnip for her.

He pointed to the tiny sink toward the front of the truck. "I asked you why you had an extra sink over there."

Confusion trickled through her. What a weird question coming from the health inspector. "Because I'm required to have a separate hand-washing sink on the truck. Frankly, I'm surprised you don't know that since the old inspector already told me that it was one of the regulations."

Max ran his hand through his hair and onto the back of his neck. "Uh, right. It just slipped my mind for a second, that's all. Thanks for the reminder."

"You're welcome. Now is there anything else you'd like to see?"

He stepped closer and peered down at her, his eyes glittering. The way he looked at her made her feel beautiful. "Everything, Jess. I want to see everything you have."

Her racing heart beat against her lungs, knocking the breath free from both of them, as her blood flowed to her limbs in a slow, sensual rhythm.

Damn those intense hazel eyes of his. With just one glance, this man had the ability to make her feel as though he'd stripped her naked and touched her intimately. As if he had reached deep into her soul and fondled her very essence.

Jesus. Maybe he was flirting with her. Which seemed almost strange since she would think it would be considered inappropriate.

Somehow, she didn't care.

The first day she'd met him, she thought he was a real jerk. A cute one, but still a jerk. Now she was surprised to find out that he was much more intriguing than she'd originally thought. Actually, he was the kind of male that was dangerous for any woman to be around. Plain and simple, the man oozed pure sex.

Jessa didn't really mind partaking in a little harmless flirting with a man who was pretty to look at. She would do just about anything to keep him on her good side at this point anyway. And if that meant flirting with a handsome guy, then who was she to complain?

Besides, it wasn't like anything was actually going to happen between them. The side windows on the truck were still wide open, and anyone passing by could see the two of them standing inside.

She licked her lips as she gazed up at him. "Which part of my everything would you like to get your hands on first?" Her sultry voice had lowered to almost a whisper.

His eyes widened slightly, and he stared at her in silence

for a moment. As if he were contemplating what to do. "Why don't you show me your, uh…food containers?"

Food containers? Well, that wasn't the least bit arousing. What happened to the great sexy-talk they were having? Jeez. "Okay, they're over here," she said, trying to keep her lackluster tone from sounding too much like disappointment.

She led him over to the low cabinet at the end of the counter and opened it for him. All of the containers were see-through, though it didn't matter since everything had also been clearly marked.

Max rummaged through the cabinet, moving things around to check that everything was in order. Which was irritating since everything *had* been in order until he'd touched it. Now she'd have to spend some time in the morning putting everything back in place before she opened for business.

Great. Like she needed more work to do.

But while he was bent down and so engrossed with messing up her organization, it gave her the perfect opportunity to check out his backside again. The dark, fitted denim jeans stretched tight across his sculpted derrière, which only made her wonder how his bare butt would look with her nails digging into it.

She wasn't surprised his hind end was as firm as the rest of him. This guy was clearly in shape. Even through two layers of shirt, she could see the dense bands of muscle bunching beneath the material with every movement of his arms. And his biceps? God, those were fantastic too. If there was such a thing as an arm porn commercial, he would probably be hired as their top model.

Max stood, reaching his full height before turning

around to face her. He rolled his broad shoulders, and the controlled movement made the bulk of his pectoral muscles strain against the front of his shirt. Then, as if she wasn't already worked up enough, he offered her an incredible smile that stirred something inside of her. "Looks like we're good here."

Mmm-hmm. "Yes, we are."

* * *

Several days had passed and Max still hadn't made any headway with Jessa. He'd shown up at her truck for the past three evenings after work, trying to come up with something that would aggravate her enough to move that damn thing. But the woman had unflappable control. Nothing he did seemed to have any effect on her.

Well, except for one thing. But damn it, he never should've started flirting with her. Now he didn't want to stop. Not only that, but it had been increasingly hard to stay on track whenever she smiled at him the way she did. Or the way she stared at him with those liquid blue eyes while batting those long lashes of hers. It was enough to make a man go insane.

To give himself some perspective and get Jessa off his mind awhile, Max decided he needed to do something normal. Something mundane that he hadn't done in a while. Like shopping for groceries. So he headed for the local farmers' market, which was held in downtown Granite near the shopping square.

The outdoor market was open every Saturday from nine to two, and farmers from all over the surrounding area showed up to sell their goods. Though Granite was a fairly small town, the farmers' market had grown into a decent-sized event. Enough so that the organizers had to ask the police to barricade the downtown streets to keep customers safe as they shopped.

Max strolled leisurely through the entrance of the outdoor market, taking in his surroundings. Loud country music pumped out of speakers somewhere nearby. Hoards of people, young and old, weaved in and out of the maze of small white tents before him. Children giggled as they rode ponies in a circle while their parents looked on.

What started out years ago as a little local weekend market had somehow morphed into a weekly festival of food, music, and fun. But Max wasn't there for the music and fun. Only the food. He'd been out of town during the past two Saturdays and needed to stock up on his produce for the next week. Otherwise, he'd be paying supermarket prices for lower quality produce.

That's what he loved most about the farmers' market. The organizers supported healthy eating and had created the event with a strong foundation of local Texas farmers who brought in locally grown and organic produce to sell at a fair price. Real food harvested from the ground or picked from a tree. Not that processed shit so many people lived on.

But as Max started to move through the crowd, his gaze snagged on a booth with a familiar name. *Sweets n' Treats? What in the hell?* Confused, Max strolled toward the booth to make sure he read the sign right and caught sight of Leah standing at the table talking to a customer. Sam leaned back in a lawn chair behind her, drinking a glass of lemonade.

"Hey," Max said, peering at Sam. "What are you doing here?"

Sam grinned. "Well, at the moment, absolutely nothing. I did my part earlier as the pack mule," he said, motioning to the tables stacked high with boxes of all sizes from his wife's bakery.

Leah waved good-bye as her customer left. "Hey, Max. I didn't know you would be here today. How was your vacation?"

"Good," he lied, remembering how he practically starved to death at his parents' house. "Couldn't have been better."

"I'm glad to hear it," she said, sitting in a second lawn chair next to Sam. "So what have you been up to all week?"

Max stilled. Shit. Had she heard something about him pretending to be the health inspector? And if so, from who? "Um, nothing much. Why?"

She shrugged. "No reason. I just wondered where you've been hiding out all week. I haven't seen you. You usually stop by our place or the bakery at least a couple of times a week for coffee."

"I guess I've just been busy and haven't gotten out much." To change the subject, he gestured to the sign with her bakery name listed on it. "Since when did you start selling things here anyway?"

"Last weekend was my first time."

"How?"

"Well, I filled out a vendor form, and I was approved by—"

"No, not that," Max said, shaking his head. "I mean, how are you selling your goods at an event that promotes healthy eating? Your desserts aren't exactly diet-friendly."

"Oh, that," she said, waving her hand through the air. "At this booth, I'm only selling gluten-free items or things made with all natural ingredients. Most everything I'm offering has been prepared using free-range eggs, freshly ground organic flour, or un-homogenized milk and butter. They allow specialty foods as long as you are consistent with their standards."

"So these items might not be lower in calories but they're a bit healthier than what you would normally serve in the bakery?"

"Basically. It's a great option for anyone who has a gluten allergy or wants to indulge in something sweet without all the added pesticides, hormones, and antibiotics they'll find in most dairy. I'm even going to start selling some of this in my bakery on a regular basis too."

"That's good." Too bad Max still couldn't eat any of it.

"So what are you doing here?" Sam asked, sitting forward in his chair. "It's your day off. I figured you'd be sleeping in or already heading to the gym."

"I'm going to go work out later. I'm just stopping by here to...uh, offer my support to our local businesses."

"Yeah, right. While you're scoping out the women?"

He grinned. "That too." If Sam wanted to think that was the reason Max was here, then that was fine by him. At least it kept him from having to tell Sam the truth about his problem with food.

It wasn't a big secret in town that Max worked out and liked to look good. Anyone with eyes could see that he was packing some muscles. And just by hanging out with him over the years, Sam had probably already figured out that he didn't eat a lot of junk food. Okay, *any* junk food. But Max had never actually explained that he had a weight problem as a child. Or that, as an adult, he still struggled with a food addiction on a daily basis.

Not only because he didn't want anyone to feel sorry for him. But because he didn't want anyone—especially Sam of all people—to treat him differently by catering to him. And they would. He just wanted everyone to look at him like he was normal. It had taken Max years to finally find a place where he fit in completely. Now that he had that, the last thing he would ever do was single himself out and put his eating disorder on display for everyone to see. Not gonna happen.

"All right, guys. I'm going to take off," Max told them. "I might swing back through on my way out though."

"Bye, Max," Leah said, stepping up to the table to help another customer.

"See ya, buddy." Sam grinned. "Good luck with the ladies."

Max shook his head and laughed as he walked away from the booth. He wasn't nearly the horn dog that Sam and his other friends thought he was. Sure, Max had had his fair share of women. But he didn't pick them up at every event he attended, nor did he sleep with every woman he talked to. *Otherwise, I might've ended up with Leah or Valerie the first night I met them.*

Sam and Logan would kick his ass if they knew that thought had even crossed his mind. But truthfully, from the moment Max had met both women, he knew the three of them would be nothing more than good friends.

Mainly because both of them worked in a bakery. And he didn't think it would be smart to date anyone who smelled like sugar all the time. For a guy on a special diet, that would've been the ultimate kind of torture.

Besides, Max had known that Sam had an interest in Leah from the get-go, one that it took him a while to admit. And Valerie had told Max straight up that first night that she was hung up on some man who wasn't the least bit interested—and apparently needed a seeing-eye dog. Undoubtedly, they were both gorgeous women. But with the added complications of the other men in their lives, Max would've never made a move on either of them anyway. Whether they worked in a bakery or not.

He'd been known to pull some crazy stunts over the years, but he wasn't the type of guy who would stoop so low as to steal another man's girl. Some things were unforgivable. As far as he was concerned, that was one of them.

Max made his way through the lines, stopping occasionally at individual booths to look over the wide range of products available for sale. Some vendors brought in new items each week, depending on the season, while some of them were just new vendors altogether. Either way, it was fun to see what each individual booth offered.

The meat booths were the largest at the market and usually drew a huge crowd. A guy wearing white rubber boots and a long yellow vinyl apron peddled his seafood while advertising it as the freshest gulf shrimp, fish, and shucked oysters you could buy. They guy in the booth next to him wore a cowboy hat and sold grass-fed, pasture-raised beef and chicken, but he also had a huge array of fresh milk, free-range eggs, and homemade cheeses that had come straight from his dairy farm.

But not everything at the market was edible. One couple from a nearby nursery offered drought-resistant plants and flowers that were free of pesticides and other chemicals. Not far from them was a lady who sold organic skin care products as well as custom artisans jewelry made from sustainable, recyclable products such as walnut and pecan shells.

None of those were booths Max usually shopped at though. He kept things simple and always bought everything he needed at one table in particular. Betty's Garden was just up ahead, and the sweet, old woman who ran it recognized him immediately. "Hey, Max. I missed seeing you the past two weekends. How was your vacation?"

"It was great, Miss Betty. Thanks for asking." He smiled at the kind woman. "How have you been? You had a cold or something coming on the last time I saw you. Did you get over it?"

"Must've been my allergies acting up again. I'm all better now."

"Good. I'm glad to hear it." He glanced over her produce on the table as Betty reached for a large brown paper bag that she had already filled before he had arrived. "What do we have today?"

"Sweet potatoes, baby arugula, vine-ripened tomatoes, cucumbers, peppers, fresh peas, heirloom green beans, bundles of carrots, and I brought out the last of my peaches for you since they're about to go out of season."

"Great, thanks," Max said, pulling cash out of his pocket and paying for his prefilled bag of goodies. He'd been ordering from Miss Betty long enough that they both knew the drill by heart.

She nodded at him. "In the next few weeks, I'll be harvesting different types of lettuce, and I'll bring in some bags of pecans for you too."

"Can't wait."

"Oh, and I almost forgot," she said, reaching behind her for something on the ground. "One of my sons took a trip down to the Texas valley this past week, and I had him pick you up a ten-pound bag of grapefruit. I know how much you like them." She placed it on the table next to his other bag.

Max grinned at her. "That was nice of you. Tell your son thanks for picking them up for me. What do I owe you for them?"

"No charge."

"No way. Let me pay for them. I appreciate you going to the trouble of getting them for me. The least I can do is pay for them."

She shook her head adamantly. "You're one of my best customers, Max. I didn't mind and neither did my son. He was driving down there anyway. Keep your money."

"Are you sure?"

She fisted her hands onto her hips and pursed her lips.

Max sighed. She was always doing nice things for him, and he knew that he wouldn't win in an argument with her. He never had in the past. "Okay," he said, putting his money away. "Well, thanks. I appreciate it."

She smiled at him. "I know you do."

He made a mental note to pick Miss Betty up a thank-you gift. She had always been generous when it came to him. Like she said, he was her best...Wait a minute. That wasn't what she said this time. When the hell had his status with her suddenly changed? "So what happened to me being your best customer? Did I lose that title to someone else because I've been gone for two weeks?"

"Well, technically yes, but you're still my favorite."

"Well, thank God for that. I was wondering who I was going to have to fight to get back into your good graces. I don't want anyone taking my place."

Miss Betty giggled at him. "It would never happen. But I do have a young woman who has been buying up a lot of produce from me for the past two weeks. I don't know how many people are in her family, but she must be feeding an army."

No way. It can't be. "Does she happen to run a food truck?"

"Hmm. I'm not sure. But I guess it would make sense. She's a short redhead with the sweetest demeanor. Do you know her?"

"Yeah, I know her," he grumbled. "Her name is Jessa Gibson."

"Oh. Well, you just missed her." She shifted to look around him and then pointed toward one of the exits as another customer walked up. "Actually, I still see her. She's right over there." Then Miss Betty moved away from him to help the newcomer.

Max glanced over his shoulder and caught sight of Jessa walking slowly toward one of the exits that led to the parking area while carrying three good-sized cardboard boxes stacked on one another. Her fingers were white from her tight grasp and her arms trembled relentlessly, suggesting that it was probably a heavy load.

No sooner had the thought crossed his mind, Jessa stumbled a little and the top box crashed to the ground. Green peppers and white onions scattered across the pavement. Jessa set the other two boxes down and began gathering the runaway vegetables and placing them back in the box she flipped right side up.

Max instantly reached for his brown paper sack and his bag of grapefruit and started for her. But then he faltered. What the hell was he doing? Was he seriously going over there to ask her if she needed help? Christ. He was supposed to be running her out of town, not loading the damn food on the truck for her.

Once all the peppers and onions had been returned to the box, she stacked it on top of the other two and frowned down at them while wiping sweat from her brow. Then she laced her fingers and cracked her knuckles before struggling to lift the boxes once more.

Max sighed. He just couldn't do it. There was no way he would sit by and watch her possibly injure herself by carrying something that was clearly too heavy for her. He admired how determined she was, but the woman couldn't even see over the boxes to know where she was going. In a busy parking lot, that was nothing more than a recipe for disaster.

He could live with a lot of things on his conscience, but Jessa hurting herself sure the hell wouldn't be one of them.

Chapter Five

Jessa could've kicked herself. If she hadn't left the dolly behind, she wouldn't be breaking her back to get these boxes to her truck in one trip. Who knew a couple of boxes of vegetables and fruits could be so heavy?

"Need a hand?" someone asked from somewhere on the other side of the stack.

She couldn't see him but she would recognize that gravelly, masculine voice anywhere. "Max?"

"Yep."

"Yeah, I'd love a hand." She adjusted her hold on the boxes and grunted. "As you can probably tell, mine are a little full at the moment."

"Here, let me take those from you."

Rough fingers brushed against hers as he gripped the edges of the bottom box, and the entire load was immediately lifted out of her straining arms. Relief swept over her as blood circulation instantly returned to each of her poor limbs. Thank God.

She shaded her eyes from the bright sun and gazed up at his smiling face over the top of the boxes he held. "Thanks. I really appreciate the help."

"No problem. But now could you do *me* a favor by carrying my bags?" He nodded down to the ground, where a brown paper sack sat next to a red mesh bag of grapefruit. "They're much lighter than these, I promise."

"Sure." She lifted them both. He was right. They weren't nearly as heavy.

He looked around. "Which way?"

She motioned to the back of the lot. "I parked at the very end. Sorry. Big trucks aren't always easy to get in and out of these tiny parking spots. But if those boxes get too heavy, I'll happily take one back and lighten your load a little."

"That's okay. I'll manage," he said, starting toward the back of the lot.

They walked side by side, and the farther they went, the more Jessa appreciated his help. She would never have made it on her own without passing out from overexertion. So as they maneuvered their way to her truck, Jessa became increasingly aware of his strength and impressed by his endurance.

As he moved much faster than she had, the veins in his forearms showed prominently, and the bulge of his biceps flexed against the sleeves of his white T-shirt. But all of that only served as an added bonus.

She glanced down to the red mesh bag with the white label. "Where did you get these grapefruit? They're huge."

Max grinned. "They were a gift from my favorite vendor. Her son picked them up for me while he was down in the Texas valley."

Wow. He still wasn't even out of breath yet. "Really? I might have to take a special trip down there just to pick some up. My regular supplier only carries the little ones. They look pitiful compared to yours."

"After tasting these, I stopped buying the ones in the grocery store. But it's too far to drive down to the valley just for a bag of grapefruit."

Jessa shook her head. "Not if they look like this, it isn't."

He glanced over at her and smiled. "I thought I was the only one in town who took my produce shopping so seriously."

"Well, you haven't seen anything yet. I was going to wait until you looked the other way and slip a couple of your grapefruit under my shirt. You would never know they're missing."

"Slick," he said with an amused chuckle. "But I think I'd notice if you suddenly developed an extra set of..." His gaze fell to her chest, and his smile faded. "Uh, never mind."

She laughed. "They're called breasts."

"I know that. But I didn't have to say it out loud to get my point across." The way he kept his eyes forward, she wondered if she'd embarrassed him.

The last few days had been quite interesting. Max would flirt with her on occasion, but whenever she flirted back, he would withdraw instantly as if she'd somehow flustered him. Though it was confusing, the whole thing was strangely endearing.

They made it to the truck, and Jessa unlocked the back door, holding it open for him as he stepped inside and placed her boxes on the counter. She stepped into the truck behind him and shut the door. "So why can't you say it?"

He turned to face her with confusion quirking his brows. "Say what?"

She smiled. "Breasts."

His gaze drifted down to her chest and then quickly lifted to her face. "I *can* say it. I just don't want to."

"Then do it."

Max shook his head. "I'm not going to say it, Jess."

"I dare you."

He rolled his eyes. "What are we—six-year-olds?" He took his bags from her and started past her.

She stepped in front of him to block his path. "Okay, fine. Don't say it then. But at least tell me why you won't."

Max stared at her in silence for a moment, as if he were deciding whether to answer the question. Then he sighed. "Because I'm a man and you're a woman."

"Um, okay. I've noticed that too. So what?"

"All right, let me spell it out for you. If we start talking about breasts, I'm going to think about yours. Not only that, but I'm going to start imagining what they look like without your clothes on. After that, things are probably going to start getting really uncomfortable between us. Especially for me." He nodded toward his groin and shifted awkwardly, as if punctuating his comment.

Her gaze went straight to his crotch and landed on the large bulge pushing against the seam of his jeans. *God, Jess. Don't look at his junk. What the heck is wrong with you?* She quickly lifted her eyes to meet his, and her cheeks heated. "Um...oh." *Oh? That's all I could come up with? Jeez.*

"See? Told you." He offered her an uneasy grin as he set down his bags and wiped away a bead of sweat trickling down his temple. "Is it just me or is it hot in here?"

It wasn't all that warm outside today, and she'd even left the air conditioner running in the truck. So no, it wasn't hot in there. But it seemed a sweltering heat wave had suddenly invaded both of their bodies. "Would you like some water? I put a bottle in the fridge before I left. It's probably not cold yet, but I can pour it into a cup of ice for you."

He swallowed audibly. "Yeah, that would be great."

Jess moved around him and reached into the fridge for a bottle of water. Just like she thought, it wasn't very cold. So she got him a paper cup and tossed some ice into it before filling it with the water. She took her sweet time in doing so just in case he needed a moment to rearrange himself.

After a few minutes, she finally handed him the water. "Here ya go."

"Thanks," he said before taking a large gulp.

"You're welcome."

As he drank his water, Max regarded her with curious eyes. His gaze seemed to be drawn to her lips. Which only made them go dry and made her continually lick them. Every time her tongue darted out, his brows rose a little higher. But the longer they stood there looking at each other in silence, the more an unbearable awkwardness crept in.

When his jaw suddenly tightened and his eyes filled

with something that looked a lot like regret, Jessa grew concerned. "What's wrong?"

"I, um..." As if he were nervous, he ran his long fingers through his thick brown hair. "Look, I can't do this anymore. I...I need to tell you something."

"Okay. What is it?"

He hesitated. "It's just that..." His words trailed off as his wide eyes flickered over her face. Then he cringed and shoved the paper cup toward her. "I'm out of water."

Hmm. That wasn't at all what she thought he was going to say. She accepted the cup from him. "Would you like some more?"

"No, thanks. I should probably get going."

"Okay. Well, thank you for helping me with the boxes. I really appreciate it. I'd left my dolly behind by accident. I don't think I would've made it back to the truck with all of those boxes on my own."

He pulled open the door and started through it. "You're welcome."

"Max?"

He stopped just outside and glanced back at her. "Yeah?"

"Will you be coming by the park later?"

He hesitated but eventually shrugged. "I don't know. I guess you just never know when or where I'll pop up." He must've realized what he said because he glanced down at his groin and cringed. "Uh, I didn't mean—"

She raised a hand to stop him. "It's okay. I know what you meant."

Max sighed again. "See ya around, Jess." Without waiting for a response, he walked away while shaking his head.

Jessa stayed in the doorway and blew out a large breath. There was something strange about that man. Something she couldn't quite put her finger on. For a moment, she'd been sure he was about to admit to being attracted to her. But he hadn't. And now she was left wondering why.

He obviously liked her. Why else would he be flirting with her and stopping by her truck every day? Besides that, what else could it be?

Maybe his job as the health inspector and her role as a business owner made it difficult for him to openly admit his attraction to her. After all, other people in town could easily view it as unethical. And that would actually explain all the mixed signals she was getting from him. Hot one minute, cold the next.

But she didn't give a damn what anyone else thought. There was something about Max that spoke to her, that made him absolutely irresistible. Sure, he was handsome and nice to look at. But that wasn't it. There was more to him than that. He reminded her of a dormant volcano. Calm and poised on the surface, but all this heat and passion bubbling inside of him. And that intrigued the hell out of her.

Whatever. She couldn't stand around trying to figure Max out all day. She needed to hurry and put everything away if she was going to make it to the park on time to open for the Saturday lunch crowd. The last thing she wanted to do was disappoint her customers.

Jessa pivoted toward the stacked boxes and reached into the top one to grab an onion. But when she pulled her hand back, she froze in place.

In her hand was a big, juicy grapefruit.

She knew she hadn't ordered any and briefly considered that she'd picked up the wrong box from one of the vendors. But then she remembered dropping this particular box on the ground and gathering everything that had fallen out of it. There had been no grapefruit in it at the time. Only peppers and onions.

She lifted onto her tiptoes and peered into the box. The peppers and onions were still inside, but several more grapefruit perched on top of them. Probably close to half a bag. She glanced back at the door where Max had stood moments before and blinked in shock.

He shared his grapefruit with me?

She hadn't expected the sweet gesture and thought it was very considerate of him. Especially since it wasn't like it was readily available to him. He'd already told her that he couldn't get more of it without traveling down to the Texas valley, which, by his own admission, was too far for him to drive for a bag of fruit.

Damn it. Why did he have to go and do something so nice?

Jessa rolled the ruby red ball around in her palm. Why had he left without mentioning it? Most people would've wanted some sort of recognition for their good deed. Or at the very least a proper thank-you. Strangely, Max had denied himself both.

* * *

Max breathed a sigh of relief as Jessa waved good-bye to her last customer of the evening. The two women had stood there chatting about who knows what for the last twenty minutes while he'd waited in the shadows for the customer to leave. Once the woman's car pulled away from the curb, Max stepped out onto the sidewalk and strolled toward the Gypsy Cantina.

He felt like a stalker. Probably looked like one too.

It hadn't really been all that dark out when he'd first arrived. But while he'd waited for his chance to approach the food truck without anyone recognizing him, the ominous curtain of darkness had fallen fast around him. He wasn't complaining though. That had only made it easier to see what Jessa had been doing inside the lit-up truck.

Max wasn't sure how many hours she'd put in during the past week, but it had to be a lot. She was always there from early in the morning until late into the evening. And she hadn't taken a single day off either. He should know. He'd been watching her every move. *Okay, maybe that did qualify me as a stalker, after all.*

Jessa would probably think so too after he'd run into her at the farmers' market yesterday. Max was still kicking himself for that one. He couldn't believe that he had actually helped her carry her produce to the truck and then left grapefruit for her. What the hell was wrong with him? He wasn't going to get rid of her by doing shit like that.

And that's exactly why he hadn't stopped by her truck last night. After their accidental run-in, it was clear that he wasn't in the right frame of mind to do what needed to be done. Which was to force her into leaving town. So instead he'd gone to the gym and spent two hours working out. In the past, that had always helped to clear his mind. And lately, his mind had needed a lot of clearing.

Max stopped just outside the truck. Through the window, Max had a side view of Jessa leaning over the grill, her arms working back and forth as she gave it a good scrubbing. Her wavy, red locks bounced around in the ponytail on the back of her head, and a slight sheen of perspiration shone on her forehead.

Focused completely on the task at hand, Jessa didn't even notice him standing there. As if she were deep in thought, her teeth chewed relentlessly on her bottom lip, pulling it into her mouth before biting down on it. Max grinned. He'd give anything to have a little nibble of those beautiful, ripe lips himself. Because if the woman tasted as good as she looked, then he would be in...

Ah, hell. Trouble. He'd be in a whole lot of trouble, that's what.

Maybe he already was.

Jessa had clearly caught him unawares. Like she had somehow slipped through his defenses, and he couldn't seem to shake her. No wonder why he'd been acting like such a confused idiot whenever she was around. *She* was what was wrong with him. The woman was pretty, kind, and hardworking. With traits like that, it made it impossible to view her as the enemy.

Not that he wanted to be mean to her. Of course he didn't. But he only had two weeks left before the end of the month, and he really needed to get her out of there before then. Unfortunately, the thought of doing so felt a lot like taking a hard fist to the gut. How the hell do you make someone leave when you don't really want them to go?

There were so many things about her that drew him in as well as surprised him. Like her great attitude, quick laughter, unrelenting patience, and ambitious nature. No wonder why he was so damn attracted to her. Jessa had everything he looked for in a woman.

God. Why the fuck did she have to be a good person?

"Max?"

He jolted, surprised by the sound of her voice. "Uh, hi."

"Why are you standing out there like that?"

He shifted uncomfortably. "I'm just…checking out your awning."

Panic flashed in her eyes. "Uh-oh. Did I violate another code?" she asked, her tone strained with worry. "If I did, I'm sorry. Let me know what's wrong with it, and I'll go buy a new awning first thing in the morning."

Well, that made him feel like a dick. Why hadn't he said he was checking out the stars or something? At least then she wouldn't be worrying that she'd violated another one of his fake codes.

He leaned against the truck with his arm on the ordering window's counter. "No, Jess. That wasn't what I meant. It's a great awning. No need to replace anything."

She exhaled a slow breath. "Thank goodness. I'm really trying to watch what I'm spending this week to keep from going over my budget."

Oh man. Was she having money problems like Pops? God, he hoped not. Especially after he'd bullied her into buying tablecloths and extra trash cans that she hadn't technically needed to purchase. He hadn't even considered her financial situation at the time. But then he noticed the tip jar in the window next to him. It was stuffed full of coins and dollar bills, and there were even some fives and tens in there.

Surely she wasn't having money issues if she made

that much in tips during only one shift. Relief spread through him, and he sighed. Thank God. He didn't want her to go broke. He just wanted her to go.

Well, actually he didn't really want that either. But he couldn't see any other way around it. If she stayed, she would continue taking Pops' customers. So there was no other choice. She had to leave. Didn't she?

Damn it, the whole situation was really starting to confuse him. It was as if her mere presence had thrown him once again. Why did this have to be so difficult?

A soft hand slid onto his arm, snaring his attention. "By the way, Max, I wanted to thank you for the grapefruit. That was very sweet of you."

His eyes met hers, and his stomach knotted. Her touching his forearm wasn't blatantly sexual or anything. Rather more of a friendly gesture. But somehow it seemed more intimate coming from her than it did with other women. In fact, every time Jessa's smooth, silky skin brushed against his in any way, an overwhelming urge to bury himself in that soft body of hers spiraled through him.

He cleared his throat to keep from sounding like a teenage boy going through puberty. "You're welcome."

She smiled and turned away as she gathered up all of her dirty kitchen utensils and set them inside a small gray tub inside the sink. "You didn't have to leave any grapefruit for me. I feel bad that you shared something that was meant as a gift for you."

Max shrugged, though she didn't see it with her back turned to him. "It's fine," he said, brushing off his good deed. It was just grapefruit. No big deal. "I probably wouldn't have eaten all of them before they spoiled anyway." Besides, he didn't deserve any praise after he'd spent the past week lying to her face. The only thing he deserved was a swift kick in his ass for doing so to begin with. Hell, she'd probably never speak to him again if she found out the truth.

"Well, I just wanted you to know I appreciated the gesture. I was so excited to try one that I didn't even wait until I got to work. I ate it while I was still in the parking lot of the farmers' market."

Max grinned. "What'd you think?"

She glanced over her shoulder at him and grinned. "It was as juicy and delicious as I thought it would be. A little bitter, of course, but it had a nice hint of sweetness. The rind was flawless, and the red pulp looked picture perfect. I'm pretty sure that was the best grapefruit I've ever eaten."

Something squeezed inside his chest. Not only did he like knowing that he could make her smile, but he could almost hear the passion for food and genuine excitement in the tone of her voice. Even if it was over something as small as a grapefruit. "I'm glad you liked it, Jess."

"I really did. In fact, I'm going to have to figure out a way of getting more so I can put it in something on my menu. I was thinking maybe a grapefruit and avocado salad or something."

Max cocked his head. Hmm. That actually sounded pretty good. He'd just been juicing the fruit or eating them for breakfast in the mornings. He never considered putting the wedges in a salad with some avocado. It was a great idea and definitely something he wanted to try. "You know, Miss Betty's son is a truck driver, and he takes scheduled trips down to the valley every few weeks to drop off some of her produce at a market down there. If you'd like, I can ask her for his phone number. He would probably be willing to pick them up for you whenever he's heading back down. I never wanted to trouble him to stop for just one bag, but if you plan on getting more than that, I'm sure he would be interested in cutting a deal with you."

"Really?" She wiped her hands on a dish towel and turned to face him. "That would be amazing, Max. I guess I owe you another thank-you."

He shook his head. "It isn't necessary."

"As far as I'm concerned, it's always necessary to show your appreciation to someone who does something nice for you. So thank you."

Nodding, Max said, "It's not a problem."

Which wasn't really true. It *was* a huge problem. Why the hell was he helping her again? This was the exact opposite of what he was supposed to be doing. Damn it. Instead of running her out of town, he was treating her like an invited guest. What was he going to do next— fluff a pillow for her and then prop her feet up? Jeez.

Somehow he'd gotten way off track with this plan. He needed to remember what he was doing this for. Or actually *who* he was doing this for. Pops. The old man had nothing left but his café. If he lost it now, it would be all Max's fault. All because he was sweet on Jessa and couldn't stop doing nice things for her. God, he was such a moron.

This was why each visit to her truck had become more nerve-racking than the last. Every time he got anywhere near her, he started doing stupid shit. That was the kind of effect she had on him. Well, among others. He'd never in his life spent so much time in the shower jacking himself off as he had in the last week.

Unless, of course, you count the time in tenth grade when Celia Rogers had squished her ample breasts against him while squeezing past him in the hallway. He'd pleasured himself for a month straight over that particular incident. Sadly, once he'd found out that her friends had dared her to do it, the inciting incident had quickly lost its luster.

Hopefully, the same thing would happen with Jessa. He just needed to figure out how to snuff out the flame growing inside of him…which he clearly wasn't going to do if he kept standing there staring at her backside all night. "Well, I guess I'd better head out and let you finish closing up."

"I'm almost done here anyway," Jessa said with her back still to him. "I'm just trying to batten down the hatches before I roll out. Everything in here has to be stowed away before I can leave. Otherwise, it'll be flying around back here while I'm driving down the road. The last thing I want to do is to replace something else."

Max gazed at the overflowing tip jar once again and sighed. Though she probably wasn't completely broke or hurting for money, he never should've forced her into buying the tablecloths and trash cans last week. That hadn't been fair. And since it was *his* fault that Jessa had spent her hard-earned money on those things because of a lie he'd told, it was only right that he pay for them.

Reaching into his pocket, he pulled out a hundred-dollar bill. It was the only money he had on him at the moment, but it would probably be enough to cover the expenses of what she'd bought at his suggestion. Without hesitation, Max leaned forward and deposited the bill inside the jar.

He'd barely pulled his hand free when Jessa turned around to face him. "Will I see you tomorrow?"

Max shrugged nonchalantly. "Probably."

"All right. Have a good night, Max."

"Thanks. You too."

Though guilt swam through him at the thought of betraying Pops, Max walked back to his truck with his hands in his empty pockets and a huge grin on his face. The deed was done, and Jessa hadn't apparently noticed a thing. He regretted that he had once again failed Pops, but Max liked knowing that he'd done the right thing. Even if he couldn't tell Jessa the truth.

Chapter Six

Jessa arrived at the commercial kitchen where she rented space to find a stocky Hispanic man in his late thirties waiting on her under a security light. As usual, Mario was right on time.

She waved at him as she backed the truck up to the doors of the kitchen and came to a full stop. It took her a moment to get out since she had to gather her money bag and all of her paperwork, but Mario didn't hesitate. He threw open the back door of the food truck and got straight to work with unloading.

She didn't know what she would do without him. Not only did he work hard for her, but he had always taken initiative and never stood around waiting for orders. She loved that about him.

When she'd first hired Mario, his job had been to help her stock the truck in the mornings. But the moment he found out Jessa had been unloading and cleaning the truck out all by herself at night, he'd started showing up then too. She had always made sure she paid him for all of his time, of course, but had to laugh when he remarked that she was too little to carry all of those boxes by herself.

Little? Ha! Short, maybe. Jessa definitely wouldn't call herself little. She had thick thighs and too many side rolls to be classified that way. But it didn't matter to her. Even though she could probably stand to lose a few extra pounds, she was otherwise okay with her full, womanly figure. Liked it even. Not every woman needed to be a size six or have a perfectly flat tummy. None of that would change her worth as a decent human being or make her a more valuable member of society.

Besides, there were plenty of guys out there who liked a woman with some meat on her bones. Sexy wasn't a size; it was a state of mind.

Arms full, she climbed out of the cab and headed for the kitchen. She reached the door just as Mario came out to grab another load from the truck. "How'd you do today, boss?" he asked with a thick Spanish accent.

"I think we did well. I won't know for sure until I figure the receipts, but it's the third day in a row that we sold out of almost everything."

He nodded his approval. "Good. I'm glad to hear it."

"Well, you probably shouldn't be. I might have to start stocking more food onto the truck."

Not one to shy away from work, Mario grinned. "No problem. Just let me know what you want to add in the morning, and I'll make sure it's on the truck."

"Thanks," Jessa told him as she continued inside to put her things down.

Once she'd done so, she headed back out to help him unload the last few boxes and food storage bins. After several trips, the truck was completely unloaded. Jessa went back inside to start on the paperwork and wash the dirty dishes while Mario finished up with the truck outside.

The used oil from the fryer needed to be drained into the grease trap, the trash needed to be deposited into the Dumpster, and every surface inside the truck needed to be washed and sanitized thoroughly. If it hadn't been for Mario's willingness to show up at night and help out, she would easily be stuck there another hour making sure it was all taken care of. The man was a godsend.

Jessa totaled all of her receipts, counted the money she had taken in, and went through all of the figures twice. All of that checked out perfectly. But something strange happened. When she counted the tip money, she found a hundred-dollar bill! She'd never found that large of a tip in the jar before, so where had it come from? The last customer who ordered from her had given a tip, but the woman had never touched the tip jar. That woman had handed Jessa her cash and told her to keep the change. And no one else came by after that. Well, except for . . . Max?

No. That's too silly to even consider. Why the heck would he tip me a hundred dollars? He didn't even order anything.

Then she remembered that he *had* been standing at the counter where the money jar had been sitting. Not only that, but at one point, she had turned around to tell him good-bye and distinctly remembered seeing his hand near the tip jar. She hadn't thought anything of it at the time, but now it seemed to make sense. But why in the world would he give her money? Especially that large of an amount. Was he insane? He had to be. Who else in their right mind would go around tipping someone a hundred dollars for doing nothing?

With questions swimming through her mind, Jessa stared absently at the wall. She didn't know how long she'd been doing so when a female voice registered in her ears. "Is it going to change colors?"

"Huh?" Jessa twisted her neck to see Valerie coming through the inside door linking the kitchen with her bar, Bottoms Up.

Valerie grinned wide, flashing her pearly whites. "The wall. Are you waiting for it to do something?"

"Oh. No, sorry. I just...well, I guess I was lost in thought."

"What's wrong?"

Jessa shook her head. "Nothing. I was just wondering about something, that's all."

"Maybe I can help?"

"I doubt it. Unless you can tell me why some guy tipped me a hundred dollars."

Her eyes widened. "Damn, Jess. How much food did he order from you?"

"Well, that's the puzzling part. He didn't order anything from me. He just slipped a hundred-dollar bill into the tip jar, and I can't figure out why." Jessa paused as what she said sank in. "Actually, now that I think about it, he's never ordered anything from my truck. At least not while I've been there. And that seems to be the only time he shows up. Mary and Lisa would've mentioned it if he showed up during their shifts."

"Maybe he likes you."

Heat crept up Jessa's neck and into her cheeks.

Valerie smirked. "Judging by the way you just changed colors, I'm assuming he's not the only one who has a little crush going on."

That only made Jessa blush more. "Well, we have been sort of flirting for the past week. But I wouldn't think that would be the reason he'd drop money into my tip jar. That seems a little creepy and inappropriate. Especially since it's not like I need the..." Her words trailed off as she remembered the conversation she had with Max earlier in the night. "Oh."

Valerie raised one eyebrow. "Oh? Oh, what? What does that mean?"

"While we were talking earlier, I mentioned that I didn't want to spend any more money this week. But that wasn't because I couldn't afford it. It was because I like to keep my food costs down for my customers. I think he might've taken what I said out of context."

"Ah, I see. So he thought he was helping you then?"

"I guess so." Max's sweet gesture filled her with warmth, but the fuzzy feelings warred with the guilt of knowing she hadn't deserved the money he had given her. "I'll have to give it back to him. It was nice of him to do that, but it wasn't necessary. I just hope he'll take it back."

Valerie smiled. "Well, if he doesn't, tell this guy to come hang out at the bar for a few hours. I'd love to serve him a thing or two."

Jessa giggled, but a man's curt voice cut through the air. "Val, you better be talking about alcohol."

Both women glanced in the direction of the voice and

spied Valerie's fiancé, Logan, standing in the open doorway connected to the bar.

Valerie laughed. "Of course I'm talking about serving him drinks. I'd love to have this guy as a customer."

Logan strolled farther into the room. "Who?"

Jessa grinned. "A really big tipper."

"Hell, then send him my way. I like big tippers too."

Valerie shook her head. "From what Jess just told me, I don't think you're his type. Actually, I'm probably not either. It seems the guy likes cute redheads who can cook."

"So who is this mystery man?" Logan asked, leaning his hip against the counter.

Jessa shrugged. "Just a guy in town that's been a little flirty. I probably shouldn't say who he is since there's a conflict of interest where he's concerned. I doubt it will lead to anything between us anyway."

Logan frowned. "He's not married, is he?"

"Logan!" Valerie's eyes widened. "That's none of your business."

He cringed at her words. "You're right. It's not." Then he gazed back at Jessa. "That was rude of me to ask. I'm sorry."

Jessa smiled at him. "It's okay. And the answer is no. As far as I know, he's not married. It's more of a work conflict, not a personal one."

He nodded. "Okay. Well, if you don't want this guy hanging around, let me know, and I'll have a talk with him. I don't want you feeling like you're in a tough spot and not able to get out of it."

"Thanks. I appreciate that," Jessa said. "It's nice knowing I have friends here who are willing to go out of their way to help me out. You two have already done so much for me. I don't know how I'm ever going to repay you."

Valerie reached over and squeezed Jessa's hand. "You don't need to repay us for anything. We love having you here. I only hope things work out with the food truck so you'll end up staying here. I would miss you terribly if you left. Even though it's only been a few short weeks, I've already grown attached to you and am used to having you around."

"I second that," Logan said, nodding.

Jessa smiled at the adorable couple.

It had taken months and months of careful planning for her idea to come to fruition. But now that it had, she couldn't believe how well everything was going. For the past few weeks, she'd been testing out her signature menu items on the locals. Gourmet comfort food with low prices was a concept that was relatively unknown in this area. But her unique take on it had been well received. She'd created a buzz in this small community, one that was even bringing in new customers from the next town over.

"No worries. I don't see me going anywhere. Business has been booming since I got into town. If this keeps up, I'm going to have enough money to open my restaurant sooner than I thought."

Valerie squealed and gave her a hug. "That's great news, Jess! I'm so excited for you."

"Congrats," Logan told her. "I'm glad you've found a home here, Jess."

She truly had. Granite was different from any place she'd ever lived before. The only thing that would make this place even more perfect was if Jessa's mother could've been here in person to see how well her daughter's food truck business was doing and share in her joy. She would've loved that. "Thank you. Really, I mean that. You two letting me rent your commercial kitchen has been instrumental in making this happen for me."

Logan shook his head. "It was just good timing all around. If I hadn't met you in the grocery store when I did, this kitchen would still be sitting here unused. I'm just glad we finally found something to do with the space."

Jessa knew Logan was just being kind. Not everyone would have gone out of their way to help out a stranger they'd just met. But he'd offered the kitchen to her as if they'd been friends for years. He hadn't even considered charging her for the space until she refused to use it unless he accepted a monthly rent and allowed her to reimburse him for the licensing fees. Only then had he caved.

Who knew she would have found such amazing friends so fast? And really, that was just the start of good things to come. She could feel it.

So yeah, she wasn't going anywhere. As far as Jessa was concerned, her moving days were over.

* * *

Max scoped out the food truck before he approached to make certain no one in line would recognize him. He knew he was taking another risk by showing up right before lunch rush, but he needed to try something different. So far, everything else he'd been doing hadn't worked.

Unfortunately, he was no closer to getting her to leave now than he had been the first day he'd met her. And that really frustrated the hell out of him.

Never in his life had he met a more compliant, more detail-oriented, more eager-to-please woman than Jessa. And it was slowly driving him insane.

But enough was enough. He couldn't sit around dropping hints and subliminal messages anymore, hoping she'd point her truck out of town and hit the gas pedal.

So if that meant showing up at her busiest time to hassle her and make things more uncomfortable, then so be it. That was exactly what he was going to do. Because it was now or never. If this plan didn't work, he didn't have anything else that would get her to leave.

He was almost to the truck when he caught sight of Jessa stepping outside in a pink tie-dye halter top, a pair of cut-off denim shorts, and white flip-flops. She was carrying a small tray of food in one hand and a soda in the other. But before he reached her, she began walking in the opposite direction.

Max quickened his pace. "Hey, Jess."

She stopped and glanced back. "Hi. What are you doing here?"

"Just came to check up on you." *And give you a hard time.*

"Again?" she said teasingly.

Max just grinned.

"Well, I'm taking my lunch break before we get too busy. Are you hungry? You could always grab something and come eat with me, if you want." She gestured to a vacant picnic table a few yards away.

He hated to sit out in the open in case someone recognized him and stopped by the table to talk, but it would probably be too obvious to ask her to eat her lunch in his truck. "That's okay, I already ate. But I don't mind keeping you company while you do."

"Great."

They walked together to the table and slid their legs under it. Jessa removed the cap on her bottle of soda while gazing over at him. "You never come by this early anymore. You usually show up at closing time."

He shrugged. "I have plans later."

"Oh." She paused before taking a sip of her drink, and her forehead wrinkled. "You...uh, have a date or something?"

Max recognized disappointment when he saw it, and for some strange reason, he wanted her to know that he wasn't dating anyone. "No, it's not a date. Just a work thing. But it's going to keep me busy all evening long." Which was his own fault since he'd gotten off work early just to come see her.

Since she was technically on her lunch break, he was going to be a gentleman and give her a short reprieve. The last thing he wanted was for anyone else to overhear him pretending to be the health inspector. But the moment she was done eating and back to work, her stay of execution was over. He wasn't exactly sure how, but he planned to antagonize the hell out of her in whatever way he could. He was sure he would think of something by the time she got back to work.

"Sorry, but you're going to have to do most of the talking. I skipped breakfast this morning, and I'm starving to death. But don't worry, I'll listen and nod in appropriate moments." She giggled as she turned her attention to her tray.

Max glanced down at her food and licked his dry lips. Damn, those tacos looked and smelled great. Pieces of cooked steak and colorful peppers were nestled inside a corn tortilla with some kind of sweet-smelling green sauce drizzled on top. The tacos looked so good, in fact, that they easily rivaled dishes he'd seen cooked by professional chefs on The Food Network channel. Impressive.

Mouth watering, he watched as she pinched the two halves of one shell together and lifted the taco out of her paper boat. She leaned forward to take her first bite, and juices dripped from beneath her chin into the container below. Max's stomach growled quietly. He didn't know why he had agreed to this kind of torture.

Once she swallowed, she hummed appreciatively. "I'm totally patting myself on the back right now, but these are so good, I could eat them all day long."

If they tasted as great as they smelled, Max really couldn't blame her. But he sighed. "While I admire your commitment, you should probably rethink that decision. And you probably shouldn't skip meals either. It's not healthy."

She squinted at him. "Did *you* eat breakfast this morning?"

"Of course. I had steel-cut oatmeal and fresh fruit."

Jessa giggled. "Would it be weird if I tell you that you eat like my grandmother?"

He grinned. "Your grandma must like to stay healthy."

"Not anymore. She died when I was ten."

"I'm sorry to hear that."

"It's okay. It was a long time ago. And she did live well into her eighties."

"Must've been all those good-for-you breakfast foods she ate." He winked to show her he was teasing.

"Probably," she said with a laugh. "So I take it you eat healthy a lot then?"

"All the time."

"No way. No one eats healthy all the time."

He shrugged. "I do. And I work out at the gym a lot too."

"I figured you did. You have a lot of bulges." She must've realized what she said because Jessa's eyes widened. "Oh, wait. I didn't mean that the way it came out. I just meant—"

"It's okay. I understood what you meant," Max said, chuckling. "And trust me, I worked hard for these...bulges."

A quick pink blush settled into her cheeks, but she smiled. "Oh, believe me, I worked hard for my bulges too." She snickered at herself. "Sorry, that was a fat-girl joke."

Max shook his head. "That wasn't at all funny."

"It was to me."

"You really shouldn't say things like that about yourself."

"Why not? It's true." She took another bite of her taco.

"I don't think so. You should be kinder to yourself. You're beautiful and have an amazing figure." When her eyes lifted to meet his, he smirked. "What? You think I didn't notice?"

Jessa swallowed and wiped her mouth with a paper napkin. "Well, I had a feeling." She set her taco down and blotted the juice from her fingers. "The thing is, I know being plus-sized bothers some women, but it doesn't really faze me at all. I'm a total foodie and enjoy eating what I want. If my size bothers someone else, then that's on them. I'm happy the way I am."

"I wish more women had that attitude about their bodies. It's a great one to have."

"Thanks," she said, picking up her taco and finishing it off.

Wait. Why was he being so nice when he was supposed to be waging war on the woman? Fuck. Okay, that was it. Amnesty hour was over as of right now.

She glanced over at the food truck. "We're getting busier already."

Damn it. The last thing he needed was someone to spot him sitting with her and then come over to talk to him. "Better hurry up with your other taco then."

Jessa nodded. "It's okay. That's only the first wave of customers. Lisa and Mary can handle them by themselves for a few more minutes."

Max glanced at the line and shook his head. There were so many of Pops' old customers in that line. He just didn't get it. "Why do so many people want to eat at a food truck anyway? Especially when they can go into a sit-down restaurant."

She shrugged. "Street food is...I don't know, sexy and appealing."

Funny. He thought the same thing about her. "But it's also very fattening."

"Not all of them are. There are plenty of trucks where you can get turkey wraps, salads, or veggie burgers. I've also seen trucks that juice fresh vegetables, make healthy smoothies, and serve cucumber water. So there are some healthier options."

"Not here, there aren't."

"Hmm. That may be true for this area. But it isn't like one higher-fat meal on occasion would ruin anyone's diet anyway. It's all about moderation." She gestured to the chalkboard on the side of the truck. "Even I have some options that aren't as high in fat and calories as others. I'm not saying they're as low-cal as they could be, but they're not all that bad for you. Maybe you should pick something off the menu and see what you think."

He didn't even glance at the menu. "No thanks."

"Oh, come on. You could at least try something, Max. As much time as you spend around here, you should at least taste the food. In fact, it'll be on the house. My treat," she said with a smile.

Max shook his head. "Thanks, but I'm not interested."

Her mouth was set in a grim line. She apparently hadn't expected him to refuse her offer of a free meal. Probably because most people wouldn't have. But he wasn't like most people.

"All right. But would you at least try a bite of mine then?" She picked up the plastic fork on the side of her tray and stabbed a chunk of steak with it. Then she lifted it to his lips as she waited for him to open his mouth. "Just one taste."

The scent of the meat under his nose was rich and intoxicating, but it only made him feel like a raging alcoholic at a whiskey convention. One taste of that and he'd be hooked and fall right off the wagon. "No," he said firmly.

She frowned. "Why not? What's it going to hurt to try it?"

"My diet." He crinkled his nose at the bite in front of him. "Sorry, but I just don't eat crap like that."

Her body tensed, and her hand fisted on the table. "Crap? Seriously?" She shook her head in disbelief as the pitch of her voice rose higher. "Don't you think that's an unfair assessment of my food since you've never even tasted any of it?"

Max wasn't trying to offend her or insult her food. The comment had only slipped out because he never ate red meat. At least not anymore. But he was a little surprised by the amount of outrage showing on her face. Wide eyes. Pursed lips. Set jaw. Hell, if he had known she would've gotten this upset over something like that, he would've done it a week ago. He wanted to grin at the thought, but he was afraid he'd get punched in the nose if he did.

Still, he felt a little bad about it. Even though he enjoyed seeing that lovely flash of fire shooting through her gorgeous blue eyes. He hadn't known she had it in her, but it took his breath away and sent sparks of pleasure straight to his balls. Too bad *she* wasn't on the menu...because Max would definitely have ordered some of that.

"I'm waiting," she said, still holding the fork up to his lips.

He groaned. "Look, I already told you I—"

Without warning, Jessa quickly shoved the morsel into his open mouth. Caught off guard by the unexpected move, his lips automatically closed around the fork as she pulled it away, which left the piece of beef behind in his mouth. The piece of steak rolled across his tongue as the juices coated his taste buds. Though he hadn't even chewed, an explosion of intense flavor hit him so hard that he nearly moaned out loud.

Holy hell.

Sadly, he used to consider himself a meat-and-potatoes type of guy. But after a big change to his lifestyle had overhauled his diet, Max now considered himself more of a protein-shake-and-baked-sweet-potato type of man. Didn't mean that he didn't miss red meat though. Still, no matter how badly he wanted to chew and swallow and get the full drugging effect of the tasty, well-seasoned beef, he just couldn't do it.

Not without ruining his diet and regaining some of his old, bad habits.

Yes, the steak morsel was insanely delicious. And yeah, it was such a small piece that it shouldn't matter. But Max knew himself well, and that one slip-up on his diet was usually enough to set him back for months. He just couldn't give in to that kind of temptation. Ever. But that didn't mean he couldn't use this as a perfect opportunity to work Jessa into more of a frenzy.

Unable to help himself, Max spit the small bite out into the palm of his hand. Then he purposely cringed and held it far away from him like it was the most disgusting thing he'd ever tasted.

Jessa's mouth fell open, and fury lit her eyes. She was clearly shocked by his reaction to the taste of her food. He'd accidentally stumbled onto a way to get her worked up. Good.

He shoved the urge to laugh down deep and glanced

around for the nearest garbage can. "Where can I put this?"

Her eyes narrowed. "Well, my second choice would be in the trash."

He lifted one brow. "Do I want to know what your first choice would've been?"

"Probably not."

Chapter Seven

Jessa thrummed her fingers on the picnic table.

Irritated didn't even begin to describe how she was feeling in this moment after seeing Max spit out her food. In front of her. Like a two-year-old. The jerk.

Okay, so maybe it wasn't real mature for her to force the bite of meat on him in the first place. He *had* specifically said he didn't want it. But instead of acting like a big baby, couldn't he just have humored her and swallowed the damn thing?

As she watched him walking back from the trash can, a fresh round of frustration coursed through her veins. That had been the first time in her life that anyone had ever turned down a free meal from her. And although she knew it was silly, it had hurt her feelings.

She had no doubt that was the chef in her talking, the one who wanted everyone to love what she made for them. She always wanted to win people over, astound them with her talent for cooking, and turn them into happy repeat customers.

She'd hoped to win Max over with her food too, but clearly that wasn't going to happen. If he had tried it once and not liked it, then that would've been one thing. But he hadn't even given it half a chance. And she really wanted him to.

Then again, what did it matter if Max didn't give her food a fair shake? Who was he to snub his nose at her dish anyway? It's not like the guy was some Michelin-starred chef or something. Why the hell did she even care that he didn't have great taste and probably couldn't tell the difference between a good piece of prime beef or an old lump of shoe leather?

She sighed. *Because I like him, that's why. And I want him to like me... including my cooking.* Damn it. "I'm sorry. I shouldn't have done that. It wasn't right for me to force you to take a bite like that."

He shrugged. "It's okay. Don't worry about it."

They sat in silence for a moment. "So, um... did you at least get a small taste of it?" *Oh God, I'm actually fishing for a freakin' compliment. How pathetic is that?*

"Well, as I stated earlier, I don't usually eat... *stuff* like that. But I can tell you that the small taste I got wasn't too bad. It almost reminded me of the food at the Pearl Oyster," he said with a smirk.

Jessa gasped, offended by the comparison. "Are you kidding me right now?"

Max shook his head, but his grin widened. "I don't know what you mean."

"Since I first came to town, I've heard nothing but

horror stories about the food in that place. Everyone constantly talks about how nasty it is."

"Have you eaten there yet?"

"No, of course not. I mean, it's not like it comes highly recommended or anything. Why would I go to a restaurant that other people warn me away from?"

He shrugged nonchalantly. "Don't knock it until you try it then."

Try it, hell. She had one customer who swore the food was so bad at the Pearl Oyster that the lady said she was tempted to burn the place down herself to stop them from ever serving another meal. At the time, Jessa had giggled about it. But now, knowing that Max thought her food was similar to theirs, she only wanted to prove him wrong. Dead wrong.

An idea ran through her head, and she bit her lip. "Fine. I will, if you will."

"Huh?" Max blinked at her, clearly not understanding what she meant.

"The Pearl Oyster. I want to try it...and I would like you to join me."

He stared at her in complete silence, as if she'd asked him to impregnate her with a turkey baster. "If you heard it's not a good place to eat, why the hell would you want to go there?"

"Because you said my food reminded you of theirs and implied it was good. But that's not what I hear from everyone else. And it's not possible for them to be as good as you claim and as bad as I think they probably are. So one of us is wrong...and I want to see which one. Are you game?"

"I...uh, can't. I mean, as the health inspector, it

would be considered unprofessional, if not unethical, to go out to dinner with you, Jess."

She held her hand up. "I wasn't suggesting a date. I understand why that would be a conflict of interest. But that doesn't stop us from going to eat together as colleagues."

Max's face paled, and a bead of sweat formed over his brow. "Um, I really don't think that would be a good idea."

"Why not?"

Wiping at his brow, Max hesitated so long that she wasn't entirely sure he was going to answer her question at all. But then he finally said, "Because I don't think the city council would approve of me going to dinner with you. I'm sure they would be against me fraternizing with a business owner in such a manner."

There was no way she was letting Max out of this one. Maybe it was her competitive nature, but she felt like she had something to prove about her food. "Okay, fine. Then I'll go in to city hall and have a talk with the mayor about it in the morning. I'm sure I can convince him that this is a business arrangement only so that he'll approve of it." Jessa smiled. "In fact, I'll even invite him to join us."

"No," Max said firmly. He closed his eyes and dropped his head forward. She wasn't sure, but it sounded like he even breathed out a curse word. "I mean, that's not necessary. I'll go out to dinner with you, but let's keep it just between us. The less people who know about it, the better."

She smiled triumphantly. "All right. I know you have to work tonight so how about we go tomorrow night? I'll

ask Mary or Lisa if they can switch a shift with me. Will
that work for you?"

"Yeah," Max mumbled.

"Perfect." She pulled a pen out of her shirt pocket and
hastily scribbled her address on a napkin, sliding it toward Max. "Then it's a date."

He lifted his head and glared at her.

"Oh, sorry." She smiled. "Or not."

* * *

Max pulled into Jessa's driveway on time, but he didn't
get out of the truck right away. Instead, he stared at the
steering wheel as he contemplated bashing his head into
it a couple of times. He couldn't believe that he had
agreed to go out to dinner with her tonight. Not that he'd
had much of a choice.

The last thing he could let her do was to talk to
the mayor about him. Otherwise, she would've quickly
found out that he wasn't who he said he was. That
would've been a complete disaster...just like tonight
would be. *How the hell am I supposed to convince her
that I like the food at the Pearl Oyster when it tastes like
shit?*

A noise caught his attention, and he gazed out his
truck's window at her house. The setting sun had already
dipped behind the small dark gray cottage with the white
trim and black shutters, but there was still plenty of light
to see her stepping outside onto the tiny covered front
porch built out of mahogany-stained oak.

Thank God he'd gone with his gut and dressed in
a blue button-down shirt, black pants, and a black suit

jacket. Because when Jessa stepped off the porch, his jaw practically hit the ground.

Not a date, my ass.

The short pink dress was eye-catching and a bit revealing to say the least. A hint of shoulder. Flirty neckline. A whole lot of leg. And not at all what he had pictured her wearing when he picked her up.

Jessa usually had more of a chic bohemian style that suited her laid-back personality and happy-go-lucky ways. But the sexy woman walking toward him was nothing like the sweet, pretty Jessa he had become accustomed to over the past week. This Jessa was an erotic vision who wore a dazzling smile...and not much else.

He couldn't help but obsess over every sensual little detail of her body as she came closer. Long, wavy red hair. The gentle curve cinching her waist. The round slope of her hips. Silky smooth legs. The bare thigh peeking out from beneath her dress.

He stumbled out of the truck to greet her and nearly fell on his face. *Sonofabitch. When the hell had I gotten so clumsy?* "Hi," he said, righting himself and moving around to the passenger side to open her door for her. "You look different...uh, I mean, great."

"Thanks. So do you," she said, accepting the hand he offered her. She slid into the cab of his truck, coming perilously close to flashing him whatever was beneath that skirt. Thankfully, she managed to hold the front of her material down to keep it from drifting higher up her legs.

Max quickly darted around to the driver's seat and climbed inside. He started the engine and pointed the nose of his truck toward their destination. "You let your hair down," Max said, wondering why that suddenly seemed so significant to him.

"I usually wear it down unless I'm at work." She fiddled with the gold bracelet on her wrist. "I don't usually wear jewelry or any other kind of accessories either. They tend to get in the way."

Max nodded. He understood that well. "I'm the same way. I only wear a watch when I'm on the construction site."

"Construction site?"

He froze. Shit. He hadn't meant to say that. "My best friend, Sam, runs a construction crew, and I visit him on site occasionally. Ya know, just to say hello."

"Oh, I see. For a second I thought you must've changed career paths on me."

Damn it. He needed to change the subject before he let anything else slip out. "So are you ready to eat?" *God, why did I have to say that? Just the thought of eating there makes me sick. Ugh.*

She smiled, flashing her straight, white teeth. "Yes. I'm dying to try this place out. This should be, ah…interesting, I think."

His gaze fell onto her short hem, and his stomach tightened. *Not nearly as interesting as that dress.*

They arrived at the Pearl Oyster a few minutes later and strolled leisurely inside. Almost immediately, the maître d' greeted them and asked them to follow him, leading them into a fancy, nearly empty dining room.

Max placed his hand gently on the small of her back, guiding her to the table in the center of the room. He pulled out an elegant, high-back chair and waited for her to sit before taking a seat of his own across from her.

Pressed white linens covered the surface of the table, which was decorated with white silk peony centerpieces and gold-rimmed place settings. The maître d' offered them menus and filled their water glasses, and then Max ordered a bottle of their best wine before the waiter took his leave of absence.

"I hope you're okay with me ordering the wine."

"Sure. Sounds great." Jessa took in her surroundings. "It's so much prettier in here than I expected. I love those opaque globe chandeliers. They're lovely."

Max gazed up at the light fixtures. Their incandescent globes looked like oversized pearls with soft twinkling lights inside of them. "They're beautiful." He should know. He had been the one who wired them into place back when they opened. Made six hundred bucks on that job.

They looked over the menu in silence until the waiter returned with the wine and took their order. With so much sophistication in such a posh establishment, anyone would undoubtedly assume that their meal was being prepared by a professional, possibly award-winning chef. But Max knew better.

The Pearl Oyster had once been a great place to dine. But once the owner's youngest son took over the running of the kitchen, things had gone downhill fast. The restaurant's dining experience—and its reputation for putting out quality food—had quickly been ruined. It was a classy place with the worst cuisine anyone's ever tasted, a fact Jessa would soon be finding out.

While waiting for their appetizers to arrive, they chatted freely and drank a glass of wine. Max was careful to only have a small one that he sipped slowly, but Jessa poured freely from the bottle and was already working on her second glass. Since she wasn't the one driving home, it didn't really matter.

The waiter finally arrived with their salads. Max had ordered his with a light balsamic vinaigrette while Jessa had ordered a creamy buttermilk ranch dressing. He watched in horror as she took bite after bite of the side salad with the calorie-rich dressing, but he kept his comments and thoughts to himself.

Besides, there was a good chance that her salad was the only thing she'd be eating tonight anyway. It apparently had been some kind of prepackaged salad mix, and the cooks in the back hadn't been able to screw that up. But Max had been here enough times to know that he shouldn't hold out hope for a great meal. It never happened anymore in this place.

When their entrées were finally served, Max wanted to laugh at how fast the waiter dropped the dishes onto their table and hightailed it out of there. Apparently the poor guy was used to getting complaints on the food and didn't want to wait around.

Jessa glared at her plate, her mouth forming an even, grim line. "Well, none of this looks very appetizing."

He glanced over at her dinner and fought the urge to grin. "What's wrong?"

"Well, for starters, they overcooked my steak and forgot the Dijon cream sauce they were supposed to drizzle it with. And then there's this," she said, using a fork to lift a soggy blob of lobster from her plate. "It looks like an old sock that they drenched in butter."

Max cleared his throat to keep from laughing. "How about your side dishes? Are they okay at least?"

She frowned. "No. There's a layer of oil over the cheesy risotto, and the fried mushrooms are nothing but grease."

"Maybe they'll taste better than they look."

"How's yours?" she asked, glancing over at his plate.

The three-quarter-inch-thick amberjack filet Max had ordered sat atop a bed of brown rice with a side of heirloom carrots and asparagus. It was the lowest calorie dish on the menu, and the grilled fish actually looked pretty good on the plate.

"Mine is fine," he said prematurely, knowing that there would most definitely be something wrong with his as well.

He raked his fork into one side of the filet and pulled away a chunk of the fish. Almost immediately, he noticed that the center had not been thoroughly cooked. Thankfully, Jessa sat on the opposite side of the table and couldn't see the raw meat. So he pushed the piece back in place to hide the center and stabbed a carrot instead and bit into it. It was way harder than he'd expected, and it crunched between his teeth.

The sound had Jessa lifting her head. "Are your carrots undercooked?"

Max swallowed the hard, bland vegetable. "Not at all. They're perfectly cooked." *If raw is what they were aiming for.*

Max tried not to cringe as he watched Jessa try a bite of everything on her plate. She chewed on a tiny piece of her steak for what seemed like forever while scrunching her nose in disgust. Then she tried the fried mushrooms, which had her shuddering. After a bite of the risotto, he was pretty sure he heard her gag. And the lobster? Yeah, she spit that out into her napkin almost immediately.

With a frustrated sound of annoyance, Jessa glanced around the room. "Where's our waiter?"

Probably hiding in one of the bathroom stalls. "Not sure. Are you sending your food back?"

"God, yes. This is the worst food I've ever tasted. It's so bad that someone could end up in a hospital getting their stomachs pumped out after consuming it. I can't eat this...crap." Her eyes met his, and she sighed heavily.

The hair on the back of his neck prickled. He knew she was remembering when he'd said that very thing about her own food. He hadn't truly meant it though, damn it. Everyone in town knew that the food here sucked. Guilt coursed through him, and he wanted to kick himself in the ass.

He felt terrible that she'd taken his comment about her dish to heart. He had wanted to rile her up, not hurt her feelings. It didn't take a genius to know that any chef who had so many repeat customers wouldn't serve anyone crap. But apparently, he'd made her second-guess herself. He hated that.

"I haven't eaten here in a while. I guess the food has really gone downhill," he said, hoping that would help to soothe the wound his previous comment had caused. "When I was comparing your food to theirs, I was going off of memory. Their food used to be a lot better than this."

And he wasn't lying. At one time, they had offered great food. Of course, that had been a long time ago. It was surprising that they were even still in business.

Jessa rose from her chair. "Well, excuse me for a

minute. I'm going to go to the ladies' room. If you see our waiter though…"

"I'll have him take your plate away."

She smiled politely and headed out of the dining room. Probably to go throw up and then wash the horrible taste out of her mouth.

While Jessa was gone, Max tracked down the waiter and got him to take both of their uneaten dishes away before she returned. Thank goodness. Because that meant he didn't have to force himself to eat any more of his horrible food either.

When Jessa finally returned about ten minutes later, she stepped up beside him with a small ceramic plate in each hand. "I brought you a little something."

He gazed up at the bottom of the plate and shivered. There was no way he was eating anything else in this place. "You were pretty grossed out with the first meal they served you. Don't tell me you're trying something else of theirs."

"Of course not. This actually isn't something of theirs." She slid a piece of strawberry cheesecake in front of Max and grinned. "It's from their dessert cart, but apparently all of their desserts are provided by Sweets n' Treats. There's a little sign on it that says so."

Max grinned. "My best friend's wife, Leah, owns that bakery," he said proudly. Then he glanced down at the delicious-looking dessert, and his smiled faded. "But I can't eat this."

"Why not?"

"Because it's not something I can have on my diet."

"At all?"

He nodded. "At all."

"Oh." Her face fell. "I'm sorry. I didn't realize."

He smiled lightly and motioned for her to sit. "It's okay. You can still enjoy yours."

She settled back into her chair with her slice of cheesecake in front of her. "Do you ever indulge in anything?" she asked, reaching for a fork.

Yeah. Sex. "Not when it comes to food."

"I don't think I could live like that. Seems too restrictive."

"I'm used to it. I like having a strict regimen when it comes to my diet and workouts. Keeps me on track."

She lifted a bite of cheesecake to her mouth and closed her lips around it. It must've been damn good because her eyes practically rolled up into the back of her head, and she gave an appreciative little moan.

Instantly, the bulge in his pants hardened against the seam. He nonchalantly reached down and rearranged himself.

"Does it ever bother you?" she asked.

At first, Max thought she meant her reaction to tasting the dessert, but he quickly realized she meant something else. "You mean the strict diet?"

"Yeah. Don't you just have moments where you want to eat whatever the hell you want? You know, just enjoy the treat and not give a damn how many calories are in it?"

"Sometimes. But when I adopted a healthier lifestyle, I knew I couldn't keep my foot in the door. I needed to either do it all the way or not at all."

"So there's no gray area when it comes to you?"

He shrugged. "Not with food, there isn't." Though the more she talked, the more increasingly anxious and dissatisfied with his choices he became.

"But don't you get cravings for certain things?" She slid another bite in her mouth and then ran her fork slowly across her full lips.

His tongue thickened, but he managed to get out a strangled, "Yes." Even though, right now, it wasn't exactly food that he was craving.

He had to physically force himself to turn his attention elsewhere to keep his dick from getting any harder than it already was. The way she licked her fork and lips was taking a major toll on his libido and driving him wild with need. She might as well have been rubbing her hands down her body in front of him.

"Do you ever do anything about those...cravings of yours?" she asked in a breathy tone that forced him to look back at her.

She slid another small bite into her mouth and then slowly licked the tine of her fork in a blatantly sexual way to get off every last bit of cheesecake. Tension simmered between them, and he forgot to answer her.

Her mouth curved with a sexy smile. "Max?"

"Yes?"

"Aren't you hungry?"

"No," he said easily, which was a lie. He was starving with the desire to touch her right now. He had to know if that smooth skin of hers was as soft as he'd imagined. Though he liked to think he had strong willpower, the impulse to wrap his arms around her was too great to ignore. "Would you like to dance?"

Chapter Eight

Jessa sighed.

Well, that hadn't gone quite the way she had hoped. The way Max had been devouring her with his eyes, she would've thought he was planning to take her home and straight to bed. Not to the damn dance floor.

Given their circumstances, entertaining the idea of a one-night stand with Max was probably not the smartest move on her part. She knew that. Unfortunately, she was having a hard time convincing her body otherwise. Especially when Max swept her onto her feet and led her out to the small inlaid oak–polished floor and wrapped his arms around her.

The dance floor was set up in front of huge twin windows with long sheer drapes cascading down each side, framing a beautiful view of the full moon. And with soft classical music humming low in the background, it was actually a pretty romantic gesture on Max's part.

He looked amazing in his black jacket and the white tailored shirt, which accentuated the tanned, smooth skin where the top two buttons were left undone. But even when he wore his regular street clothes, which seemed to usually consist of jeans and a nice button-down shirt, the man always looked great.

Max pulled her into his chest and looked down at her, gazing directly into her eyes. It took her breath away. *God, could he be any more handsome?*

His low voice came out rough, almost strained. "Jess?"

"Yes?"

"Are you having a good time tonight?"

"Of course," she said, smiling.

The hand on her hip moved slowly up her back, stopping between her shoulder blades while the other one held her hand gently and directed her dance motion. "Good. I'm glad to hear it."

His rough palm rasped against the soft skin of her hand, and she nearly shivered. She loved the way his strong, manly hands felt on her body. Even if it was a little strange for a man who worked in an office environment to have calloused hands. But then again, he had said that he visited his buddy's construction site sometimes. Maybe it wasn't so strange, after all.

"What are you thinking right now?"

She smiled. "I was thinking about how much I love your hands."

One of his eyebrows rose, as if he hadn't expected her to admit something like that to him. "Oh yeah? What do you like about them?" He skated his fingers across her back so lightly that she barely could discern the movement.

"How they touch me."

Tension rolled off of him, and there was a controlled intensity behind his eyes. "You like it when I touch you, Jess?"

They swayed to a slow rhythm, but her pulse began to race. "Yes, I do."

His eyes smoldered with heat. "Good to know."

Good to know? What did that mean? She thought for a second maybe he would try and kiss her the way the conversation was going. Apparently not.

God, she really wanted him to kiss her.

Instead, Max released her and spun her around in a slow circle. Then he pulled her back against him, his hand suddenly much lower than it had been before. It wasn't on her butt though. Not really. It was more on the slope leading down to it.

Her hand left his for a moment so that she could push a piece of loose hair out of her face. But the second she reached for it, he beat her to the runaway red strand and tenderly brushed it back away from her cheek. Almost like they were now in sync and had connected on some different kind of level than before.

She pressed her cheek to his chest, listening to the steady beat of his heart and taking in his masculine scent. Maybe it was a weird thought to have since she wasn't in any actual danger, but she felt safe and protected in his arms. Like he'd never let anyone do anything to hurt her. It was a feeling she hadn't had since her mother had died, and it only made her feel closer to both of them.

After a couple of slow songs passed, Max swallowed audibly. "Jess, it's getting late."

Her throat tightened. Guess their date was over. "And?"

"And I...well, I think it's time I take you home."

Though he hadn't said the actual words and she didn't have a clue why he was suddenly in a rush to leave, she hoped he meant he was going to take her home...to bed. Probably a stupid thing, but well...Her breathing increased slightly, and she bit her lip. "Okay," she agreed.

The moment he took a step back from her, she suddenly felt way too cold and already missed his warmth. She hadn't realized how much of his body heat had been detectable through his clothes. But apparently the man burned hot.

He extended his arm to her. "We just need to wait for the waiter to bring us the check and then we'll go."

"All right," she said, allowing him to guide her back to their table.

Max flagged down the waiter and asked him to finalize the check. Then they sat there in uncomfortable silence, taking turns staring at one another while waiting for their server to return.

Her palms dampened. She really wanted to know what he was thinking right now.

Thus far their only relationship had been a friendly yet professional one. Had that somehow changed tonight? The thought had anxiety twisting in her stomach. God, she hoped so. Because, although it probably was idiotic to get involved with someone who could ruin your livelihood with a snap of their fingers, Jessa couldn't seem to stop herself from wanting to.

Then a revelation impaired the flow of blood to her brain. Jessa wanted Max. She wanted his heated body once again pressing into hers...this time without the barrier of clothing keeping them apart.

But the question was, did he want her in the same way?

* * *

The moment the waiter set the check down on the edge of the table, Max reached for it at the same time as Jessa did.

"I've got it," he told her, stealing it out from under her hand before she could grasp a good hold on it.

She shook her head. "It's okay. I don't mind taking care of it."

"Neither do I."

"Well, then how about we split the difference?"

He slid his credit card into the holder and passed it back to the waiter before gazing back at Jessa with a sly grin. "How about we don't?"

"Okay, fine," she said with a smile of her own. "But can I at least take care of the…tip?" Her tongue darted out to wet her lips.

Jesus. For a brief second, he considered saying yes just because of how dirty it sounded coming out of her pretty little mouth. "Thank you, but no. Like I said, I've got it covered."

Her eyes blazed a trail down to his lap. "Hmm, okay. Let me know if you change your mind."

His cock jerked in his pants, and he sucked in a slow breath. They were obviously not talking about the same thing…though he liked her version of the conversation much better than his.

While they danced, she'd pressed her gorgeous body so tightly against his that he was sure she'd left an imprint. Her fingers had played with the short hair on the back of his neck, while her breathy little pants had forced him to shift his groin away from her to keep from embarrassing himself. But the highlight of the entire evening had been watching Jessa eat her dessert. He'd gotten more pleasure out of that one piece of cheesecake than he'd ever had before...and he hadn't even been the one eating it.

Her sudden thirst for him had definitely not gone unnoticed. Actually, he'd been aware of it most of the night. But unfortunately, Max wouldn't be able to quench her desire because there was still a huge conflict of interest between them.

It wasn't like he hadn't thought about it throughout the evening. He definitely had, and his level of interest had been rising by the second, seemingly along with her skirt. But no matter how much he would love to have her in his bed for the night, he couldn't incorporate sex into their working relationship...even if it was a fake one.

That would be a dick move on his part. On any guy's part.

In her eyes, he was the health inspector. That meant he held the position of power. So if he touched her, if he dared to lay a hand on her, he'd be taking advantage of her in a way that no woman should ever be taken advantage of. Although Max had never been much of an angel, he damn sure wasn't a bastard.

Yeah, they were two consenting adults. And yes, they both apparently had a mutual interest in taking off each other's clothes. But that would be nothing more than a giant stumbling block in the wrong direction on a very slippery slope that he had no right being on to begin with. And he wasn't about to participate in something like that. Even if he was in too deep with the whole health inspector impersonation bit.

Once the waiter returned with the receipt, Max scribbled his name across it and rose from his chair. "Ready to go now?" he asked, offering Jessa his hand.

She nodded and accepted it.

They walked hand in hand out into the moonlit parking lot, her feminine scent swirling in the air around him as the light breeze ran its fingers through her hair. Max helped her into the passenger seat of his truck but casually held his breath to keep from taking her right then and there.

Unfortunately, that move also created a raging war between his dick and his brain, and though he struggled to turn his overanalyzing brain completely off, his futile dick lost the unsung battle.

As he walked around to the driver's side, Max ran a hand through his hair. This was all his fault. When he'd flirted with her for the past week, he'd done so to hopefully make her feel uncomfortable enough to send her packing. It was unintentional, but clearly, all he'd done was issue her a green light.

Max climbed into the cab and glanced over at her. She had put on her seat belt and was smiling at him as she traced a finger down her upper thigh. As if it were a damn invitation.

Sonofabitch. He wasn't going to be able to keep ignoring those kinds of signals for much longer. If he was going to keep his sanity, he needed to come up with a plan B. One that would leave her hot and bothered...but not in a good way.

An idea sparked in his head, but it was so devious that it made him wince. It involved Max giving Jessa more than she bargained for by making her a licentious offer she'd never accept: one night in bed with him and he'd leave her food truck business alone for good. But was it scandalous enough to send her on her way? That was the question.

To him, Jessa had come across as a woman who wouldn't appreciate that kind of raunchy behavior from a man. Hell, *he* didn't even like it. If he could've put a boot in his own hind end for thinking it up, he would have. So it really wasn't a huge leap to think that she—or any other woman—would balk at it too.

But could he really do that to her? Could he let her believe that he was that big of an asshole?

Max had always been a mischievous guy who pushed things too far. Whether he was pulling a prank on someone or just harassing one of his buddies. Apparently, this wasn't going to be any different. He hated the idea, and the whole thing sounded insane, but yeah…he could do it if he had to.

And right now, it didn't look like he had any other options. Not if he was going to get her out of town before the Empty Plate Café closed down for good. And he was running out of time. He had less than two weeks left.

No doubt he'd feel rotten about it afterward. He'd enjoyed spending time with her and would miss seeing her around. But he'd promised himself that he would help Pops, and he planned to make sure he did no matter what. Even if that meant making him look like the biggest prick there ever was to a woman he'd come to like.

"Everything okay?" Jessa asked quietly.

Max's jaw tightened. "Yeah. Peachy." He started the truck and pointed it in the direction of her house.

They drove in silence all the way there. He didn't know if she hadn't said anything because she could feel the thick tension in the air emanating from him, but she'd stayed quiet until they'd pulled up in front of her little cottage. She apparently left the porch light on when they'd left earlier, and one inside as well so that she didn't come home to a dark house alone. Smart thinking.

But she wasn't really alone. She had Max with her. Which, with the way he was feeling about himself at this moment, was about the same as having some creepy, weird guy in the bushes who was about to whisper dirty things to her. At least it felt like the same thing.

They walked up the sidewalk together, but Max's mind was far away. And when they reached the porch and stopped in front of her door, the two of them just stared at one another again in silence.

Do it now. Get it over with already.

But the words teetered on the edge of his lips, unable to take the leap and descend to her ears. He didn't like that he was having to resort to such dirty tactics. God, she was going to hate him afterward. But if he was going to be able to do this, then he would just have to think of it as a controlled experiment... even if not a damn thing was actually under his control.

There was always a slight chance that Jessa wouldn't be as disgusted as he was with what was about to come out of his mouth. Hell, she might even take him up on his offer. That would instantly destroy the lines of right and wrong that sat between them—you know, the ones he'd been blurring from the first day they'd met.

All he knew was that he had to keep her from inviting him inside. Because if he got anywhere near a bedroom with her, it would be all over. He wouldn't have the strength he needed to stop himself from taking her against the nearest flat surface. Actually, he didn't really give a damn if the surface was flat. He'd fuck her on the highest peak of a triangle if it meant getting to feel her inner muscles convulsing around his dick.

Damn it. Thinking of shit like that wasn't helping his situation any. He shifted his position a little to keep from having to reach down and rearrange himself in front of her. Then he sighed. It was now or never. He needed to say something before she—

"Would you like to come inside?" she asked, her eyes glittering up at him.

Great. Much to his chagrin, the woman beat him to it.

Chapter Nine

Jessa hadn't meant to invite him in.

Damn it. She knew that sleeping with the health inspector would be a very bad idea for both of them. Yet the constant flirting and thick sexual tension lying between them made her forget all about those frustrating little details.

She wanted him. And judging from the way his intense eyes focused on her, letting his gaze roam over her body, she was pretty sure he wanted her too. Thank God for that. She'd never before spent an entire evening pulling her virtual panties back up because they were involuntarily creeping down her legs every time her date's eyes met hers.

Until Max.

If he had that kind of naughty effect on her mind with just a simple look, she could only imagine what he'd do to her body with a single touch. So she'd taken a chance and asked him inside. But he hadn't answered her yet, which was starting to worry her a little. "Well? Would you like to come in or not?"

Max hesitated once again, shifting uncomfortably. "Maybe we could just talk out here for a few minutes instead."

Huh. Weird. Had she read the situation between them wrong? Maybe he hadn't been interested at all and it had been just wishful thinking on her part. "Um, okay."

He backed away from her and leaned against the hand railing with his hip. "So how do you like living in Granite?"

Really? That's what he wants to talk about? "It's nice," she said, trying not to let her disappointment color her tone. She was horny as hell, and this was the last thing she wanted to discuss at the moment. But she continued on anyway. "I love the people here. Everyone has been really welcoming. Now all I need is a friend to...occupy my spare time."

Sheesh. Could you be more obvious, Jess?

His gaze traveled over her body once more before landing on her face. "I'll be your friend," Max said with a lazy, sexy drawl.

The way he was looking at her was a hell of a lot more than friendly. "Of course. I'm happy to be friends with you too. I mean, that *is* what we are, right?" Her gaze lowered to the rock-hard bulge pressing against the seam of his pants. "Just, ah...friends."

Jesus. She was totally fishing again. Tossing out a line while hoping he'd take the bait so that she could reel him in. Pathetic.

"Jessa."

"Yes," she breathed out, her tongue running across her bottom lip.

"If you don't stop looking at the bulge in my pants while licking your lips, things between us are going to get a lot more friendly than we mean for them to."

Her eyes lifted back to his. "Would that be so bad?"

Max breathed out a sigh. "I can't...er, I mean, we probably shouldn't."

Jessa blinked rapidly, and heat rushed to her face. "Oh, I'm sorry. I guess I just thought..." She shook her head so hard that dizziness swamped her, and her stomach tied itself in knots. God, she couldn't believe she'd misread his signals the entire night. "Never mind. I'll just stop talking and go inside before I make an even bigger ass out of myself."

His voice was low, demanding. "Jess, wait."

"No, it's okay," she said, quickly unlocking her door and stepping inside. "I just misunderstood, that's all. But don't worry, Max. Things are perfectly clear now. Drive safe."

She started to shut the door, but a hand shot out and kept it from closing. From behind the door, she cringed and said, "Good night, Max."

The hand stayed put. "Open the door, Jess."

"No."

"I'm not leaving until you do."

She inhaled a deep breath and swung it open until he could once again see her face. "Did you need something?"

His gaze swept over her face, and his eyes deepened in color. "Yes. I need you to invite me inside again."

Great. Now he apparently felt bad that she'd gotten

the wrong idea. Or he was a vampire. Hopefully it was the latter. "It's okay, Max. I'm fine."

He stepped closer. "Invite. Me. Inside."

She shook her head adamantly. "Look, I think it's sweet that you're afraid you hurt my feelings, but I promise I'll live. It's not the first time I've been turned down, and I'm sure it won't be the last."

He placed both hands on the frame of the door and leaned forward, his face looking more serious than she'd ever seen it. "I am normally a nice guy, Jess. But don't you ever make the mistake of thinking I'm a gentleman. Because unless you invite me in right now, I'm going to pull you out here with me and take you on the goddamn porch."

Her mouth went dry, and something tugged low and deep as the heat of his words swirled through her. "Um, come inside?" Her voice cracked slightly.

A sinful smile curved his mouth. "Don't mind if I do," he said as he swept past her.

She closed the door behind him and released a shaky breath. But she'd barely managed to turn around before he shoved her back against the door and his mouth came crashing down on hers.

Christ. A little warning next time.

Actually, who was she kidding? She loved it when a man took her mouth by force. After, of course, he'd gotten permission from her. Which he clearly knew he had after their embarrassing conversation on the porch.

Max lifted his head. "Stop thinking." Then he grasped her wrists and held them over her head against the cold wood of the door as he lowered his mouth once more and slid his warm tongue inside hers.

With his hips pinning hers, he bent his knees until his rock-hard cock prodded suggestively against the cleft between her shaky legs. Then he undulated gently, causing the friction of her panties to rub over her in the most sensitive of places while her breath caught in her throat and hot flames of desire seared through her.

Her body shivered, and a moan caught in her throat.

She longed for him to slip his fingers into her panties. To touch her in a more direct way that would ease this burning ache that was smothering her from the inside out. Then he could shove the material aside and enter her hard and fast, screwing her into oblivion.

Releasing her wrists, Max let his hands fall to her face and then clasped his fingers around the back of her neck, with each thumb making light circular motions at her jawline beneath her earlobes. He nibbled at her lips, teasing and tasting them for the longest time before deepening the kiss once more.

Then everything slowed down even more as he took a step back from her. "Okay, that's it."

What? The hell it is! She opened her mouth to say those words exactly, but he grasped her by the hand and yanked her into the living room.

Max paused by the couch and took in his surroundings. She didn't know what he was looking for, but she hoped like hell it had to do with a bed and some sheets they could get tangled in. "Max?"

"Hold on a second," he said calmly, still surveying the room.

It was only a one-bedroom cottage, so there really wasn't much to see. Almost everything she owned was within view from where he stood. But she watched his gaze move from the sectional sofa, its large fabric-covered ottoman, the matching recliner, and then finally onto the small dining room table just off the tiny kitchen.

"Over here," he said, leading her toward the solid wood table.

She waited patiently as he pulled out the end chair and set it to the side. But when he turned back toward her with a sly grin on his face and a twinkle in his eye, her heart began to pound, and her pulse raced.

Max threaded his fingers into her hair, tugging lightly until she moved forward enough that her lips were back on his. She was so caught up in the kiss that she didn't even realize their feet had been moving until her butt bumped into the table that was somehow now behind her.

Without warning, he broke the lip lock and twisted her body around until she faced away from him. Then he placed a large hand on her upper back and gently pushed her forward until she bent at the waist. He reached around her and grasped her hands, flattening them on the table.

His low, sexy voice rumbled in her ear. "Keep them there."

She did as he ordered, but her body vibrated with anticipation as his hands trailed up her arms, over her back, and down toward her bottom. Her legs shook as he lifted the back of her skirt and smoothed his rough hands over the satiny panties covering her rear end. And when he gave them a little tug downward and let the silk flutter to the floor, her lungs seized her breath, holding it captive.

Have mercy. The man was going to screw her sense-less while she was bent over her dining room table.

The thought alone caused a tingling sensation to spread throughout her lower body. She would never be able to eat at this table again without thinking about him and the way he was making her feel. He wasn't even inside of her yet, but her nerves were already shooting off like fireworks.

Spreading her legs apart with his foot, Max leaned over her, brushing his large hand between her inner thighs and over her sex. His fingers dipped between the folds and swirled through the wetness, probing lightly at her entrance, as if he was testing whether or not she was ready to accept him.

She definitely was.

But he didn't enter her. Instead, he slid one arm under her waist, pulling her back firmly against him and whispered, "Do you know your neighbors?"

At the strange question, she glanced over her shoulder. "Not yet. Why?"

A smug grin lit up his face. "Because they're about to know *me* really well. By name. Repeatedly."

Jessa started to laugh, but the sound turned into more of a gasping moan as he tunneled two large fingers inside of her.

* * *

Max nearly came in his pants right then.

The strangled sound Jessa had made shot scorching fire through his veins and hot lava into his aching balls. The heavy, unexpected pressure of his fingers sliding into her tightness had forced her onto her tiptoes and lifted her hips higher as she flattened her body against the wooden table beneath her. That provided the perfect angle for what he wanted to do to her.

But first things first.

Max kneeled down behind her, and the subtle scent of her arousal filled his nostrils. Something dark and intense moved through him, and his cock twitched against his leg, spiking his edginess to the next degree. *Fucking hell. Not yet.*

For the past week, he'd longed to know how she tasted, how she would feel quivering against his tongue, wanted to hear her scream his name as he brought her to climax. And that was damn sure what he was going to do.

He loved the power he felt while pleasuring a woman. He loved the sleepy, relaxed look in their eyes after they came so hard that they felt it all the way to the core of their soul. And he was absolutely determined to make sure Jessa experienced that. Even if he had to do this all night.

Not to be conceited, but he was a fairly well-hung man, and she was tight as hell. His two fingers fit her snugly, but he planned to take his time, making sure she was wet and ready for him. Because he damn sure was ready for her.

Tilting his hand, Max moved closer and pressed his mouth to her sensitive bundle of nerves just below, sucking the nub into his awaiting mouth. They both moaned at the same time—her, from the overwhelming sensations he was causing, and him, from the sweet taste of her warm nectar. His fingers slowly pumped in and out of her with accuracy and precision, gliding over her G-spot with every pass.

It didn't take long at all before her soft murmurs grew louder and her inner muscles clamped down persistently on his fingers, begging him to move them faster. Jessa was so damn close to letting go that he thought she might burst at any second. Normally, he would've happily obliged and sent her flying over the edge, but his cock was so hard and revved up that he knew if he did, he would never make it inside of her before he shot off a load himself. And he wanted them to climax together.

So he pulled away and rose to his feet behind her.

Almost immediately, she released a sound of disappointment, expressing her impatience at having her gratification delayed. Which only made him grin.

Max hurried to remove his clothes and pulled out the condom he'd put in his pocket before leaving the house earlier that evening. Okay, yeah, so maybe he was a bastard after all. "One second, baby. I promise I'll make you feel good."

"I have news for you," she panted out. "I was already feeling pretty damn good until you stopped what you were doing."

The condom wrapper made a crinkling sound as he ripped it open, and his dick swayed with anticipation. "You will again, I assure you," he said, rolling the latex on his length. "I want you to come on my cock. I need to feel you pulsing around me."

She moaned under her breath. "Mmm, I like the sound of that."

Thank God. Because the last thing he wanted to do was admit that she was making him feel like a teenager again. Not that he ever got laid all that much back then.

All those years ago, he recalled thinking about having sex with a beautiful woman much more than he'd actually done it. Which only made him glad that he was no longer so young and dumb when it came to females anymore. Not usually anyway.

Max positioned the blunt head of his cock at her entrance and inched forward slowly, giving her time to become accustomed to his girth.

Jessa tensed, and her hips lifted higher. "Uh, Max?"

Knowing what she was thinking, he grinned. "Don't worry. I'm going to go slow, I promise."

"Are you sure you'll fit?"

Max stifled a chuckle. "I'll fit. I'm just being careful so I don't hurt you." His fingers were already causing a depression in her skin where he was hanging on to her hips for dear life. As the crown of his penis slipped fully inside of her, his vision blurred and a groan left his throat. "Sweetheart, you tell me if it's too much and I'll stop, okay?" His voice was strangled, as if the life was being choked out of him. And as tight as she was, it definitely felt that way.

"If you dare stop, Max, I'll kill you dead with my bare hands."

"Deal." He slid a little farther inside of her and grunted from the extreme amount of pressure around him.

Max was eager to explore the silken vise that wrapped around him so tightly. Every fiber of his being pleaded with him to thrust forward, but his sensible side knew that the journey to this new, unfamiliar territory would be even more rewarding the slower he went. For both of them. So he calculated the angle of entry and rocked gently into her, inch by inch, until he was fully seated inside of her.

With the back of his hand, he wiped a bead of sweat from his brow. "Still doing all right?"

She gave an unintelligible moan and a firm nod, which was good enough for him. So he slid one hand under her and touched her intimately as he began to rock in and out of her at a slow, dragging pace. He concentrated on pleasuring her with his hand, grinding his palm against her and scissoring her clit between his fingers. All the while, keeping a steady, unhurried rhythm that seemed to suit them both just fine.

As her breathing quickened so did the speed and strength of his thrusts. Her hips writhed against him, rising and falling in time with him as her inner muscles clasped him tighter. Urging him on. Demanding more of him. Then Jessa did something that nearly sent him over the edge prematurely. She hoisted one of her legs high onto the table, causing him to drill deeper into her depths than ever before.

His blood bubbled in his veins. "Christ, you're flexible as hell."

"I...do...yoga," she said simply as her breaths panted out of her with the power of his thrusts and the surge of her body.

Of course she does. "Don't stop," he suggested, hoping to God she listened to him. Because that little move of hers was fucking hot.

Moments later, when Jessa gripped the edges of the table and arched her back, Max removed his hand from her and sharpened all of his focus on pumping faster and harder, pounding her from behind as he felt her shiver.

"Oh God, oh God. I...I'm..."

"I know, babe. God, you're so tight. It feels amazing."

In between the deep moans, the tortured gasps of pleasure, and the twitching shudders racking her body, she screamed his name several times, which only stimulated his libido more. It was beautiful music to his ears, and Max had never been more aroused by a woman than he was in that moment.

He clutched at her hips as his wound-up body convulsed behind her, his cock jerking inside her as his release came. He grunted loudly with each spasm, letting himself go inside of her as the slope of her soft cheeks slapped against his hard thighs. Spent, Max stilled his movements.

Bracing his hands on the table around her, he leaned forward, motionless. Although breathing was difficult for him just yet, he wanted to make sure she was all right and that he hadn't hurt her. "Jess, you still doing okay?"

She purred and stretched like a kitten after a long afternoon nap. "God, yes. Couldn't be better."

Max ran his hands over her soft curves and blew out a hard breath. Now that all the blood wasn't rushing straight to his groin, his senses were coming back to him.

And that wasn't a good thing.

Chapter Ten

Jessa didn't have a clue what to say.

While Max had been in the bathroom disposing of the condom, she'd slid her panties back on and returned the dining room chair back to its rightful place. She planned to sanitize the table too, but he returned before she'd gotten the chance. Now he was just standing there staring at her with a bleak expression and a look of regret and disappointment in his eyes.

If he was waiting for her to say something to make this moment any less awkward, then he would be waiting a long damn time. Her mind was a complete blank, and her brain had stopped functioning properly the moment he'd bent her over the table.

Finally, he broke the silence. "We need to talk."

Oh, hell no. Anytime a guy wanted to talk about something right after sex, it was rarely a good thing. Usually, it meant that he was going to explain that it was a one-night stand, that it didn't mean anything, and how it couldn't possibly happen again. Or something to that effect.

Well, fuck that. She didn't want to unlock his innermost thoughts and hear that kind of bullshit from him. He could just keep that stuff to himself. "No, we don't."

"Jess, we need to talk about what just happened here." His shoulders sagged as if something was weighing heavily upon them. "It's important."

She shook her head furiously. "Seriously, Max. We don't have to talk about anything at all," she said, starting past him. "I'm good."

Max grasped both of her shoulders, turned her to face him, and then held her in place with a gentle grip. "You're good? What the hell does that mean?" He glared at her.

She spoke fast, nervously waving her hand through the air as if it didn't matter. "Oh, come on. Don't make me spell it all out for you." When he lifted one curious brow, she sighed. *It's just a little adult conversation, Jessa. Get a hold of yourself already.* "Fine, here's the deal. You're a single guy who isn't looking for a relationship. I understand that. I knew what this was from the beginning. There's no reason for us to talk it out."

His eyes narrowed. "Are you trying to brush me off?"

"No. I'm just saying I get it."

He frowned, and his brows lowered over his eyes. "No. I really don't think you do."

She sighed heavily. "Max, listen. I didn't ask you for anything more than coming inside...and we both knew exactly what that would entail. If you're thinking I'm now waiting for rose petals on the bed, cute little notes by the coffeemaker, or sweet nothings whispered in my ear, then you don't have anything to worry about." She smiled lightly to show him there were no hard feelings. "There. Are we clear now?"

"About as clear as a brick wall."

Jessa shook her head. "Well, then I don't know what you want me to say."

"Why do you feel the need to say anything? I needed to tell you the truth about something, which is why I wanted to talk to you. I wasn't expecting you to say a word."

She shrugged. "Oh, I'm sorry. I'm not an expert at one-night stands. I just thought this was how they worked. Sex and then an awkward conversation afterward."

Max dropped his hands and fisted them at his sides. "Okay, hold on one goddamn second. Who the hell ever said this was a one-night stand?"

She blinked rapidly. "I just thought—"

"What? Were you really expecting me to up and leave after what we just did?"

"I...I don't know. I guess." Her cheeks heated, and she turned away from him.

He grasped her arm gently and turned her back around. His eyes softened. "Did someone do that to you, Jess?"

Oh God. That was the last thing she wanted to talk about right now. Max was already looking at her as if she were some kind of wounded animal. She wasn't, damn it. But unfortunately, she wasn't a liar either. "Yes. Once. It happened years ago." The whole thing had been so embarrassing that she hadn't told anyone about the incident...up until now. She waved her hand dismissively through the air. "It doesn't matter anymore though. I got over that a long time ago."

"It still matters," he said with a terse nod. "Look at me, Jess. Do I look like the kind of guy who would do something like that?"

She gazed at the sexy, good-looking man standing in front of her. He'd been stripping her naked with his eyes for a solid week and shooting her all kinds of mixed signals, and then he'd practically pounced on her at the door after she let him in. It hadn't stopped her from having sex with him anyway, but yeah, he did seem like the kind of guy who would do such a thing.

Her eyes lifted to his. "You don't want me to answer that."

He released a hard breath. "Okay, fine. Fair enough. But now that you've gotten to know me on a more personal level, do you really think I would do that to *you*?"

Well, when he put it that way... "No. Probably not."

He sighed with relief. "Thank goodness for that. For a second there, my opinion of myself was really going downhill fast."

"I apologize. I wasn't trying to offend you. Maybe I'm still a bit jaded." She lowered her eyes. "I guess what that jerk did to me all those years ago still affects me in some way after all. It was just that...well, he made me believe that there was more to us than what there actually was, got what he wanted from me, and then walked out and left me standing there alone like a fool. I hate feeling foolish."

Max lifted her chin and leaned his forehead into hers. "I'm not going to do that to you, Jess."

"Promise?"

He nodded. "I promise."

Relief washed over her, and she managed to smile. "Okay, then. So what did you want to tell me?"

"Huh?"

"You said you needed to tell me the truth about something."

"Oh, um. Yeah," Max said, running his hand over the back of his neck. "I, uh…need to confess something. I…don't know how you're going to take it though."

Jessa stared at him warily. She didn't know what the hell he was going to say, but she didn't like the sound of it already. The suspense alone made her palms sweat. "Just say it already. I'm a big girl. I can take it."

He sighed and lowered his head. There was a long pause before he finally said, "I'm using you for your bathtub."

She froze mid-breath. Had she heard him right? "My…um, bathtub?"

"Yeah. I know it's a horrible thing to do, but I don't have a garden tub at home. Yours is so much bigger than mine," he said, his eyes crinkling with mirth. "So I thought that by sleeping with you, I'd have access to yours. I'm sorry if I led you on."

Her lips twitched with amusement. "I see," she said, knowing Max hadn't been in her bathroom until *after* they'd had sex. "Well, do you feel any remorse for your actions?"

He shrugged lightly. "Not really. I mean, the sex was pretty fucking hot and definitely something I'd like to do again. So I was thinking maybe we could just share the bathtub."

She crossed her arms and raised one brow. "I don't know. I mean, it's a pretty awesome tub meant for only me."

"I'm betting we'd both fit."

She smirked. "Maybe we should find out for sure."

* * *

Max had made a mistake. A big one.

He hadn't meant to have sex with Jessa, nor did he think calling it an "accident" made for a very good excuse. After all, it wasn't like he'd tripped and fallen dick-first in between her legs.

But it was true. It *had* been an accident.

His plan to proposition her for one night in her bed in exchange for him leaving her food truck alone had been a good one. He knew Jessa would never have gone along with it in a million years. She would've thrown his ass out onto the street faster than he could've gotten the words out, which was exactly why it had been such a perfect plan.

Unfortunately, he hadn't been able to follow through with it.

Well, part of it anyway.

All of his hopes of her leaving town had relied on the indecent proposal coming out of his mouth. It was despicable and downright unethical for a health inspector to proposition a food vendor like that. She would recognize that. And once she had turned him down, he had hoped she would have moved on. Because no one in their right mind who owned a food business would stay in a town where the health inspector had it out for them.

But he'd never even gotten that far. Not before he'd found himself bending her over the table and pumping in and out of her with slow, sensual movements.

God. The sounds she'd made when she came around him.

Max couldn't stop thinking about it. Which made it real damn hard to feel guilty about any of it. Maybe he never had intentionally meant to go through with getting her into bed. But hands down, it was the best sex he'd ever had.

He'd never meant for things between him and Jessa to go this far. He never would've lied to her or deceived her in any way if he had known it would lead to this.

And he definitely hadn't done any of this just to get her into bed. *Or on the table.*

He doubted she would look at it quite the same way now that the situation had drastically changed between them.

Max needed to tell her the truth. But how could he?

The fact was that he had not only lied to her about who he was, but he'd also now slept with her while under the pretense of being the health inspector. No matter what he said, nothing was going to change any of that.

All Max knew was that he was screwed. In more ways than one.

Now he just needed to figure out what in the hell he was supposed to do about it. And at the moment, he had no clue. He just knew he couldn't keep sitting there obsessing over how the tactical error had occurred. It wasn't helping.

"Would you mind unzipping me?" Jessa asked, turning her back to him in the bathroom.

"Sure." He grasped the zipper and ran it slowly down her back. The dress parted, baring more of her velvety smooth skin that Max couldn't wait to get his hands on.

"Can you turn the water off for me? If it gets any higher, it's going to overflow the sides of the tub when we both get in."

Max did as she asked. Then he unbuckled his pants and shoved them down his legs and kicked them off, along with his underwear. He stepped into the large bathtub and sank down into the warm water, letting his elbows rest on the sides of the tub.

His gaze fell on Jessa, who had just finished clipping her wavy red hair up onto the back of her head, though short wispy tendrils still framed her gorgeous face. She turned toward him as she pulled her arms from the sleeves of her dress and skimmed the tight pink material past her hips to puddle on the tile at her feet.

Standing there in only a white strapless bra and matching panties, her eyes lifted to his. He waited for a blush to color her cheeks, but it didn't happen. Instead, her mouth curved with a genuine smile as she wiggled out of her undergarments and dropped them to the floor as well.

Damn, her body was stunning. Her beautiful breasts were perfectly shaped with large nipples that tightened into peaks under his gaze. Full hips and a curvy waist accentuated her hour-glass figure. Soft womanly thighs led downward to muscular calves. At the apex of her thighs was a little slice of heaven.

He knew that for a fact since he'd been there only fifteen minutes before.

Jessa held on to the tub with one hand as she stepped over the side and began to lower her foot into the water.

"Careful where you step," Max warned, reaching down with his hand to protect himself from permanent damage.

"Oops. Sorry," Jessa said with a giggle. "I can't see through the bubbles. Where do you want me?"

Well, hell. If that wasn't a loaded question, he didn't know what was.

His heated eyes trailed up her body, not stopping until they reached her sweet face. Because she was so much shorter than he was, he always felt like he was looking down at her. This was different, and he rather liked the new angle. "On my face."

"Max," she said, her reluctance evident in the pitch of her voice.

"I'm not kidding, Jess. On my face. Now."

He grasped her lush hips and helped her put both legs into the tub, positioning her feet on either side of him. Then he ran his wet hands around to her magnificent rear, gathering her closer to him before pressing his mouth against her. Her knees shook against his shoulders, threatening to buckle, as a loud feminine moan echoed through the bathroom.

After she'd nearly taken out his manhood with her foot, his manhood had shriveled to semi-erect. There was just something about a threat to a guy's junk—even an accidental one—that dulled a man's desire. But the moment he tasted the sweet, succulent flavor of her flesh against his tongue, his cock instantly roared back to life.

Feasting on her, Max used his tongue, teeth, lips, and even his fingers to bring her pleasure. He was like a cat with a new wind-up toy, one he couldn't stop playing with. The more he wound his little mouse up, the more she rocked against his face and the louder and longer she squeaked.

When the persistent clamping of her inner muscles around his fingers signaled her impending release, he tugged her more firmly onto his face and buried himself there. She shuddered, her body twitching against his mouth as he licked faster, tasting every bit of her orgasm on his tongue.

A vein throbbed in his temple, and he reached down to fist himself beneath the surface of the water to keep from letting himself go. He'd never come just by tasting a woman before, but he was damn close to doing so now. Once her convulsions died out, she levered herself up and off his mouth before drifting downward to straddle him.

His cock pressed unerringly against her entrance, and he sucked in a deep breath. "Condoms. Please tell me you have some, baby. I only had one with me."

She shook her head. "I don't, but... well, I'm on the pill."

One eyebrow rose. "You sure?"

"Well, since I take them every day, I'm pretty damn sure."

He grinned. "Um, that's not quite what I mean. I was asking if you're sure you want to do this without a condom? We don't have to go bare. We can always do a rain check."

"Are you responsible?"

"Yes, I'm responsible. I've never actually gone bare with a woman before, and I get tested regularly. It's the only smart thing to do nowadays. But I don't expect you to take my word for it. Why don't we put this off for another day? I'm okay with that, if that's what you want."

"It's okay." She smiled. "I trust you, Max."

Damn it, that stung. If she had any idea that he'd been lying to her, she wouldn't trust him one bit. "Maybe you shouldn't."

"The fact that you're saying we can put it off and that I shouldn't trust you only makes me trust you more. So you lose."

Max chuckled. "I wasn't aware this was a contest."

"It's not anymore. I won, remember?" She tilted her hips forward, rubbing herself against the length of his hard cock.

His hands automatically reached for her, and he grunted. "Somehow I'm thinking we both just won."

She reached into the water and wrapped her fingers around him. Lifting up slightly, she positioned the head of his cock at her entrance and sank down enough to take the crown. Inch by inch, she slowly accepted more of him. Max sucked in a sizzling breath through his teeth as if she were slowly torturing him to death. Which she was definitely doing, even if it was unintentional.

"Too slow?"

He shook his head and closed his eyes. "No, you're doing fine."

But she obviously didn't agree. With the last few inches to go, Jessa dropped her weight onto him, impaling herself and making his penetration abrupt and almost forceful.

His eyes shot open. Fireworks exploded in his groin in an array of sensation. Colorful words blasted from his mouth. Water splashed over the edge of the tub and onto the tile floor.

Sonofabitch. What was the woman trying to do—kill him? He locked his large hands on her thighs. "Christ. Don't move."

An innocent smile touched her lips. "Too much, too fast?"

His voice was guttural. "Jess, I don't want to hurt you."

"You didn't," she said, wiggling her hips as much as his hands would allow. Which wasn't really much at all.

He tightened his grip even more and shook his head. "That couldn't have been very pleasant for you."

"Mmm. Wanna bet? If you hadn't been blindly cursing, you would've noticed just how much I enjoyed it." She ground herself against him, and his body tensed. "The feeling of being filled by you so fast is amazingly erotic."

Max blew out a hard breath. "Be careful what you say to me or I'll stop being gentle."

"Who asked you to be gent—"

Before she could finish the word, he wrapped his arms around her, hoisted her up a little without coming out of her, and sucked one hard pink bud into his mouth.

She gasped. "Oh."

Fascinated by her large nipples, Max traced his tongue first around one, then the other. Then he pressed her breasts together so that he could nibble on both without having to choose between them. Some lovemaking positions were more convenient for this than others. This was one of them.

She moaned and started to move, rising and falling on his length. Rotating her hips in a circular motion and then working her body back and forth. Her inner muscles quivered around him, causing warm sensuous vibrations to wrap around his balls. God, she was driving him wild.

Grasping her neck, he pulled her forward until her mouth fused to his. His tongue stabbed into her mouth, rolling against hers. She strained against him, feminine softness pressing into masculine hardness. His hand slid down into the sloshing water, finding and touching her where the two of them were joined.

The press of his fingers against her must've electrified something in her. Because she arched her back, lifted her arms over her head, and rode him hard and long.

He hadn't expected it. Not from her. Everything he thought he knew about this woman pointed at her being a giver, not a taker. But this beautiful, full-figured woman was taking charge of her own pleasure—as well as his. Fearless. Uninhibited. Unrestrained. And it was totally fucking hot.

His fever spiked higher, and his eyes clouded over. Desire pooled in his gut, and his balls rioted for release. His heart pounded against his ribs. Breaths panted out of him at a fast rate. More water splashed out onto the tile floor. Fuck.

Finally, Jessa cried out, her body convulsing around him as her insides gripped his cock and milked him hard. *Thank God.* He'd been so goddamn close to speaking in tongues that it wasn't even funny.

Without hesitation, he lost himself in her. He grunted his release, spilling himself deep inside her as the intense waves of his climax shook him to his core.

As far as fantasies went, this one was at the top of his list.

Chapter Eleven

Max scrubbed at his prickly chin.

He needed to go home and shave before going to work, but he didn't want to wake the woman who was sleeping so soundly on his arm. His dead arm. The one that went completely numb an hour ago.

He didn't mind though. He liked waking up with her next to him. Her hair cascaded over his shoulder and smelled like the lilac shampoo he'd noticed in the bathroom the night before. He lay there mute, sniffing the great-smelling scent while listening to her soft breathing. In. Out. In. Out. Then she snorted in her sleep.

He laughed out loud, which instantly woke her. "Max?"

"I'm right here," he said, still chuckling. "Go back to sleep."

"I can't. I have to work this morning." She leaned up

and glanced at the clock. "Oh crap. I'm already running a little late."

Max watched as she jumped out of bed and ran into the bathroom. He was still reclining on the bed with a sheet over his waist when she returned, her wavy hair clipped onto the back of her head. He rubbed at his tingling arm. Thank God he was finally getting some feeling back in it. "Maybe we could call in sick and stay in bed all day."

She stood in her closet doorway, riffling through her clothes. "You're cute and all, but I really can't." She tugged on a pair of green capris and buttoned them, then slid on a white top before turning to Max. "If I don't go, I don't make any money."

He grinned. "I could pay you by the hour to stay home and let me—"

"Stop right there. Because if you say what I think you're about to say, you're going to lose cuteness points with me."

He laughed. "You know what I mean."

She walked closer to the bed and reached down for her sneakers. But Max grabbed her arm and yanked her on top of him. "Come back to bed with me. I need to have you again."

"I never thought I'd say this, Max, but I think five rounds of sex in a twenty-four hour period of time would be overkill."

"But I want to make you feel good."

"You did. Four other times."

He shifted her a little to let her feel how hard he was for her, but he didn't say anything.

Her breath quickened. "I know what you're doing, and it won't work."

"I'm just trying to prove to you that I can make it worth your while if you stay." He waggled his brows.

"No need. I have no doubts about your abilities. But I really can't. Sorry."

He frowned at her. "What's the fun of being a business owner if you can't even take an unplanned day off once in a while?"

"It's not that. I have other people relying on me. I have to get down to the kitchen and help Mario get the truck ready to roll out. Otherwise, I'll miss the lunch rush."

His brow furrowed. "Who's Mario?" He didn't mean for his tone to come out so possessive...but it did. Damn it.

She smoothed a finger across his brow and grinned. "He's just one of my employees."

Confusion washed over him. "Wait a minute. I thought you only had two women who work on your truck with you."

"I do. Mary and Lisa. But Mario and Mrs. Howard work at the kitchen that supplies my truck with the things I need."

Max didn't know Mario, but he was very familiar with Mrs. Howard. She was a retired schoolteacher who liked to get into everyone else's business. The busybody.

"So you have an actual kitchen too?"

"Well, sort of. I rented a commercial kitchen that wasn't being used by anyone else. The owner had no plans for it. It's small but it works for what I need it for. Also, the owner lets me park the Gypsy Cantina at the back of the lot, which comes in handy." She glanced away for a moment as if she was thinking about something and then said, "You know, you should get dressed and come with me this morning."

So he could run into Mrs. Howard and she could out him in front of Jessa? No fucking way. "I can't. I have to work too."

"Then that's perfect. The old inspector passed the kitchen already, but it hasn't been checked again since we've been up and running. Just like the food truck had been. So it's a good opportunity to do that. Besides, you can make sure I'm on the up and up." She winked at him.

He shook his head adamantly. "That's okay. I really don't need to. I trust that you have everything in order."

She sighed. "Max, that's sweet. And while I appreciate what you're trying to do, you can't just disregard it. It's your job as the health inspector to visit my kitchen, and I expect you to do your job. Just because we slept together doesn't mean I want you to give me any leniency when it comes to the rules. No special favors. That wouldn't be right."

Great. Of course she thought he was doing her a favor. "It's fine, Jess. Really."

"No, it's not. Now get dressed. You're coming with me." She rolled off of him and started putting on her shoes.

This is what you get for lying to her, dipshit. Just tell her the fucking truth already... before someone else does. "Jess, I need to, uh..."

She rose to her feet and fisted her hands on her hips. "Max, I'm not kidding. You aren't letting me get out of this. It wouldn't be fair. If you don't agree to come with me today, I'm going to go up to your office at city hall and fill out an inspection request form just to force you into it. Don't think I won't."

Fuck. If she went to city hall, she would find out he'd been lying to her anyway. "Okay, fine. I'm coming."

Begrudgingly, he shoved the sheet off of him and slid out of the bed. Jessa's eyes lowered, blatantly gazing with interest at his swinging manhood as he reached for his clothes. She even licked her lips.

His brow rose. "You sure I can't interest you in—"

"Max."

He sighed. "Okay, okay. It was worth a shot."

She grinned. "If it makes you feel any better, I was tempted to say yes."

"Still could, ya know?"

She shook her head but grinned as she headed to the bedroom door. "I'm going to grab some breakfast before we leave. Do you want anything?"

At the mention of food, his stomach growled. They'd burned off enough calories last night that he was sure he could eat a small horse. "What are you having?"

She stopped in the doorway. "Cold pepperoni pizza. I have some leftover in the fridge."

Jesus. This woman and her poor eating habits were going to be the death of him. He pulled on his pants and buttoned them. "No, thanks. I need to run home and change so I'll just grab something while I'm there. Then I can meet you at the kitchen. Where's it located?"

"Are you familiar with Bottoms Up?"

He nodded as he swung his shirt over his shoulders and stuffed his arms into the sleeves and began rolling them up. "Yeah, that's Logan and Valerie's bar."

"Oh, are they friends of yours?"

Max shrugged. "Yeah, mostly. Logan and I have a love-hate relationship though."

"Why?"

"Well, when the two of them were getting together, I may have pretended to hit on Valerie to make Logan jealous."

She gave him a teasing smile. "Ah, so you're a troublemaker?"

"Sometimes," he said, waggling his brows as he buttoned his shirt. "So your kitchen is near their bar?"

"No, my kitchen is *inside* their bar."

He squinted at her. "What are you talking about?"

"The bar has a commercial kitchen in it. But since Logan and Valerie didn't have any plans to use it, they let me rent it from them. It's been a huge help."

Shit. So now he had to worry about running into them too? He was so screwed. "Are either of them normally there during the day?"

"Not usually. But today is delivery day so I know Logan will be."

Perfect. So not only was he going to a kitchen where the town's lead gossip would be, but he would also have to come face-to-face with the one guy who would love to rat Max out the most. Just fucking great.

* * *

Jessa rode her bicycle into Bottom Up's parking lot and coasted around the back of the building. As usual, she tapped her brakes and stopped near the light pole, leaning her bike up against it. Then she looped a security chain around both, locking them together.

She didn't think anyone in town would actually steal her bike, but since it was her only mode of transportation beyond the food truck, she refused to take an unnecessary chance. Weird considering all the chances she had taken over the course of the last several months.

Jessa usually thought of herself as pretty levelheaded. Maybe it had been her free-spirited late mother guiding her decisions from the other side. Because, on a crazy whim, she'd decided to move to Granite and bought a food truck to take along with her. She knew how small the town was, so she hadn't seen much of a point in keeping her blue sedan. So instead she sold the car on Craig's List and got herself a bicycle.

It had actually been a great investment.

Since the area was well known for its sandy soil, she'd bought a beach cruiser type with wide, oversized tires, a wire basket affixed to the handlebars, and a large, cozy seat. It was built for comfort rather than speed, but it got her from one place to another without any problems. It wasn't the coolest ride ever, but at least it was functional...and way better on gas than a car.

When she'd moved to town, the bike had fit easily enough inside her food truck, along with all of her other belongings. After all, Jessa's mother had taught her the importance of traveling light. They'd never stayed in one place long and always rented fully furnished apartments. So all Jessa had come to town with was her new bike, her clothes, some personal items, and an old cedar chest that held photos and her mother's traveling journals.

A thick, familiar accent broke the silence. "Mornin', boss."

She glanced up to see Mario carrying a box of food supplies to the Gypsy Cantina, which was parked close to the kitchen entrance, ready for loading. "Good morning, Mario. Sorry I'm late. I...um, overslept."

"No worries. Mrs. Howard is almost done with the food prep. I'm just waiting for her to finish up the last box and then I can load it for you."

"Great. Thank you."

He nodded his response and stepped into the truck.

She didn't know how long it would be before Max would show up, but she couldn't stand around out here waiting. She had things to do. Thankfully, she'd already given Max instructions to park around back and use the kitchen entrance to get inside. If all else failed, Mario would surely see him and could point him in the right direction.

Just as she went to rap on the side of the truck to get his attention, her mother's likeness caught her eye. Every time she looked at the mural on the side of the truck, she remembered how beautiful the woman truly was. Everyone always said that Jessa looked just like her mother since she'd inherited her long waves of fiery red hair, pale skin, and brilliant blue eyes.

The only differences between them had been the light scattering of freckles on Jessa's nose and their clothing size. Her mother had been sick though. Terminally ill. While Jessa had always maintained a healthy glow. Sadly, that only served as a gentle reminder that being thin didn't equal vitality any more than being heavy equaled lethargy.

Sadness washed over her, but she pushed it away. "Hey, Mario?"

He poked his head around the side of the truck. "Yeah?"

"I have a friend stopping by soon. When he gets here, will you point him in my direction?"

"No problem."

"Thanks," she said, heading inside.

Mrs. Howard stood at the stainless steel prep table shredding cabbage for the slaw. Though she only worked a few hours every morning, she was in charge of accepting food deliveries, preparing produce ahead of time, and marinating the meats that would be stored overnight in the walk-in cooler and used the next day. She was Jessa's right hand... and sometimes her conscience.

The whirring sound of the shredder slowly wound down. "You're late," the woman said in an admonishing tone that she probably used a lot during her teaching days.

"I know. Sorry about that. I... overslept." *With Max. Four times.*

The old woman clucked her tongue. "You know, it doesn't look good for the boss to be late at her own place of business. That kind of behavior could make her employees want to lollygag as well."

Jessa lifted one brow but offered a teasing smile. "Mrs. Howard, were you planning on lollygagging?"

"Hmm. Maybe not... as long as you get here on time tomorrow," she said, wiping her hands on a towel. "I might need a good role model to keep me in line."

Jessa laughed. Leave it to this woman to try to use reverse psychology on her. Mrs. Howard had probably done the same with her students. "I'll be here on time tomorrow, I promise."

Mrs. Howard's mouth crinkled around the edges. "Good." She turned toward the large washbasin and grabbed the hanging water nozzle and began spraying the dirty pans in the sink. "I'm just going to wash up these few dishes before I leave."

"That's okay. Why don't you go ahead and go. I can do them for you."

"It's not a problem. I still have half an hour before I get off. Mario's going to load the bucket of shredded cabbage onto the truck, so there's really nothing left for me to do anyway."

A loud banging sound came from the other side of the wall. Both women jolted, and Mrs. Howard's hand flew to her chest. "My goodness. What in the world?"

Jessa walked over to the wall and touched it. Something from the other side bumped the wall once again, making it vibrate beneath her fingers. "I think the bar's storeroom is on the other side of this wall." She dropped her hand and shrugged. "I know it's delivery day. They must've dropped off Logan's liquor order already."

Mrs. Howard glanced at the clock on the wall. "This early?"

Hmm. Good point.

The kitchen received early morning deliveries only because Jessa ordered most of her meat, eggs, and produce from the local farmers in the area. But Logan probably wouldn't receive an alcohol delivery this early. At least he never had in the past.

Mario stepped inside just as something else thudded against the wall. A puzzled expression warped his face. "What's that noise?"

Jessa shook her head. "We don't know. It's definitely coming from the bar though."

Worry creased Mrs. Howard's forehead. "Do you think someone broke in? Maybe we should call the police?"

Unconcerned, Mario lifted the bucket of shredded cabbage and carried it toward the door. "No. Logan's definitely over there. I saw his truck out front." Then Mario disappeared through the open doorway.

"Maybe Valerie is with him," Mrs. Howard said, winking. "The two of them can't seem to keep their hands off one another."

Jessa giggled at first but then remembered something worrisome. Max would probably be showing up there any minute, and he'd already told her that he and Logan had a love-hate relationship. If the sound coming through the wall was actually Logan and Valerie getting it on, Max could possibly close down their bar. He was the health inspector, for Christ's sake.

Damn it. Maybe inviting Max to inspect her kitchen today wasn't such a good idea after all. Not if it was going to get Logan and Valerie in trouble with the health department. If either of them actually started moaning while Max was there, he would surely know what was going on.

God, why hadn't she thought to warn them first?

Maybe she still could. "I'll be right back. I'm going to go over and let them know that we can hear them before the sounds escalate into something more."

Mrs. Howard continued washing the dishes but nodded. "That's probably wise. I definitely don't want to hear what's going on over there."

Jessa pulled out her keys and used them to unlock the door leading into the bar. She traipsed down the employee hallway toward the storage room but paused at the door when she heard something slide across the floor. What the hell was Logan doing to Valerie in there— screwing her so hard she slid across the floor?

She knocked on the metal door. "Hello?"

There was a slight pause. "Hey, Jess. Is that you?"

"Yeah, I just wanted to let you know that the walls are really thin." The door flew open, and her hand instantly slapped over her eyes.

"Um, Jess?"

"Yes?"

"Is there a specific reason as to why you're covering your eyes?" Logan asked, his voice radiating confusion and maybe a bit of humor.

"I, uh... Are you decent?"

"Yeah."

She peeked through her fingers to see a fully dressed Logan standing in front of her. Thank God. "Where's Valerie?"

"She's at home. Still sleeping, I believe. I just came up here early to rearrange the storeroom before the delivery truck gets here. Valerie said she wanted to do it this evening, but I didn't want her lifting all of these heavy boxes."

"Oh, that's sweet. And now everything makes sense too. We kept hearing weird noises coming through the wall on the other side. We thought for a minute that you and Valerie were, uh..." Her cheeks heated.

Logan chuckled. "I have to say, I like your version of my workday way better than my actual one."

"Sorry. I'm glad it wasn't what it seemed like. Even if it was, I wouldn't normally...ah, interrupt. But I needed to warn you that I invited the new health inspector to come check out the kitchen. I hope you don't mind."

He leaned against the doorjamb and crossed one booted ankle over the other. "I hadn't even realized the guy started yet. What's his name?"

She blinked at him. "You don't know?"

"Why would I?"

"Because you're friends with him. Well, sort of. He mentioned that you two have a bit of a tepid relationship."

He shook his head. "Jess, I don't have a clue who you're talking about. Who's the new health inspector?"

"Max Hager."

Logan's face went blank. "Is that some kind of a joke?"

Jessa cringed. "No. Max...uh, I mean, Mr. Hager...stopped by my food truck early last week and introduced himself. I guess he had just started. But he found some issues with the truck. Lots of them actually." *Stupid ones too, but whatever.* "So I spent the whole week correcting all the code violations he'd pointed out."

"Really? And you're sure that this is the Max Hager I know?"

She didn't know why he would ask her such a weird question. "Yes, he told me that he knows you and Valerie. If I had known that earlier, I might've dropped your name to get him to leave me and my food truck alone."

The look of disbelief on Logan's face turned to one of irritation. "So he was messing with you?"

"I guess. As much as any finicky, arrogant health inspector would, I suppose. It wasn't like I was doing anything seriously wrong. It was just little things that he kept pointing out. Things that didn't seem to matter."

"Like what?"

"Well, for one, I had to cover all the picnic tables in the park with tablecloths and buy some new trash cans."

His forehead crinkled. "But those don't belong to you. Those belong to the city."

"That's what I said!"

Logan shook his head in disgust. "What else?"

"My truck tires apparently need to be exactly ten and three-quarter inches from the curb at all times. He actually measured them."

Logan barked out a laugh. "Are you kidding me? That's the stupidest thing I've ever heard."

She couldn't help but grin. "Thank goodness someone agrees with me on that. I thought it was just me. But he seemed adamant that he was going to make sure I followed all the rules. I just hope he doesn't find anything wrong in the kitchen."

A strange smile spread on Logan's face. "Oh, trust me. I guarantee he's not going to have a damn thing to say about that kitchen."

Chapter Twelve

Max couldn't believe he'd agreed to show up this morning.

Was he trying to get himself caught in a damn lie? Because if he got anywhere near Mrs. Howard with Jessa around, that was exactly what the hell was going to happen.

He liked Mrs. Howard. He really did. The dear old gal reminded him a lot of his late Grandma Bess. It had never mattered how big he was. Or how old he was. With just a simple look, that woman always made him feel like he'd just been spanked.

Mrs. Howard had that same gift. As well as a big mouth.

Of course, it was probably no bigger than his own since he'd been the one to get himself into this whole mess in the first place.

Idiot.

After leaving Jessa's house earlier, Max had taken his sweet time driving to his own house across town so that he could change his clothes. Then, while he was there, he'd made himself a quick breakfast of microwaved egg whites, fake bacon, a dry slice of whole-grain wheat toast, and a vanilla protein shake. Yeah, he couldn't cook worth a damn, and breakfast had basically sucked.

But it wasn't like he could've eaten at Jessa's house. Well, unless he'd been able to convince her to come back to bed... which hadn't happened. So his only option had been to go home to eat. Because, unfortunately, cold pepperoni pizza didn't coincide with a healthy lifestyle. At least not in his way of thinking.

And that sucked too.

Max pulled his truck into the bar's parking lot and drove around the back. He parked next to her food truck and then walked over to see if she was inside. A short Hispanic male with stocky shoulders and big biceps glanced over at him. "You Mario?" Max asked.

"Who wants to know?" the guy asked warily.

"I'm a friend of Jessa's."

The guy gave Max a once-over and shrugged one shoulder. "Yeah, she said you'd be stopping by. She's in the kitchen," he said, pointing toward a solid metal door at the back of the building.

"Thanks," Max said, heading for it.

He opened the door quietly, poked his head inside, and caught sight of Jessa standing alone in the kitchen. Thank goodness for that. Maybe he wouldn't have to worry about running into Mrs. Howard, after all. "You busy?" he asked, stepping fully inside the room.

Jessa's head snapped up. "Oh. I almost thought you weren't coming."

"I told you I would."

"Yeah, but that was earlier when I still had time to show you around. Now I've only got a few minutes before I have to head out on the truck."

"Sorry about that. I got…held up." By the shitty breakfast he'd made for himself…and his conscience. "I guess we'll just have to reschedule for another day."

Out of his peripheral vision, a figure moved into view, and a scratchy older female's voice asked, "What is it that you need to reschedule?"

Mrs. Howard had apparently been bent over a counter on the other side of the upright freezer, so he hadn't noticed her standing there. Just great.

Jessa smiled. "Oh, it's nothing. Max was going to inspect the kitchen for any problem areas."

Mrs. Howard's mouth drooped at the corners. "Is there something wrong with the electricity that I don't know about?"

Shit. Jessa opened her mouth to respond but Max beat her to it. "I'm sure everything here is perfect," he said quickly. "I was just going to have a look around. But since Jess has to leave soon, we'll do it another time. Right, Jess?"

The elderly woman looked over at Jessa and shook her head. "That won't be necessary. I can stay and show Max around for you. I know exactly where the circuit panel is, as well as the outside electrical box."

Jessa cocked her head at Mrs. Howard. "Why would he need to look at those?"

Damn it. He was so busted. There was nothing he

could do now to stop Mrs. Howard from throwing him under the bus and running him over with it. Twice.

Mrs. Howard's mouth quirked up with amusement. "Well, Max *is* an elect—"

"Electrifying individual," someone blurted out from across the kitchen.

Max's head snapped up, and his eyes fell on Logan Mathis entering the room from a door that apparently separated the bar from the kitchen.

As if things weren't bad enough?

"Logan," Max said with a cordial nod.

"Max."

Super. Just what he needed. This smug jerk to witness his embarrassing demise. If Max was going to go down in flames in front of someone, why did it have to be Logan of all people? Damn it. "What are you doing here?"

Logan propped his hip against the counter and grinned. "I own the building."

"I know that," Max said, stifling the urge to roll his eyes. "But why don't you stay on your own side of it?"

"Max," Jessa blurted out, her eyes pinned to him. "That was rude."

Logan grinned. "It's okay, Jess. I know Max is just kidding around. Just like that time he kissed my girlfriend's neck. Yeah, funny stuff."

Max let loose a sardonic chuckle. "Still pissed about that, huh? Valerie wasn't your girlfriend at the time. She was as single as I was, and what happened between us is none of your business."

Logan's heated gaze sliced into Max. "Nothing happened between the two of you. I know because Valerie said so."

He was absolutely right. Nothing *had* ever happened between Max and Valerie. But that didn't mean he couldn't still get on Logan's nerves about it. "Maybe."

Valerie's pissed-off fiancé took a step toward Max. "There's no maybe about it, asshole."

"Logan Mathis!" Mrs. Howard yelled in that stern tone she'd perfected over the years. "If I hear you use that kind of language in front of us ladies again, I'm going to…to…call your mother."

Logan winced and his shoulders relaxed. "Uh, sorry, Mrs. Howard."

Max grinned. Thank goodness he hadn't been the one to curse in front of them. Mrs. Howard didn't know his mother, but the last time he'd slipped up in front of her, the old-fashioned schoolmarm had given him a twenty-minute lecture about cleaning up his vulgar vocabulary. And all he'd said was shit.

"Well, this has been lots of fun," Jessa said sarcastically. She glanced at her wristwatch. "But I've got to hit the road so I can get there on time and start setting up. Max, why don't we just do this another day? I really don't want to inconvenience Mrs. Howard. It is quitting time for her, and she was just getting ready to leave."

"Works for me," he replied. The last thing he wanted to do was spend the next hour listening to Mrs. Howard drone on and on about her women's poker night or something even worse. Like her bunions.

But Mrs. Howard raised one wrinkled hand. "It's no bother."

"Actually," Logan said with a pompous grin, "why don't you let me show him around the kitchen. I need to discuss something with him anyway."

That piqued Max's curiosity, but he shook his head. "We don't have anything to talk about."

Logan grinned again. "I beg to differ. I have a few things I need you to...inspect," he said, emphasizing the last word. "And since that's apparently your job now, I think you might want to reconsider your position."

Sonofabitch. The bastard knew something about what was going on. But if that was true, then why wasn't Logan outing him in front of everyone, including Jessa? Surely Logan would love the chance to get back at him, and it wasn't like Max could blame him.

Max nodded firmly. "All right. Then I guess it's just you and me, buddy." Though the words came out friendly, the tension between the two men was palpable.

"Um, okay," Jessa said, her high-pitch tone lending some inconsistency to her agreement. Her eyes trained on Max. "But I'd like to have a word with you first, if you don't mind."

"I'll wait for you at the bar, Max," Logan said, heading to the inside door that led to his side of the building. "I'm pretty sure that we're both going to need a strong drink for this conversation."

The moment Logan disappeared through the doorway, Mrs. Howard turned to Jessa. "Dear, do you think it's wise to leave these two alone together? Especially while they're drinking? I'm pretty sure nothing good will come from that."

Jessa shrugged. "Well, they're two grown men. I think they should be able to have a simple conversation without it turning into a full-out brawl. Don't you?"

Mrs. Howard laughed as she looped her oversized

purse on her frail, skinny arm. "Good luck with that," she said, heading out the door.

Once they were alone, Jessa turned her concerned gaze onto Max. "I know you and Logan don't have the best relationship, but I hope you'll be on good behavior today while you're talking to him."

"Define good."

"Max."

He grinned. "Okay. I won't kill him. How's that?"

Jessa sighed. "I guess that's about the best I can hope for."

"It'll be fine," Max assured her. He glanced around the kitchen at his surroundings. "How did you even meet Logan anyway?"

"I ran into him after I got into town. I was in the grocery store talking to one of the cashiers as she rang me up. I had asked her if she knew where I could rent some kitchen space, and she suggested I check with the owner of Sweets n' Treats. But that wouldn't work out."

"Why? Leah wouldn't be able to help you?"

"I don't know. I never asked. Unfortunately, bakeries just don't have the right kind of equipment that I need. When I said that to the cashier, Logan happened to be standing behind me in line and overheard the conversation. We got to talking, and he mentioned that he had a fully equipped kitchen at his bar that he wasn't even using."

"That was pretty convenient, I bet."

"I know. I couldn't believe my luck!" Her face brightened. "It was as if fate had stepped in and the stars had all aligned perfectly. Like we were meant to be."

Irritation settled in Max's gut. He didn't like hearing

her talk about another man like that after she'd spent the night in his arms. "You do know that Logan's off the market, right?"

She stared blankly at him. "You're kidding me."

"No. Logan is really engaged to Valerie. They're getting married soon."

She scowled at Max. "Not about *that*. I meant you're kidding that you seriously think I'm interested in Logan in that way. God, Max. We're just friends. Nothing more. Logan has been very kind to me and went out of his way to help me out. And I know he's engaged to Valerie because she and I are friends too. They're adorable together."

He hesitated thoughtfully. "Okay, then what was up with the whole fate and stars bit?"

"You don't believe in stuff like that?"

Max shrugged. "I don't know. I guess I never really thought about it. But I take it *you* do."

"My mother believed in it wholeheartedly. And well, yeah, I guess I do too since I said all of that without even thinking about it. I guess I just find it pretty amazing how one person can come into your life and affect you so much without you or them even realizing it. Then before you know it, you're attached to them and it's too late to do anything about it."

His heart thumped in his chest. Hard. "Yeah. I know exactly what you mean." As strange as it was, he was starting to feel that way about Jessa.

She smiled and glanced at her watch again. "Anyway, now I'm really late. I have to go." She grabbed her keys from the table. "Will I see you later tonight?"

Max hesitated, knowing he should put a stop to all

of this now. But remembering how great last night had been, he couldn't seem to do it. "Sure," he said, glancing at the closed door to the bar. "If I'm still alive, that is."

She smirked lightly. "I'm sure you two will be able to find some kind of common ground. Who knows? Maybe you will even become friends."

"Yeah. Maybe." *Don't hold your breath.*

"Just try, please." She leaned up on her tiptoes and brushed her lips firmly against his. "If you won't do it for yourself, then do it for me."

He cupped his hand around the back of her neck and brought her mouth back to his. When he broke the kiss, he said, "That's a lot to ask, ya know?"

"I'll make it worth your while when I see you later tonight," she said with a wink.

That one little gesture foretold all the dirty, delicious things she would do to him. Maybe he believed in this fate and stars shit, after all. "You're on. I'll keep my hands off Logan. But later with you? That's going to be an entirely different story. Count on it."

"Good to hear," she said with a smile, and then headed for the door. "By the way, Mario will be locking this door up when he leaves. So just have Logan let you out when the two of you are done."

"Okay. Drive safe."

"Always do," she replied, waving as she walked out.

The moment she started her truck and drove away, Max headed into the bar to find Logan. It wasn't hard to do since he was exactly where he'd said he would be. Max walked straight up to the bar and slid onto the black vinyl stool. "Okay, so what is it that you know?"

Logan grinned wide. "I know it's early in the day, but I'm going to drink a beer anyway. Want one?"

"Okay. Give me a Bud Lite and then start talking."

"Maybe it's *you* who should start talking," Logan said, grabbing Max a bottle of beer and popping the metal cap off before sliding it toward him. Then he grabbed himself a Corona and did the same. "You want to tell me what the hell's going on between you and Jessa?"

Max took a long pull from his beer. "None of your damn business, that's what."

"Bullshit. You made this my business the moment you showed up at the building *I* own pretending to be something you're not." He chuckled. "Isn't that right, inspector?"

Max ground his teeth together. He had a feeling Logan had somehow figured it all out. "It's not what you think, damn it."

"Funny seeing how I don't have a clue what to think. I have my reservations about you, Max. Always have. But I've seen how you are with Valerie and Leah, and never in a million years would I think you're such a lowlife that you would use a job title to get into a woman's pants. So why the hell would you let Jessa believe that you're the new city health inspector?"

He sighed. "It's a long story, but the summed-up version is that I was trying to get her to leave town because she was taking Pops' customers away from him and he's about to go out of business."

Logan lifted a brow. "Pops is that old guy who owns the Empty Plate Café, right?"

"Yeah, he's a good friend of mine."

Logan smirked. "You sure about that? I still find it hard to believe that anyone other than Sam actually likes you."

"Very funny, smart-ass." But Max grinned. It was probably true. "You want to hear this or not?"

"All right. Go on."

"Okay, so here it is. The old man is a friend of mine and he's losing money every day because the Gypsy Cantina has been parking across the street from his restaurant. He won't be able to stay open much longer so I told him I'd pretend to be the new inspector and run the truck off. I was just trying to help him out."

"By hurting Jessa?"

Max shook his head furiously. "No. I didn't know that she was running the food truck at the time. And by the time I figured it out, it was too late. I'd already put my foot in my mouth. But I haven't done anything all that bad. I've made up some ridiculous fake city code violations and told her to fix them. Other than that, I didn't do anything to hurt her."

"Yet, you mean? You haven't done anything to hurt her *yet*. I saw the way she was looking at you in that kitchen, Max. There's more going on than you just lying to her about your profession."

Lord, were they really going to talk about this? "Look, *Dad*, if you dare ask me what my intentions are with her, I'm getting up and leaving."

"I'm just saying that it wasn't a *we're-just-friends* kind of look. She obviously likes you a lot, and you're sitting here feeding her a bunch of bullshit. Don't you think she's going to figure it out at some point?"

Max ran his hand through his hair. "Yeah, I do. That's

why I need to tell her the truth before she does. I just…don't know how to. I'm working on that."

"Well, you better work faster. Because if you don't tell her soon, I'm going to."

Anger simmered in Max's blood, and his eyes narrowed. "Like I didn't know that already? Of course you'd look for any excuse to send me up shit creek without a paddle. I'm not the least bit surprised, Logan. In fact, I don't even know why you didn't let the truth come out in the kitchen a few minutes ago instead of covering for me. I'm sure you would've loved seeing me in hot water."

Logan set his beer down and swallowed. "I didn't do it for *you*. I don't give a shit if you get yourself in hot water or not. You've always been an instigator, and yeah, payback would've been a bitch for you back there. But there's only one reason I stopped it from happening and that was for Jessa's sake. She's a sweet girl. The last thing she deserves is you fucking with her head like this. So you need to fix this shit. Now. Or I'm going to."

"First off, I already planned on it. Second, Jessa's not a girl. She's a woman."

"Yeah, but she's short and sweet and has those freckles, which makes her seem more vulnerable somehow. That only makes me want to protect her more… especially from the likes of you."

A grin stretched Max's lips. "Yeah, well, I felt the same way about Valerie. We're good friends, and I only wanted the best for her. Unfortunately, she had shitty taste in men. It is what it is."

There. Now they were back on solid ground.

Logan chuckled and clanked his bottle of Corona against Max's Bud Lite. "Touché."

"Great talk," Max said, taking another swig from his bottle. "We're good, right?"

"Yeah, we're good," Logan agreed. "But you know Valerie's brother, Brett? He still hates your guts."

Max smirked. "What can I say? Feeling's mutual."

* * *

Jessa awoke to something touching her thigh.

It was a...hand. A very large, very warm one. And it didn't belong to her. *Holy hell. The man is insatiable.*

She couldn't move so she didn't even bother to try. "Again? So soon?"

Max chuckled. "You up for it?"

Well, no. Not entirely. When Max had arrived earlier in the evening, she'd opened the door and started to ask him how things went with Logan. But before she could, Max had covered her mouth with his, kicked the door closed with his foot, and began yanking off her clothes. Her legs still felt like jelly from where he'd taken her up against the wall an hour before. Afterward, they'd collapsed on the bed, their limbs intertwined while they dozed off.

"One more hour," she said, yawning. "Then I'm all yours."

But Max apparently had other ideas. His hand continued up her inner thighs, massaging lightly, while his fingers shifted upward. "I don't think I can wait another hour. I'm selfish like that. Open up," he said, giving her leg a nudge.

She giggled. "Okay, but I'm warning you now. I'm just going to lie here. I'm too tired to move. I had a long day and spent most of it on my feet."

Max leaned over and kissed her mouth softly. "You can lie there. I just want to taste you again. That doesn't really require any effort on your part."

She smiled. "Should I give an occasional moan to let you know that I'm still awake?"

A smile spread across his face, and he winked at her. "It certainly would be appreciated." He moved down her body and positioned himself between her legs. "Though if what I'm about to do to you doesn't have you screaming my name at the top of your lungs, there's something seriously wrong with the both of us."

Jessa laughed. "I'm sure my neighbors hate you already."

Propping each of her legs over his strong shoulders, Max nuzzled his head between them. The stubble on his unshaved jaw scraped lightly against the sensitive skin of her inner thighs, and she squirmed a little in response to the sensation.

"So you *can* move."

She grinned. "Looks like I'm gaining back some of my abilities."

"Hallelujah, it's a miracle!"

She started to laugh, but without warning, he nestled his face into the apex of her thighs and found her with his warm mouth. The laugh came out more like a strangled gasp, and her hips jerked involuntarily at the sensation.

His hard, muscular arms wrapped around her soft, pliable thighs in a death grip, holding her in place as he began his onslaught. Without a doubt, he wasn't going to let go until she fully surrendered everything she had. And that thought only made her nipples peak and her breath quicken.

His tongue slid over her in a sensual rhythm, gliding through her wet folds and teasing her clit. Sharp teeth lightly grazed over her, nibbling on that sensitive little bud, then sucked on it until she began to pant harder.

Jesus. She hadn't felt this good in... well, about an hour.

Max slid his fingers into her. First one. Then another. And after pumping them in and out for a while, stretching her, he finally added a third. The overwhelming sensation of fullness and pressure against her inner walls only brought her closer to the edge. But it was when he started rubbing against her G-spot that the exquisite heat pooled in her abdomen, radiating out to her limbs.

Her hands fisted in his hair. "Oh God. Oh my God! Oh... I'm going to..."

He firmed the pressure of his mouth and thrust his fingers faster. Her head thrashed back and forth on the pillow. Desire coated her with wetness. Need flooded her system. Spasms of raw pleasure spiraled through her belly, making her body twitch in delight.

When the glorious convulsions finally subsided, Max lifted his head, his lips glistening with her arousal. He licked them. "So fucking good."

Her eyes were closed at half-mast, and she sighed contently. "I'm sorry, but I'll need another hour before I can return the favor."

"Like hell you will," Max said, moving swiftly between her legs and lifting her hips until his erection prodded at her. "I think we're about to witness another miracle."

Chapter Thirteen

The next day, Max stalked into the Empty Plate Café and plopped down at his usual table. Pops had been sweeping the floor over by the front windows, but he abandoned his broom and came right over.

"Hey, Max. You're here early today. What can I get for you?"

"A brain," he grumbled under his breath.

"What was that?"

Max sighed. "Nothing. I'll have the special."

His curt tone must've caught Pops' attention because the old man rocked back on his heels and crossed his arms. "What's bothering you?"

Everything. "Nothing," he snarled. "I'm fine."

"You don't look fine."

Max breathed out hard. "Just hungry, I guess."

"And grouchy as a bear," Pops said with a grin. "You want to talk about it?"

"No."

Pops nodded. "All right, that's fine. I'll just go fix you up something to eat. But if you aren't in a better mood by the time I return, you're going to tell me what's bothering you . . . whether you want to or not."

Max rolled his eyes. He wasn't in the mood to take orders. "Or what?"

"Or I'm not going to bother washing my hands next time I make your lunch." Pops raised one brow, daring Max to say something else.

"That's blackmail."

"Yeah. So? What are you going to do about it—tell my other customers?" Pops chuckled to himself as he headed for the kitchen.

Max shook his head as the old man vacated the room. Of course he wasn't going to tell the other customers. "There's no one else here to tell," he said out loud though he knew Pops hadn't heard him. The place was as dead as ever.

But within seconds, the doorbell chimed as someone entered through the front door. Guess he had spoken too soon.

Sam stepped into the dining room. The moment he spotted Max, he marched straight over to him, anger flashing in his eyes and a grim expression on his face. "What the hell is wrong with you?"

Max leaned back in his chair, propping one arm on the chair next to him. "Me? What the hell is wrong with you?"

"My problem right now is you."

Max shrugged. "Then why are you here?"

"We always eat lunch together on the weekdays, dipshit. Or did you forget about that?"

"No, I didn't forget. But it's not lunchtime," Max said sarcastically. "Besides that, I don't eat with traitors."

"Traitor, my ass."

"What else would you call it when your best friend kicks you off his construction site?"

Sam's jaw tightened. "I wouldn't have asked you to leave if you hadn't been throwing shit around all morning and cussing out anyone who came within hearing distance of you. I gave you two warnings."

"That didn't mean you had to fire me in front of the entire crew. What were you doing? Using me to set an example for the rest of them?"

A smug grin tugged at Sam's mouth. "First off, I didn't fire you. I told you to take the day off and not come back until you had worked out whatever the hell was wrong with you. Second, you're damn straight I used you as an example. I'm not going to allow anyone to behave that way on one of my job sites and get away with it. Not even you." He turned a chair around and straddled it. "Now tell me what's got you so pissed off."

"Nothing," Max grumbled.

"Bullshit. I know you better than that. You've never gotten that twisted up at work about anything before. And there's only one thing I can think of to make you act like you haven't got any sense left in you. So who is she?"

Damn it. The sonofagun nailed it. "I don't want to talk about it."

Sam narrowed his eyes. "I don't give a damn what you want. Start talking. Otherwise I'm going to fire you for real."

Jeez. What's up with all of my friends trying to black-mail me?

Max hesitated to answer, but the determination in Sam's eyes told him that he wasn't going to give up easily. "Fine. The problem is that I did something that I shouldn't have, and now I can't get out of it."

"What'd you do?"

Max shook his head. He couldn't bring himself to tell Sam the whole story. "Doesn't matter. But it's put me between a rock and a hard place. No matter what I do to try to fix it, someone is going to get hurt in some way."

"Does it have to do with two women?"

He gave Sam a *yeah, right* look. "Of course not. I'm not that big of a jerk. It's only one woman. I, uh, sort of lied to her about something."

"So tell her the truth."

"Easier said than done. Especially since I've made things worse by sleeping with her. I've spent the past couple nights in her bed, and if I tell her the truth now, she's probably never going to speak to me again."

"Is it something she's going to find out eventually?"

"Yeah."

"Then you better be the one to tell her. If she finds out some other way, it's only going to make things worse."

Max nodded. "I know."

Whether he liked it or not, Sam was right. Max needed to be the one to tell her and hope like hell that she would allow him a chance to explain himself. Jessa was a kind, sweet individual. But how forgiving was she? That was something he wasn't entirely sure of. Especially since he knew she was still affected by the last guy who used her and moved on. Not that that prick deserved her forgiveness.

Hell, maybe I don't either.

Sam rose from his chair. "All right. I need to get back to work. Get some rest today and be ready to work tomorrow."

"So I can come back to the job site?"

"Nope. Until you get back in the right frame of mind, I don't want you anywhere around my crew. But tomorrow you can start rewiring that old house over on Hickory Lane. The demolition has already been done on the inside, and the wiring has to be installed before my guys can put up Sheetrock. That'll keep you busy, and since you'll be there alone, your bad attitude won't rub off on anyone else."

Max shrugged. "Fine by me. I don't feel much like being around anyone anyway."

"I figured as much," Sam said with a nod. "But do me a favor. Spend this week getting your shit together. The problem isn't going to go away if you ignore it or let it keep happening. Trust me, I know this from personal experience. Right after you left, the plumber busted another pipe, and I fired him on the spot. My problem is now solved. Or it will be when I get back to the office and find a replacement for him. Now it's your turn to resolve your own issue."

"I'm going to." *Somehow.*

"Good. But the next time you need someone to talk to, just come to me. Don't start throwing hammers at the damn wall."

Max grinned. "It was a better option than banging my own head into it."

"Yeah, but it seems to me you've already been doing that anyway."

Pops stepped out of the kitchen carrying a tray of food. "Hey, Sam. You here to eat?"

"Depends. Do you have any of the special left?"

"Nope," Pops said with a grin.

"That's what I thought," Sam replied. "That's okay. I have to get going anyway. Just stopped in to talk to Max for a minute."

"All right," Pops said as he slid the tray in front of Max. "Here's your special, grumpy ass."

Sam laughed. "He must've given you lip too, huh?"

Grinning, Pops nodded. "Yeah, but I bet he won't do it again."

Max sighed. "Sorry, fellas. I didn't mean to take it out on either of you. It won't happen again." He gazed at the turkey sandwich on wholegrain bread with the side of baby carrots and peach slices, and then glanced warily at Pops. "You washed your hands, right?"

Pops chuckled. "Would you believe me if I told you I did?"

"Probably not."

"Then yeah, I washed them."

Sam burst out laughing. "Maybe I won't come back later, after all." He gave them a teasing grin and headed for the door. "See you guys later."

The moment Sam exited the building, Pops turned to Max. "You think he's onto us about the special?"

Max shrugged. "Probably. But I kind of hope he isn't. It's fun making him think you hate him."

"You're a rotten scoundrel, Max."

Memories of the past two weeks flooded his mind.

"Yeah, tell me about it," he said, regret coloring his tone.

Pops gazed at him for a moment, and then the old man did something that Max had never seen him do before. He pulled out a chair and sat down at the table. "Why don't you tell me what your problem is. Maybe I can help."

"That's just the thing, Pops. You can't help. I was actually trying to help you."

Confusion settled into the fine lines around Pops' eyes. "Trying to help me? What do you mean—" The corners of his mouth turned down. "Don't tell me you're still messing with that young woman from across the street?"

Max winced. "Well, sort of."

"Damn it, Max. I thought maybe you learned your lesson that first day when you went flying off the handle. Why would you keep screwing with her like that?"

"Like I said, I was trying to help you. I thought if I could just aggravate her enough to make her leave, then you could keep your business and things would go back to the way they were. But then...I don't know what happened." He scrubbed a hand over his face.

Pops leaned back in his chair and tapped his fingers on the table. "You fell for her."

Max blinked. "What? No. I just...I, uh...okay, maybe. But I didn't mean to."

The old man grinned. "Does she know?"

"Well, yeah. That's sort of what is complicating the matter."

"So what you're saying is that the two of you have been intimate." It wasn't really a question, rather a statement of truth.

"Yeah. But she still thinks I'm the health inspector."

"I see," Pops said, nodding. "You plan on telling her the truth?"

"Yes, but I don't know how to do that just yet. I've lied to her so much in the past two weeks that I doubt she's going to just laugh it off and pretend it doesn't bother her. The only thing she will know for sure about me is my name and that I've done nothing but lie to her from day one. I doubt she'll forgive me."

"Do you want her to forgive you?"

Max squinted at his old friend. "What kind of silly question is that? Of course I want her to forgive me. Why wouldn't I?"

"Because you've always had a bad habit of keeping everyone—especially women—at arm's length. It's about time you finally let someone else in."

He just shrugged. "Yeah, maybe."

Pops stood and pushed his chair in. Then he gazed down at Max. "Secrets always have a way of coming out. If I were you, I'd sleep on it and consider how you're going to break the news to her, and then tell her. Don't wait any longer than that. Telling her soon is important. Sometimes accomplishing the task is more significant than doing it perfectly."

Max nodded. "I know. And I'm going to tell her. I'm just trying to work up the nerve to do so."

"Good," Pops said, squeezing his shoulder. "Like me, you don't have any family that lives here in town, but if you're ever in need of some fatherly advice, I'd be happy to be the one who provides it. You're the closest thing I have to a son, ya know?"

Max's throat tightened. "I feel the same way about

you, Pops. No one has ever supported me like you have. I can't tell you how much it means to me. I'll never forget it for as long as I live."

Pops smiled at him and then glanced toward the kitchen. "Well, I guess I should go find something to do while I wait for Sam to show up for lunch. In the meantime, you sit here and eat while you start thinking about how you're going to resolve your issue."

Max nodded in agreement. "I'll do that. Thanks for the advice."

"You're welcome." Pops headed for the kitchen door.

"Hey, Pops?"

The old man stopped and glanced back. "Yeah?"

"We haven't been fishing in a while. You want to go next weekend?"

"You bet, son."

* * *

Max headed directly for Jessa's truck.

It was weird. He'd never felt all that guilty about lying to people in the past. Like when he'd told Sam that he needed a wingman and had hooked him up with Leah. Or when he'd lied to Logan about buying the bar with Valerie's money. Or the countless times he'd lied to cover up his issues with food.

But this was different. The more time he spent with Jessa, the more he longed to tell her the truth and not have this issue hanging over their heads. Yeah, he did something shady to her in order to help Pops. But damn it, he had a good reason.

Then again, was there any good excuse to lie? Would

she even consider that he'd done so for the right reasons? The last thing he wanted was to lose her.

And that in itself was a huge problem. Because whether she forgave him or not, if Jessa stayed in town, he wasn't sure where that left Pops and his café. Maybe once he explained the problem to Jessa though, the three of them could work together to find a solution. Well, if she was still talking to him by then.

He had no doubt she would be pissed at him. At least at first. But maybe once she cooled off, she would realize that he'd only lied to help out a friend and that he hadn't meant to cause her any real harm. He just wanted her to move her truck. It's not like he wanted her to be permanently out of business. Surely that counted for something, didn't it?

Either way, he would soon be finding out.

Max knocked on the door and waited for her to open it. It was lunchtime, and they were busy, but since she usually had the other women working with her, he was hoping Jessa could spare a few minutes for the two of them to talk. And he didn't really have to worry about anyone recognizing him since he planned on taking her away from the truck to have this conversation.

But it was the older woman with short gray hair who cracked open the door. "Yes? Can I help you with something?"

He tried to peer around her. "Maybe. Is Jess here today?"

"Yes," she said, opening the door a little wider. "But right now she's eating lunch with Harry."

Max's spine straightened, and his stomach twisted into a knot. Who the hell was Harry? Jessa hadn't at all mentioned that she was still dating other people. Not that he'd asked. But since he'd been sleeping in her fucking bed the last couple nights, he basically figured he didn't have to.

What kind of shit is that? "Who's Harry?"

The older woman gestured to the other side of the park. "Harry is the homeless man who's been camping out behind that rusty old Dumpster for the past few weeks."

Max stared off in the direction the woman had gestured to, and sure enough, he spotted Jessa sitting on the edge of a broken concrete curb with a big, bearded man...by the Dumpster...near a wooded area. Because that was real fucking safe.

Jesus. What the hell was she thinking?

The woman smiled politely. "Do you want me to tell her you stopped by?"

"No, that's okay. I think I'll just go over and say hello. I could use the walk." Because he damn well needed to burn off some of the steam that was filling his head and about to blow out of his ears.

Max headed off in the direction of the trash receptacle, keeping both eyes on Jessa at all times while a persistent vein throbbed in his temple. Why would she put herself in a possibly dangerous situation like that? The guy could be a serial killer. The woman shouldn't be hanging out with some strange man that she didn't know.

Then he almost laughed at the thought. It dawned on him that that was exactly what she'd been doing with him...though they'd been doing a hell of a lot more than just hanging out by a Dumpster ever since the other night. But that was different though, wasn't it? Max had credentials as the city health inspector. Sure, they were fake and all, but it wasn't like Jessa knew that.

Fuck. That only proved his point. You never knew who you could trust nowadays.

Even more worried than he'd been seconds ago, Max marched across the park a little faster. He thought it would be too obvious if he ran toward her waving his arms and telling her to run for safety. So he kept the pace steady so that he didn't look like a lunatic.

But it was too late. The moment the two of them caught a glimpse of Max heading in their direction, they both rose instantly to their feet. Before he even made it over to them, Jessa began moving toward him while Harry headed off in the opposite direction on an old rusty bicycle.

As Max approached her, he said, "Everything okay?"

Jessa stopped and shielded her eyes from the sun's glare. "Sure, why wouldn't it be?"

"Your ... friend left awfully fast. Did I scare him off by coming over here?" *Damn serial killers.*

"Not at all. Harry just likes to keep to himself most of the time."

Yeah, except for when he's planning some innocent woman's murder.

"We had just finished eating when I saw you walking toward us so quickly. I thought maybe Mary or Lisa asked you to come and get me. They like to boss people around," she said with a giggle. "I think it's the mother persona in them."

One of his brows rose. "Do they order you around?"

She waved her hand through the air, as if she were brushing something away. "Only in a sweet way that shows they care. Nothing ever mean spirited, if that's what you're asking."

That only proved how naive and gullible Jessa truly was. Her own workers apparently tell her what to do while she made excuses for them. Great. Apparently she needed protection from them as well.

"So if Lisa or Mary didn't send you, then what were you doing here?"

"I just wanted to make sure you were all right." He glanced in the direction Harry had gone, but he didn't see him anymore. "I was worried."

Jessa followed his gaze, and one corner of her mouth drooped. "You mean because Harry is homeless?"

Max gave her a *yeah, right* look and shook his head. "No, I mean because he's a strange man that you don't know very well. It has nothing to do with him being homeless. Whether or not a person has a home isn't a requirement in order for someone to drag you behind a Dumpster and kill you."

Her eyes widened. "Jeez, morbid much?"

"It happens all the time, Jess. You need to be more careful."

"I appreciate your concern, Max, but it's unnecessary. It's broad daylight, and there are people all over the park. What did you think Harry was going to do to me—stab me to death with a plastic fork?"

Okay, maybe it did sound stupid when she put it like that. "Of course not. I just want you to remember to be careful, that's all. I don't want anything to happen to you."

She smiled. "Always watching out for someone's health and safety, aren't you, inspector?"

His jaw tightened. "Something like that."

"Well, then I should probably forewarn you that I try to eat lunch with Harry several times a week. It's sort of our thing."

Max gazed at the ugly black trash container. "This may be a silly question, but when you say you eat lunch with him every day, you mean..."

Jessa smiled, as if the idea of her Dumpster diving for a meal humored her. "I make us both a lunch and sit with him while we're eating. Harry seems to enjoy the company."

Thank God. That was what he was hoping she'd say.

"Well, I don't like that the guy took off so fast when he saw another man approaching. Seems odd. I'd like to check him out just to be on the safe side."

She giggled. "That's funny. He said the same thing about you."

Max's head snapped up. "What do you mean? You were talking about me to that guy?"

Jessa gave a nonchalant shrug. "A little."

"Why?"

"Because he asked me if I was seeing anyone."

So the old guy had been hitting on her? *That son-ofabitch.*

A muscle in Max's neck twitched, and his eyes narrowed. "And just what the hell did you tell him about us?" His tone came out way more hostile sounding than he meant for it to, damn it.

She apparently noticed because her brow rose instantly. "I only told him that I was dating you." She stared at him blankly. "But clearly that bothers you, so I'm sorry I said anything. Don't worry. It won't happen again." She started past him.

Shit. He hadn't handled that well at all. "Jess, wait."

She turned back and crossed her arms. "What?"

"I'm sorry. I didn't mean to imply that we weren't—"

"It's fine," she said, holding up a neutral hand although her frosty tone very clearly stated otherwise. "It's not like I thought you were my boyfriend or anything. I only told Harry we were somewhat involved because I thought it was more polite than telling him that we were...just...just screwing."

Max cringed. He had no doubt she'd only used the crude language to make a point. But really? "We're not 'just screwing,' Jess, and you know it."

"Then what *are* we doing?"

He paused. *Good question.*

Max had never meant for anything to happen between them. But he liked Jessa a lot. Actually, he probably liked her more than he should, seeing how every minute he spent with her was one of betrayal. Not only to Jessa because of his lies, but also to his friend Pops who only recently found out that Max had been sleeping with the enemy. Unsure of what to say, he sighed. "I don't know."

"Well, great. Glad we cleared that up. If you'll excuse me now..."

He reached for her hand, stopping her from walking away. "Look, I don't know what this thing is between us probably any more than you do. It's new. It's attraction. It's fun. And it's...well, complicated. Maybe all of that rolled up in one."

She shook her head. "I guess it doesn't seem all that complicated to me. But it's fine, Max. We never set any rules or limitations. I guess I'm just the kind of person who wants to have those boundaries in place before getting in over my head." She smiled. "Just goes to show that we don't really know each other all that well. It's okay though. Forget I said anything. Let's just keep things simple and uncomplicated."

"You're wrong about that. I do know you, Jess. You're adorable and kind. Funny and sexy as hell. Brave and ambitious too. Do you want me to go on?"

She giggled. "You're sweet, Max, but throwing out a bunch of adjectives that could describe almost anyone doesn't mean you truly know me."

Why the hell did this crazy woman keep saying that? Sure, he didn't know *everything* about her, but they'd only just met less than two weeks ago. That was what time was for, wasn't it? Getting to know the person you're with.

Frustrated beyond belief, he curled his hand around her neck and drew her closer, her lips a breath away from his. "I know you, all right. Every damn inch of you, in fact. For the past two nights, I've been doing nothing but studying your lovely expressions, learning the curves of your gorgeous body, and figuring out all of your wants, needs, and desires. And trust me when I say that I *do* pay attention."

Her mouth dropped open slightly, but she didn't speak at first. Only blinked in rapid-fire succession. Then finally, she swallowed and said, "Go on."

He grinned. "I know you, Jess. Intimately. I know where and how you like to be touched in all of those secret, special places of yours. I recognize the scent of your arousal and can tell exactly when you're soaking wet and ready for me. I can recall every sound you've ever made when I'm sliding my cock into you. Every. Single. One.

And I've memorized the flavor of your orgasms every time you've allowed me to capture that sweet essence on my tongue." He leaned forward, his lips brushing against hers as he spoke. "I can still taste you on my lips even now," he whispered, his voice low but insistent.

She swallowed audibly.

Max backed away and gazed into her eyes, making sure she understood him completely. "But most of all, Jess, I know your heart." He punctuated his words by flattening a hand on her chest, feeling the thudding organ beating beneath his palm. "And this is what matters the most."

Chapter Fourteen

The next night, Jessa sanitized the stainless steel countertops as she wiggled her butt to the tune of a song she was singing. It wasn't like she could sing well, but it sure beat listening to the sound of crickets outside that had started their nightly chorus since it was almost dark.

"Ahem."

She spun toward the sound to find Max standing in the doorway. "Oh, hey."

"What are you doing?"

Crap. "Um, singing. Got any requests?"

"Yeah," he said, grinning in amusement. "That you turn on a radio."

She laughed. "I would, but my radio isn't working." She bumped his hip with hers. "Besides, you love my horrible singing."

"I can fix it," he said.

"My singing?"

He grinned. "No, sorry. Some things can never be fixed. But I can take care of the radio."

"Jerk," she said playfully. "Knock yourself out with the radio." She nodded to it sitting on a shelf directly over the refrigerator. "There's a screwdriver over there already from earlier where I was trying to get it to work. As you can plainly see, that didn't happen."

He headed straight for the small silver radio, rolled up his sleeves, and started tinkering with it. "Busy day?" he asked, not bothering to look up from the task at hand.

She went back to wiping the counters. "Yeah. I'm thinking I'm going to start having to prep and load more product before heading out in the mornings. Thank goodness it didn't happen until later in the day, but we ran out of almost everything on the truck."

"That's good," he said absently, still checking over the radio.

"Do you know what you're doing over there?"

He shrugged. "Well, I once burned myself on a plug that threw sparks and left blisters on my hands for almost a week. But I mostly know what I'm doing."

"Eh, maybe we should leave the radio to a professional? Or I could actually just buy a new one. They're cheap enough. I don't want you to hurt yourself."

He laughed. "I'm not going to hurt myself, I promise. I will need to run out to my truck though. I think I figured out your problem. There's a loose wire in the back, and I have something in my toolbox that should fix it. Be right back."

"Okay," she said, noticing that he was taking the electronic device with him. "Just don't steal my broken radio. Because, believe it or not, I will call the cops on you." She grinned wide to show him she was teasing.

He chuckled as he stepped out the door. "I wouldn't dream of it."

Jessa continued to work on cleaning up the truck while Max went out to his. By the time he returned, she was just finishing up. "I'm almost done. Just need to throw the cleaning supplies inside the kitchen and lock up the truck for the night."

"Good. I'm done here too." He plugged the radio in and turned it on. Rock music blasted from it briefly before he shut it off again. "I was right. It was just a loose wire."

"I can't believe you repaired that so easily. You're really good with electronics."

"Uh, yeah. I get by." He didn't look like he took that as a compliment. "By the way, is that a new screen door on the truck? I never noticed it before."

Jessa glanced to the doorway. "Yep. The weather has been nice and cool with all of these fall breezes so I'm hoping to take advantage. With the metal door completely shut, we have to run the air conditioner in here, but it's an older one. It doesn't always keep up with the heat coming off the grill."

"Who put on the screen door?"

"Oh, Valerie gave me the number to a contractor she trusted, and he came over and put it on the same day. Really nice guy."

"Was his name Sam?"

She blinked at him. "How did you know that?"

"Sam is my best friend. I'm pretty sure I mentioned him before to you. I've been buddies with that guy for a few years now. Ever since we started working to-gether."

Huh? "Working together? You're in two completely different job fields. Why would the two of you work to-gether?"

Max paused. "Oh, um...well, Sam had a job to do working in a restaurant and I had to inspect the place once he was done."

"Ah, gotcha. That makes sense." She smiled. "For a second there, I thought I had misunderstood what you were talking about."

He nodded. "I just meant that Sam and I have history, that's all."

"Well, he seems like a good friend to have. He did a great job on the screen door. Makes it a lot cooler in here now."

"You know, I could've done it for you if you would've asked. I'm pretty good with my hands." He waggled his eyebrows.

She smiled. "Mmm. I agree. I definitely wouldn't re-port you to the Better Business Bureau."

Max let loose a boisterous chuckle. "You better not or your backside is going to meet my hand."

"Promises, promises."

He stalked toward her with a sexy smirk on his face, and the urge to back away took over her feet. The truck's kitchen was small though, so only a few steps backward had her butt coming into contact with the counter be-hind her. He placed his hands on either side of her, flat on the counter, and his arms automatically caged her in. "You know, you weren't nearly this feisty when I first met you."

She smirked. "Oh, I was. You just didn't know it because I was being extra nice."

Max leaned into her with his warm body, the heavy weight of him pressing against her in the most delicious way. His firm lips found her neck, nibbling and sucking, and she cocked her head to the side to give him better access. He moved upward until his lips were at her ear, and then he whispered, "Would you like that, Jess?"

Maybe it was the way he was making her brain fuzzy, but she didn't have a clue what he was referring to any longer. She liked everything he was doing to her though, so she was pretty sure her answer would be the same no matter what. "Yes."

He groaned. "Baby, you giving me permission to spank your sweet little ass is making me hard as a rock."

Oh, that. Shit.

Whatever. She was down for anything when it came to Max. He had always been gentle with her, except for when he wasn't. And those times were usually because she was screaming incoherent things, loud enough for her neighbors to hear. And she had loved every minute of it. "You might want to hold that thought until we get back to my place. Logan and Valerie are working in the bar tonight, and sometimes they come over to say hi and check on me."

"Damn. That's too bad." He tilted his hips toward her, and she felt the stiffness in his jeans.

Her breath hitched, and her heart pounded in her chest. "No kidding. But let's save that for later, shall we? I still have to stop by the grocery store on the way home or I'm not going to have anything to eat all weekend.

Also, I really could use a shower. I probably smell like I've been battered and fried."

He sniffed her hair. "Actually, you smell more like grilled steak. It smells good...even if I don't eat it."

"That's not comforting in the least. I've had you between my legs. The last thing I want to do is smell like something you won't eat." She waggled her brows back at him.

Max chuckled. "I don't think that you have to worry about that. Anytime you open those gorgeous legs of yours, I'm going to be begging to get my tongue in between them."

Holy hell. The man knew just what to say to make her throb with desire and clench with need. "If you keep talking like that, we'll be going straight back to my place and I'll have to live off of cheese and crackers the entire weekend."

He grinned. "Okay, fine. I'll just wait until I get you naked and then talk dirty to you."

"Deal." She leaned up and kissed him quick, trying to keep it from becoming a full-blown make-out session. Because once it got started, she doubted either of them would want to put a stop to it. "Let's get ready to go then."

Jessa put away the cleaning supplies and locked up the kitchen and the truck while Max loaded her bicycle into the back of his truck. She hadn't known he was going to stop by, but she was glad he did. It beat trying to carry all of the groceries home on her bike any day.

He held her hand in the truck as they drove to the grocery store, which only made her wonder if that meant they were an item. Like an actual couple. She felt like they were, but it wasn't like he'd referred to her as being his girlfriend. Yesterday, he'd told her that he knew her—like really knew her—which was nice but not exactly the same thing as being a couple.

When they arrived at the grocery store, she thought he would just wait in the truck for her. But instead, he followed her in and walked slightly behind her as she pushed the shopping cart down the aisles.

She glanced over her shoulder at him. "Max, you really didn't have to come in with me," she told him. "I'm just grabbing a few things. I won't be long."

He shrugged. "It's okay. I don't mind staring at your fantastic rear while you shop. Besides, I'll be here in case you need any heavy lifting done."

Laughing, Jessa said, "You're such a gentleman."

"Not even close. I'm just trying to hurry you along so that I can get you home and into a bed and stripped down to nothing." He grinned. "I'm sure you already knew that though."

"I figured as much. But you better behave yourself in here or you're going to have to bend me over one of the nearest sale displays."

She lifted onto her tiptoes and stretched out her arm to grab a jar of olives from a high shelf, but it was still just out of reach. Before she could ask Max to get it for her, he was practically on top of her, one hand at her waist, towering over her from behind. His warm body enfolded hers as the rock-hard bulge in his jeans pressed errantly against the small of her back. She sucked in a sharp breath.

Max grasped the jar easily and handed it to her, but she almost dropped it when his tongue traced the shell of her ear. "You really need to hurry or you're going to get your wish," he whispered, his breath tickling her neck.

She shivered and breathed out, "I'll make it quick."

"Good." He backed away from her slowly. "By the way, you'll never hear me say those words to you."

Her pulse quickened. No, Max wasn't the type to rush sex. When he made love to her, it was gloriously slow. He took his time and made sure to find all of those secret places he'd mentioned yesterday. Then he spent a great deal of time touching them. To her delight, of course.

Lord, she wanted to fan herself. If she thought he wouldn't laugh at her reaction, she might've actually done so. How was it possible for one man to have so much testosterone...and stamina?

Not that she was complaining. If anything, she was a damn fool for not jumping on his offer sooner. "Maybe we should just go. I can always come back to the store another night."

* * *

Max grinned as he took the jar of olives from her, setting it down in the metal shopping cart. "You can't live off of olives over the weekend. It's okay. Grab what you need. A few more minutes won't kill us. It'll...build the anticipation."

Ha! Anticipation, his ass. His dick was already standing straight up, hard as steel, and longing to drive hard and fast into her. Not that he would allow that to happen. Max had always been a patient lover who liked to take his sweet time in pleasuring a woman's body. Especially *this* woman's glorious body.

It was an exquisite kind of torture listening to her release sharp gasps as he filled her, her slow sighs as he played with her sinfully delicious curves, her breathy moans as he extended their lovemaking, and finally her desperate cries as she reached ultimate satisfaction.

But God. He was just a man, one with strong needs. If she didn't hurry and get him back into her bed, he probably wasn't going to make it out of the parking lot before he reached for her and started peeling off her clothes. "Let's talk about something else while you're shopping."

"Okay." She paused for a moment as they started down the aisle. "Where were you today?"

Huh. Weird question, but all right. "At work. Why?"

"Because I went by the city hall today to see you."

Panic surged through him, dropping like a lead weight in his stomach. "You did what?"

"Uh, went to city hall."

"Why in the hell would you do that?" Damn it. He hadn't meant to sound like such a jerk.

Her eyes widened slightly. "Well, I had to go there anyway to drop off some paperwork, so I was going to stop by your office to say hi."

Max's body stiffened. He didn't have an office at city hall. Hell, he didn't even have an office. Period. He had a workshop at his house with tons of electrical supplies in it, which was why he always spent the night with her rather than the other way around. Fuck. "You went by . . . my office?"

"No, I was going to. But on my way inside, I ran into Logan. He said you'd already left for the day. That's why I asked where you were. I thought maybe you stopped by the Gypsy Cantina and we missed each other."

Thank God for Logan. Max never thought he'd be thinking that in a million years. At least the tension ebbed, and his body relaxed a little. "Oh, um, no. I had a...doctor's appointment scheduled for this afternoon. That's why I left work early."

"Are you getting sick?"

He rubbed the back of his neck. "No, nothing like that. It was just an annual physical."

"Ah, I see. Well, maybe I'll catch you the next time I'm there."

Shit. He frowned at her. "Jess, you really shouldn't stop by my office unannounced like that. It's hard to...catch me there during the day anyway. Even if you did, my working hours right now are chaotic and busy as hell. I wouldn't have much time to talk."

Her face paled a little at his tone. "I'm sorry. I wasn't planning on taking up much of your time. It was just going to be a quickie."

Christ. She wanted to have sex with him at city hall? Normally, his response to something like that would be, "Hell yeah, sign me up." But since he was lying about having an office at city hall, he couldn't very well allow her to show up there looking for him. "My...uh, secretary is there all the time, and we wouldn't have any privacy for that."

She blinked. "I didn't mean an actual quickie. I wasn't stopping by to have sex with you, Max. I just meant I was going to poke my head in and say hello to you."

"Well, I'd really rather you didn't. The last thing I need is for everyone at city hall to start gossiping about me because they find out that we're sleeping together. I could get fired, ya know?"

"Jesus, Max. I wasn't planning on announcing that. It was just going to be a simple hello before I left to go back to work. But, trust me, it won't ever happen again." She shoved her basket forward and stormed into the next aisle.

Damn it. That was just great. Now he'd made her mad.

Max scrubbed a hand through his hair and then went after her. He caught up with her halfway down the next aisle and grasped her arm gently, halting her forward motion. "I'm sorry, Jess. What I was trying to say didn't come out right. I was out of line."

She huffed out a breath. "You're damn straight you were. I wouldn't do anything to cause you to lose your job. If anything, you should already know that about me since you *know me so well*." She made air quotes with her fingers.

He nodded. "You're right, and I do know that. I was just being paranoid, and it was a poor reaction on my part. I didn't mean for it to come out the way it did. I'm sorry. Please forgive me."

She didn't respond.

"Jess."

She hesitated but then finally sighed. "All right, but you're carrying my groceries inside for me when we get to my house." Then she smiled to show him all was forgiven.

Man, this woman was unbelievably amazing. Her ability to forgive him so easily for being such a jerk astounded him. It also filled him with optimism. Because if she could forgive him for something like this so easily, maybe there was a chance for them after all once he finally told her the truth. One could hope.

He drew her to him and tucked a strand of hair behind her ear. "Thank you. By the way, you're letting me off too easy. I was planning on doing that for you anyway."

"Hmm, then maybe I'll come up with a different punishment for you," Jessa said with a grin. "Maybe it won't be me who gets the spanking, after all."

"Oh no, babe. That's definitely going to be you."

Chapter Fifteen

Jessa climbed back into bed, pulling the covers up over her waist.

Almost instantly, a large hand slid over her hip, palmed her rear, and pulled her toward the center of the bed where a warm male body lay waiting. God, she loved it when Max stayed the night with her.

"What's wrong?" he asked, his sleep-induced voice barely a whisper. "Can't sleep?"

"Not really. I think you made me burn too many calories earlier with all your sexcapades so I got hungry. I went to the kitchen and found something to snack on."

"Peanut butter?" he mumbled groggily.

She glanced at his moonlit face. His eyes were still closed and his breathing deep and slow as if he were half-asleep still. No way had he snuck out there to see what she'd been eating. "Well, it was in cookie form, but yeah, they were peanut butter. How did you know?"

"I can smell it on you from here."

"Oh, sorry." She giggled. "Do you want me to go brush my teeth?"

Max's bulky arm slid up her back until his hand reached the back of her head and he pulled her toward him. He gave her a quick peck on the mouth as she leaned over him and then nuzzled his face into her hair at the side of her face. "No. It smells good."

She was surprised to hear him say that. "Really? Do you even eat peanut butter? Or is that something you can't have on that strict diet regimen you're on?"

"I ate it a lot when I was a kid, but I don't anymore," he said, releasing her and closing his eyes once more.

She got the distinct impression that he didn't want to talk about it so she didn't push the issue. Or maybe he just didn't want to talk period. "Are you still sleepy? You sound a little grumpy."

"Sorry. I've been under a lot of stress and worked late several nights this week to catch up on another job I was doing."

Confusion swept through her. "But isn't your job always the same? I thought a health inspector had a nine-to-five gig?"

His body tensed, and he rubbed a hand over his tired face. "Sorry, baby. I'm still half-asleep. I don't know what I'm saying right now. When I said job, I meant...a new place of business that I had to do some paperwork on. That is what's been keeping me at the office so late."

"Paperwork? Oh. Don't tell me you had to close someone's business down."

"No. Nothing like that. Just my...uh, regular paperwork that I have to do after every inspection."

"Well, that's good. I'd hate to think of someone losing their livelihood. Have you ever had to close anyone down before? I'm sure you have. I can't imagine—"

"Babe."

Her eyes squinted at his interruption. "Yeah?"

Max flung the covers back and lifted his body into an upright position. His well-defined muscles flexed as he propped some pillows against the headboard and leaned back into them. He yawned as he ran a hand through his rumpled hair and then rubbed at his eyes. "I don't want this to come out the wrong way. If you're just wanting to have a conversation, I'm all for it, but can we please talk about something else besides my work?"

Ouch. Okay, that stung a little. "Why? What's the big deal?"

"There's not one."

"If that's the case, then why would you ask me not to stop by city hall to see you anymore?" Yeah, she'd forgiven him earlier, but that didn't mean it didn't still bother her some. The whole thing was just a little odd.

"Sweetheart, if you haven't noticed, I have a hard time concentrating on anything except for sex when you're around. You're just too much of a distraction for me."

She squinted at him. "But you stop by my truck all the time when you're working. Maybe it's just me, but I don't really understand the difference."

Max sighed loudly. "Are you trying to pick a fight with me tonight?"

"Of course not. I'm just trying to figure out why your job—"

"Because I don't want to talk about it, okay?" He pinched the bridge of his nose between his fingers.

"Look, can't we just drop the whole subject and talk about something else? Anything?"

Jessa pursed her lips. She wasn't sure why talking about his job was a big deal, but it made her wonder if there was something else going on. Something he didn't want her to know about. "Are you sleeping with your assistant? Or maybe someone else at city hall?"

His head snapped up. "What? Come on, Jess. Why the hell would you even ask me something like that?"

"Max, I'm not playing around. I really want to know what we're doing here. I'm not trying to sit here and accuse you of cheating or anything like that. We should've made this clear from the start, but we didn't. I'm as much to blame for that as you are. But I'm asking you now, and I'll take whatever your answer is at face value. All I want is for you to be honest with me because the last thing I need is to be made to look like a fool."

"Come here," he said, wrapping his arms around her and easing her closer. When she settled in next to him, he cupped her jaw and lowered his head to gaze into her eyes. "Sweetheart, I'm not sleeping with anyone but you. I wouldn't do that, I promise." He kissed her mouth and ran his thumb along her jaw. "And I would never purposely do anything to make a fool out of you. I just…can't talk about work stuff with you right now."

Oh. She hadn't even considered that there might be a legal reason as to why he couldn't talk about it. It made sense though since, as a business owner, she wouldn't want him talking to others about the operations of her food truck either. "Sorry. God, you must think I'm an idiot making such a big deal out of all of this."

"Not at all. And I'm sorry if I made you feel that

way. I just don't want to think about work when I'm with you. I'd much rather focus all of my attention on you." He settled her against his broad chest and then kissed the top of her head before leaning his back against the headboard. "Now, let's just talk about something else for a while."

Jess craned her neck to look at him. "Like what?"

Yawning, Max said, "Why don't you talk about yourself, and I'll listen."

She laughed. "That's not a conversation. That's me giving a speech. Probably a really boring one."

He rubbed a hand over his face and yawned again. "It's okay. I'll comment occasionally to let you know I'm paying attention."

Yeah right. He was so going to fall asleep on her. "Okay, well, what do you want to know about me?"

"Let's start with an easy question," he said, leisurely stroking her collarbone with the tips of his fingers. "Do you like traveling?"

Jessa sighed. She loved when he touched her like that. "Not really. It was fun when I was little and I was doing it with my mom. And I enjoyed it somewhat when I traveled for work for a few years. But not anymore. Now I'm much more interested in staying in one place."

"How come?"

She tried to shrug, but the weight of his heavy arm over her shoulder made it ineffective. "Different reasons, I guess. Mostly, I think I either grew out of it or just got tired of it. For a couple of years, I'd worked and trained under a celebrity chef who moved from one major city to the next. He specialized in pop-up venues, so we never stayed in one place very long before moving on."

"I think I saw something about those on television once. Don't they call those supper clubs or something like that?"

"Not exactly. Those are actually a bit different from a regular pop-up venue. There are some parallels between the two of them, but there's also a big difference. From my understanding, supper clubs aren't usually legal because they don't follow any rules or regulations. The guy I worked for was legitimate. He was a young, talented chef, but he had a bit of a bad-boy complex when it came to the ladies... and the media."

"Did you and him ever, ah... you know?"

She sat straight up and stared at him blatantly. "What? No, of course not. My God, he was my boss. I'd never— oh." She winced and her forehead wrinkled. "Okay, I get it. So you think I slept with him only because I'm sleeping with you? Is that it?"

Max shook his head adamantly. "No, Jess. I know I'm sounding a bit grumpy since it's the middle of the night, but I swear that's not why I was asking."

"Okay, then why?"

He shook his head. "I was just wondering if I was going to have to kill him for touching you, or if I could let him keep living. Apparently, he's safe... for now."

Jessa laughed at his remark. "Yes, he's safe." She settled back into the nook of Max's arm but gazed up at him. "You know, I wouldn't blame you if you did think that. I mean, I am lying in bed right now with the health inspector who oversees my food truck business. I hate to admit it, but it looks bad."

"Wrong," he said, his tone filled with frustration. "It's not even close to being the same damn thing. I'm not..."

His words faded out, and a pained look took over his face.

"You're not what?"

He hesitated. "Nothing. Forget about it."

"No, tell me." She scrambled into a sitting position to get a good look at him. God, why was he acting so weird tonight? "Max, you can't start to say something and then stop like that. What is it?"

A muscle ticked in his jaw. "I'm not...someone who is going to make a snap decision about you for something like that. I know you said you didn't sleep with him, but even if you had, it wouldn't matter. I'm not going to judge you either way. Just like I hope you wouldn't judge me if you found out I did something that wasn't very smart to do."

"Of course," she said, leaning up to kiss his chin. "We have all done things that we aren't proud of. I'm just glad that, for me, my old boss isn't one of them." She nudged Max with her elbow. "Not that I was ever really tempted. He was such a huge playboy with zero respect for women. That's part of why I didn't want to work for him anymore."

"And the other part?"

"I wanted to cook whatever I wanted, and I couldn't do that as long as I was having to work off of his menus in his restaurants. I had my own creative ideas about the dishes we served and wanted to implement them. Unfortunately, I couldn't do that working for someone else."

"So that's why you bought the food truck?"

She nodded. "Sort of. Owning a food truck has given me the opportunity to cook what I want and how I want without having to work for someone else. So that has definitely been a bonus. But it's not the entire reason why I invested in one."

"Ah, so you had another motive."

"I guess you can say that. I want to open my own brick-and-mortar restaurant."

"Really? Then why didn't you just put the money you spent on the food truck down on a restaurant instead?"

"Because it wasn't enough. Starting up a food truck business is actually a lot cheaper than opening a restaurant. The amount I spent on the truck had only been a quarter of what I needed at the time."

"But couldn't you have worked for another chef in a different restaurant?"

She shrugged. "Sure, I could have. But I love the control that comes with me owning my own business. I can whip up whatever I want, experiment with different flavors and textures, and test out my concept all at the same time. Besides, I needed to establish a name for myself as a chef that produced cutting-edge cuisine at an affordable price."

"You should think about adding some healthy dishes to your menu. Then maybe I could eat there."

"Actually, I've already thought about that. I'm working on adding several healthy options. They should be on the menu by next week. You'll have to swing by and check them out."

"Sure, I'd love to," Max replied with a yawn. "So how did you end up in Granite anyway? You're not from around here, right?"

Jessa shook her head. "No. I actually wasn't sure where I would end up living. I planned to travel around for a while and figure it out. But then I remembered all the stories my mother had told me when I was a little girl about this small town called Granite. She'd told me many times that we would one day move here, but we never got the chance."

"Yeah? How come?"

A sharp pain squeezed her chest, and her throat tightened. "Because she died."

Max pulled her closer to him. "I'm sorry to hear that, sweetheart."

She shrugged. "It's okay. Well, actually it's not, but you know what I mean. We can wish all we want that things were different, but life doesn't work that way."

He nodded solemnly. "Can you tell me what your mother was like? If it's too painful to talk about, I'll understand."

"No, it's fine. All I have left is my memories of her, so I don't mind sharing them with you." Moisture flooded her eyes, but she gave him a smile. "Just ignore the tears. I'm not going to be able to talk about her like this and not cry a little. It makes me sad, but it's good to let it out, ya know?"

He brushed one finger under her eye, capturing a drop that was about to fall. "I'd never ignore your tears, Jess. They're part of you. Just like you shouldn't avoid talking about your mother just because it makes you sad. You were part of her."

Jessa snuggled closer to him and laid her head on his chest. "I miss her every day. I hate that she died and won't be around to see me get married or have her grandbabies." She paused. *Oh, jeez. Why did I say that to him?* "Sorry. I hope you didn't take that as a proposal or an offer for you to be my baby daddy."

She felt a quick chuckle vibrate through his chest. "No, I know exactly what you meant."

Of course he did. God, I'm such a dork. She sighed. "My mother had cancer around her liver, the fast-growing kind."

"How old was she at the time?"

"She was only fifty-eight when she received the diagnosis, but she passed away the following year. The cancer was really aggressive and had metastasized, spreading to her lymph nodes and several of her other organs."

"Damn. That's not good. Did she have any chemo or radiation treatments?"

"No. By the time the doctors realized how far her cancer had already progressed, they basically sent her home and told her to enjoy the time she had left. Otherwise the quality of what life she did have would've diminished to nothing. According to them, she couldn't be saved."

"That's terrible." His arms squeezed tighter around her. "I'm so sorry."

"Me too," Jessa said. "She was the only person I had left in this world."

"What about your father?"

"I don't have one."

"Correct me if I'm wrong, but isn't that how babies work? A man and a woman conceive a child together and—"

"Okay, so I had one, smart guy," she said, shaking her head. "I just never knew him. He had no interest in being a part of my life. So the moment my mom died, I've been alone ever since."

"You're not alone, Jess."

"No, I guess I'm not. I've actually made a lot of new

friends since I moved here, but no one yet that I feel comfortable talking about this kind of stuff with. Other than you, I mean. It's easy for me to talk to you about it."

"Oh yeah? Why's that?"

Her smile was quick, and she beamed up at him. "Because I trust you, of course."

* * *

Her words shook Max to the core.

Christ. What the hell am I doing?

Not only had he been sleeping with Jessa nonstop for the past few days while lying to her, now he'd gone and earned her trust, all the while knowing that he'd be the asshole breaking it in the end. What kind of a sadistic bastard did that to a woman he cared for?

Me, that's who. God, he was such a stupid son-ofabitch.

All of this had gone way too far. He should've told her the truth when he'd had the chance. Like before he'd started sleeping with her. Now, every time he imagined himself doing so, the words stuck in his throat like a splintered chicken bone.

As lovely as she was, he hadn't meant to ever put his hands on her. He'd even promised himself that he wouldn't go there. But not only had he gone there, he couldn't seem to form any definite plans for coming clean any time soon.

So much for just one night. Idiot.

Damn it, the last thing he wanted to do was hurt her. But now that he'd started sleeping with her, he couldn't seem to make himself stop. And as good as it was, the sex wasn't the only thing between them. Not if he was being completely honest with himself. And he had to be. Because he damn sure wasn't being honest with her.

Sometime in the past two weeks, something else had begun to form between them. Max had started developing a strong attachment to her, one that was only complicating matters that were already difficult enough.

What had started out as a forbidden attraction to a customer-stealing vendor soon had turned into him caring about this vibrant young woman and wanting her to do well in everything she did. Unfortunately, that also included her food truck business and her dream of opening a restaurant. After all, she deserved it since she ran the Gypsy Cantina like a champ.

But he still couldn't help but feel torn in half. Jessa's success would mean Pops' failure, yet he would only succeed if she left town. So either way, one of them would lose...which meant Max lost too.

Still, he meant what he'd said to her. Jessa may have lost her mother, but she wasn't alone in this world. No matter what, she had *him*. He wasn't quite sure what that meant at the moment, but he hoped he'd figure it out soon.

"Tell me more about your mom," he said, wanting to give her the chance to talk freely about something she wouldn't talk about to anyone else. "What was she like? Was she like you? Did she enjoy cooking too?"

Jessa laughed. "Um, no. My mother couldn't even warm up green beans from a can without burning them. She was a horrible cook. I think that's why I became so good at it. I grew tired of eating frozen dinners from a box or cold turkey sandwiches every night when I was younger. It made me a fast learner."

Max grinned. "I can't cook either and have had my fair share of sandwiches for dinner. Don't think I've ever burned canned green beans though."

"Good. Trust me, you don't want to. It's the worst smell you can imagine. She forgot them on the stove for so long that all the liquid had cooked out of it, leaving only a scorched mess in the bottom of the pot. We didn't even bother scrubbing it clean. We just threw the whole pot away."

"So I take it she didn't like doing dishes either." He grinned.

Jessa giggled. "Mom only loved two things in her life. Her daughter and traveling. And traveling had actually been her first love . . . until the cancer had taken that away from her."

"That must be horrible not to be able to do something you love so much."

Her eyes filled again. "When my mom got too sick to do it anymore, she'd lie in bed and read her old traveling journals. Her oldest ones were all the way back from when she'd graduated high school. That was the first time she'd set out on the road to see the sights in different places. She once told me that she had been afraid she would one day forget all the wonderful places she'd gone, so she started writing everything down."

"Do you still have them?"

"Yes, all of them. Even the one she wrote for Granite."

He was surprised to hear her say that her mom had actually been there before. "When did she come through here?"

"I'm not sure. It was sometime before I was born, I believe. I grew up listening to her talk about this great little town that seemed like the perfect place to live. Since she always said she was going to return and bring me with her but we never got the chance, I decided to move here. I guess I sort of felt like I was fulfilling my mom's last wish."

"Well, I hope her description in her journal matched up with what you found when you got here. It would be terrible to realize that the town was no longer anything like what your mother had loved about the place back then."

Jessa nodded. "That's true. But since I've never read that particular journal, I wouldn't have any idea whether it matches or not."

He blinked at her. "So you just moved here without even reading what she'd written? You know who does insane stuff like that? Crazy people."

Laughing, she replied, "I know it probably seems nuts for me to pick up and move to a strange town where I knew no one. But I swear I can feel my mother here. And honestly, I haven't really had the nerve to read the journal entries she wrote about Granite. I don't know why. Maybe I feel like the town would be completely different from what it was when she was here, and I...well, I wouldn't be able to feel her presence anymore."

"Aw, sweetheart. You're always going to have your mom with you. It's not the town," he said, placing a hand over Jessa's heart. "She's right here. No matter where you go, she'll always be a heartbeat away."

A single teardrop rolled down Jessa's cheek. "Thank

you. I wish you could've met my mom. She was an amazing woman."

"I have no doubt that's where you got it from." He smiled at her. "Do you have a picture of her?"

"I do, but I haven't unpacked them yet. Since I rented a furnished cottage, I put everything of mine in the attic. I'll pull some out the next time I'm up there." Then she grinned. "But technically, you have already seen my mom's face. You look at her every time you see my truck."

Max squinted in confusion. "The redheaded gypsy woman?"

Jessa nodded. "That's my mom. Well, her likeness anyway. The painter did a great job on it. It really looks a lot like her."

"She's beautiful, but I... well, I just assumed it was supposed to be you. So you both had red hair then?"

"Yep, that's where I get it from. We looked just alike. Everyone always said so."

"And the gypsy thing?"

She smiled. "My mom was born of gypsy heritage, so I guess it was in her nature to travel so much. Strong bloodlines."

"What about you?"

"I'm only half-gypsy, so maybe that's why I don't have the urge to roam like she did. Mom never could sit still while I was always fine with staying in place. We looked a lot alike, but our personalities were complete opposites of one another." She sniffled. "And then she got cancer and wasn't ever the same again."

"I'm sorry you had to watch her decline. That had to be hard. I lost my grandmother to cancer too, but that's not nearly as bad as losing your mother. Especially with you still being so young and not having a father in your life."

She nodded. "It was hard, but the worst of it was watching her take her last breath and not being able to do anything to bring her back. I'd never felt so helpless in my life. She was just…gone, and there was nothing I could do about it."

The dam that had been holding back the waterfall finally broke free, and tears dripped down her cheeks. Max gathered her into his arms, not knowing what to say to comfort someone who had watched their mother die right in front of them. He couldn't even imagine how hard that had been. So he just held her in the quiet darkness of the night until her sobs faded out.

Once she'd regained control, he lifted her chin and kissed her soft lips. "Jess, I think you should read your mother's journals. At least the one for Granite, if nothing else. I have a feeling you'll sense her presence more than ever and have an even stronger connection to her. If she wanted you here in Granite, then I think you need to know why she thought this would be the perfect place for you to live."

"I don't know if I'm ready for that. It still hurts too much."

He brushed his knuckles over her cheek. "It's all right to feel that way. There's no rush, baby. Just do it when you feel comfortable with it. I don't want you to have any regrets about it one way or another."

She shook her head. "I never have regrets, Max. Maybe I get that from my mother, but life is too short to second-guess all of your decisions. Even back when I was homeless, I didn't—"

"You were homeless?" His heart skipped a beat. The thought of her being on the streets without any place to go or anyone to protect her horrified him to no end.

"Yes. I mean, it was only for a few months, but I lived in my crappy blue sedan. After my mom passed away, my life had sort of spun out of control. I was in a depressed state most of the time, and I had a tough time pulling out of it. Nothing went my way, I wasn't working, and I ended up going through a very rough couple of months."

"Is that why you help the homeless guy in the park?"

"Harry? I guess." She shrugged. "I mean, I get it. Life isn't always easy, nor is it always kind. Stuff happens, and it sometimes takes a while before a person can stand on their own two feet again. But I don't think of me feeding Harry lunch as a handout. It's more of a hand-up. It's up to him what he does with that."

Max kissed the tip of her nose. "You're a good person, Jessa Gibson. Most people would pass by a guy like Harry and not think twice about ignoring his current living situation."

"It's hard to ignore a situation that you recognize and have been in yourself."

"True. So what happened that changed that for you?"

"Well, I guess I received a hand-up of my own. Though I didn't have a place to live, I kept my post office box. Thank goodness for that. Because I finally received a check from my mother's life insurance policy."

"Life insurance? I always thought it was nearly impossible to get approved for a policy if you had cancer. They wouldn't cover my grandmother at all."

She shrugged. "I'm not sure, but in my mother's case,

she had her policy years before she was ever diagnosed. So they paid out the policy, and that check was what got me off the streets."

"I'm glad to hear that. I don't like the idea of you being in that kind of bad situation."

"This will probably sound a bit crazy, but it was almost like my mother had reached out beyond death and had offered me a helping hand."

"I don't think it sounds crazy at all. I'd probably look at it the same way if it had been my mother. Your mom would've wanted to help you so maybe she did."

"Maybe." Jessa yawned sleepily.

"Getting tired?"

"Yeah. I think my emotions are wearing me out."

He leaned her against his chest, and his hand slid beneath her shirt and up her spine to the center of her back. "Then get comfortable on me and go to sleep. I'll rub your back for you."

She shifted a little, and then her eyes flickered up at him. "But aren't you going back to sleep too?"

"I will soon."

Right after he figured out what the hell he was going to do about Jessa. Because he was pretty damn sure he was falling completely in love with her. But even that wasn't going to stop her from hating his guts when the truth finally came out.

Chapter Sixteen

The next day, Jessa whistled happily as she strolled down the cracked sidewalk.

Ever since she first arrived in town, she'd been dying to visit some of the charming little shops that made up the town square. Now that Lisa and Mary were able to handle the food truck on their own during a busy lunch rush, Jessa simply couldn't pass up a chance to do so.

She'd already hit the farmers' market this morning and told her workers that it would probably be several hours before she returned. Then she walked the quarter of a mile into town. Since her bicycle was sitting outside of Logan's bar and her employees were manning the truck, she hadn't really had much of a choice.

It didn't matter though. The walk would do her good, and she enjoyed the gorgeous fall weather they were having right now. The bright sun was high in the sky, but a cold front had blown through sometime during the night, leaving behind a light cool breeze that kept her from breaking a sweat.

The town square was centrally located in the small downtown area of Granite and seemed to be the true heart and soul of this great community. It reminded her of a quaint little village since it was home to a host of curio shops and specialty boutiques with old wooden awnings.

It was amazing how all the residents supported their local businesses. People milled about, shopping and chatting, while some waved to familiar, friendly faces from across the way. Most of which she recognized as her customers.

At one merchant's store, a scruffy black dog greeted her at the entrance. She scratched his floppy ear and waved to his elderly owner behind the counter in passing. Then Jessa moved from one aisle to another while perusing their handmade goods. Bird houses in all shapes, sizes, and color. Seashell wind chimes that spiraled downward. Colored glass bottles. Metal yard sculptures. And just about everything in between.

But Jessa wasn't really much of a trinket gal. So she moved to a wall display and picked out a small rosemary-scented candle that was much more her sort of thing. Then she headed for the counter to pay for her purchase.

As she waited for the cashier to ring her up, she spotted a miniature tape measure key chain that reminded her of Max. She smiled and, on a whim, went ahead and bought it for him. He would probably think it was a silly gift, but she didn't care. It reminded her of how they met, and she cherished the memory regardless.

With her purchases bagged up, Jessa headed off for the next store. But as she strolled down the sidewalk, someone yelled her name. She turned to see Valerie and Logan standing outside the popular Sweets n' Treats bakery. "Hey."

"Hi," Valerie said, eyeing her bag. "Doing some shopping?"

"A little. What are you guys doing?"

"Nothing much. We're just meeting up with some friends for coffee. Do you have a few minutes to spare? Maybe you could join us."

Jessa shook her head. "Oh, that's okay. I don't want to intrude."

"Not at all. It's fine. We'd love to have you." Valerie glanced up at Logan. "Wouldn't we, Logan?"

"Of course," he agreed, nodding.

"All right. Sounds good."

Jessa followed them into the bakery, and the scent of cinnamon and warm caramelized sugar filled her nostrils. She inhaled deeply, breathing in the heavenly aroma, as she followed Valerie and Logan over to a corner table where two people sat drinking coffee. She immediately recognized Sam, who was sitting with a pretty brunette who had the most gorgeous green eyes she'd ever seen.

Valerie cleared her throat to get their attention. "Hey, guys. Sorry we're a few minutes late. *Someone* didn't want to get out of bed today," she said, tossing a telling look over her shoulder at Logan.

Sam shook his head. "Lazy bastard."

Logan grinned. "Actually, there was nothing lazy about it. I worked up quite a sweat in that bed." He nodded to his fiancée. "And don't let Val fool you with that innocent act. I'm not the one who started it."

Valerie giggled. "I didn't hear you complaining at the time."

"Nope," Logan said, shaking his head. "And you won't hear me complaining now either."

Sam laughed and then turned his attention on Jessa. "Hey, Jess. Nice to see you again. Have you met my wife, Leah?" He motioned to the lovely green-eyed woman sitting next to him who was smiling politely at her.

"Oh, sorry," Valerie cut in, cringing. "I was thinking everyone had already met."

"It's okay," Jessa said with a smile. She hadn't known it at the time, but she had actually met Sam's wife in person before. Well, sort of. "You were mostly right." She turned her gaze onto Leah. "You're the turkey melt with the spicy avocado sauce. Extra toasty, right?"

Leah's brows rose. "Holy crap. I can't believe you remember that. I ordered that last week."

Jessa laughed at her shocked expression. "Well, unfortunately, I can't remember what everyone orders, but yours stood out to me for some reason. Probably because of the extra toasty part."

"Do you remember what I order?" Logan asked curiously.

That was an easy one. "Of course. You're the fried oyster sandwich with Fresno peppers and the chipotle drizzle."

Valerie quirked a brow. "What about me? I bet you don't remember mine."

"Well, that's because you change your order all the

time. But yesterday you got the savory sausage roll and a side of jalapeño cheddar fries."

"Valerie!" Leah shrieked. "You aren't supposed to be eating that. You said you would go on a diet with me."

Valerie laughed and shook her head adamantly. "No, what I said was that I would *think* about going on a diet with you. But I decided I don't need to diet any more than you do. Life's too short to go without cheese fries. And, holy hell, that sausage was good."

Leah rolled her eyes. "You're ridiculous."

"Actually, it's my brother who's ridiculous. He loves Jessa's take on bacon mac n' cheese so much that he asked me to sneak into the kitchen at the bar and see if I could steal her recipe." Valerie's gaze flew back to Jessa. "I refused to do it, of course."

She laughed. "I don't mind giving you the recipe. It's a pretty easy one to follow. I use three kinds of shredded cheese: goat cheese, mozzarella, and Muenster. He'll need butter, heavy cream, and a touch of garlic to mix in, along with his cooked pasta, and then add some chopped, pan-seared prosciutto before throwing it all in the oven until it's bubbly hot. Remind me later, and I'll write it down for him."

"Oh, Lord, don't do that. Then he's going to want me to make it. My brother can't cook. Hell, he can barely make himself a bowl of cereal. I'd rather him just order it straight from you. That way you make the money off of it, and it saves me the headache. Win-win, if you ask me."

Jessa grinned. "Well, okay. But the offer still stands if you change your mind."

The bakery door chimed as someone entered behind

her, but she didn't get a chance to turn around because Sam grinned at her and said, "Okay, since you're doing everyone else, now you have to do *me*."

A growl rose from behind her, and a very husky male voice asked, "What did you just say to her?"

Jessa spun around, her eyes widening, to see Max standing behind her. He glared at Sam with intensity and something that looked a little bit like... rage? Apparently, he'd caught the tail end of Sam's comment and hadn't liked what he'd heard.

"Oh, um... hi," she said, walking toward him and then stretching onto her tiptoes to kiss him on the lips.

It was just a quick, friendly kiss, and she hadn't thought twice about doing it, but Max's entire body stiffened and his mouth instantly became rigid against hers.

For a second, she thought maybe she'd caught him off guard or something since he'd never shied away from her like that before. If anything, Max would normally have slid his arms around her waist, pulled her even closer, and deepened the kiss. But not this time. Instead, he seemed almost shocked that she'd offered him any sort of a public display of affection.

And as strange as it was, everyone else in the room looked just as surprised as Max. All of their mouths had fallen open, and they each had a wide-eyed stare pointed in her direction.

Why had kissing Max caused such a weird reaction? It wasn't like she'd tried to slip him some tongue or something. *Jeez. Lighten up, people.*

Though she hated to admit it, Max's reaction to the kiss troubled her the most. She found his underwhelming response to be lacking any enthusiasm, and he hadn't kissed her back at all. Then she remembered what Max had said about not wanting anyone at city hall to find out about the two of them.

Was that it? Was he worried about losing his job? Or maybe he was just more of a private person than most and didn't want anyone else to know his business. Either way, it would certainly explain his obvious level of discomfort and why a simple kiss had thrown him into a broodingly silent state.

She hadn't meant to embarrass him. And she hated to think that she'd unwittingly caused him to worry about them being seen together in public as a couple. But they'd been sharing the same bed for the past four nights now...and doing a hell of a lot more than sleeping. Or kissing for that matter.

"Well, this is a new development," Valerie said, still blinking at them. "Jess, I didn't even know you had met Max, much less that there was something going on between you two. Was Max the guy you were talking about last week?"

Jessa's face burned hot. Crap. What was she supposed to tell her? "Oh, no. I was talking about...someone else. Max and I know each other, but, um...it's not like *that*."

One of Valerie's eyebrows arched higher. "Really?"

Jessa glanced back at Max and noted how red his face had suddenly become. Damn. She must've embarrassed him again. "Sure. Max and I are...just friends, that's all."

"Uh-huh," Valerie said, her sardonic tone making it clear that she wasn't buying a word of it. "Do you go around kissing *all* of your male friends on the lips like that?"

"No, of course not," Jessa said, shaking her head furiously. Beside her, Max expelled a hard breath, as if he were relieved she hadn't said yes. He knew as well as she did that Valerie's own fiancé was one of those male friends of hers. So Jessa did the only thing she could and added, "Only the single ones."

"The fuck you do," Max blurted out, his words filled with aggravation.

What the hell is he doing? "No, uh, really. Max, you know I do. You aren't the only guy I kiss on the lips."

His eyes narrowed. "If you don't stop saying that, I'm going to prove you wrong."

She blinked at him. "Excuse me?"

"You heard me."

Jessa didn't know what Max was talking about, but his friends seemed to. They were all grinning like crazy as they watched the weird exchange between Jessa and Max. But she couldn't very well back down now without looking like a liar to all of them...which actually would've been a fairly accurate description of her at the moment. So she said, "Max, stop being silly. You know you aren't the only guy I kiss on the lips like that. There are lots of others."

Reaching for her, he threaded his fingers into her hair and tilted her jaw up until her lips were a breath away from his. "Last warning, Jess. Tell them the truth."

The way he had grasped her and was now looking at her was wickedly sexy, but she was even more confused about what she was supposed to say. So she stuck to her guns. "That kiss...meant...nothing."

"Wrong answer," he growled out before crushing his mouth to hers.

Her hands flew to his bulky shoulders to push him away, but touching this man was like touching a live wire. Her hands seized up, and she couldn't get them to work properly. His warm lips took hers, molding and shaping her mouth with his, as his tongue caressed its way inside, leaving a trail of burning desire. Before she knew it, instead of pushing him away, she began pulling him closer, as if she couldn't get enough of the exquisite sparks he shot through her.

The moment her demeanor changed, so did his. His firm grasp on her loosened, and the passionate kiss turned into more of a lazy, unhurried exploration of her mouth. It reminded her of the way Max made love, and need and want pooled low and deep in her belly.

Jessa couldn't help herself. She desperately wanted to get even closer to him and tried to climb the man like a tree. But he wouldn't allow it. Max broke the kiss off and slowly backed away, and she tried to follow. He chuckled softly and caressed her cheek, setting her back in her own place to keep her from pursuing more pleasure and enticing him to kiss her again.

God, she wanted him. Right now. Later. Forever. Always. Her body was relaxed, her lips swollen, her panties wet, and she wanted the man to take her up against the nearest flat...

She glanced around and saw Sam, Leah, Valerie, and Logan staring at them with open mouths and wide eyes, as if they were weirdly fascinated by what just happened. *Shit.*

The kiss had been indecent. Something two lovers did when they were alone in a bed, tangled between sweat-soaked sheets, and straining their naked bodies together.

Not while standing in a bakery surrounded by other couples.

Valerie fanned herself. "Um, Logan, I think we can officially mark orgy off our list. That was close enough to one for me."

Leah blinked. "Jesus. It wasn't even on our list, and I'm mentally marking it off."

Jessa didn't know what any of that meant, but Sam and Logan seemed to and they both just shook their heads and laughed.

This whole thing was really awkward, and she felt like she needed to say something. "I...um..."

But Max beat her to it. "We're dating, in case you guys haven't already figured that out by now."

Sam nodded. "I'd say you're probably doing a hell of a lot more than just dating after what we just witnessed."

Heat flooded Jessa's cheeks again, and she glanced up at Max. "Sorry. I thought you didn't want anyone to know about us."

"No, that's not it. You just caught me off guard. Actually, I think you caught all of us off guard," he said with a chuckle. "But they're my friends, Jess. I'd much rather them know about us than for you to make them think you're out kissing a bunch of other men." He shook his head. "If you thought I was going to go along with that, then you're crazy. I wasn't going to let you look bad, and they all know damn well that I don't share."

His possessive words sent tingles through her. "Good. Because I don't share either." She grinned as the others laughed. Max wasn't the only one who could stake a claim on someone.

Thankfully, everyone seemed to recover from their

initial shock, and things quickly went back to normal. Well, mostly.

Sam cleared his throat. "So, Jessa, you never answered my original question before this Neanderthal decided to make you eat your words."

Jessa laughed. "Oh, yes, that. You always order the grilled shrimp tacos with slaw and green tomatillo sauce. Is that right?"

He nodded. "Yep, you nailed it. Damn, you've got a good memory. And the shrimp tacos are killer, by the way."

"Thanks."

Max rubbed at the back of his neck. "So...uh, what are you doing here? Shouldn't you be at work?"

She shrugged one shoulder. "Lisa and Mary have the truck covered for now, so I took a few hours off to do a little shopping. Speaking of which, I bought you a little something." Everybody watched curiously as she dug into her small bag, pulled out the miniature tape measure on a key chain, and held it up for him to see. "Ya know, in case you need to measure my tires again," she said, giggling.

He reached for it and smirked. "It's a little small, don't you think?"

Sam chuckled. "You could always use it to measure your dick," he said, making the others laugh.

Max rolled his eyes at his buddy's remark and then gazed back at Jessa. "Thanks for the gift," he said softly. "That was really thoughtful of you."

"You're welcome."

Valerie headed toward the coffeepot. "Anyone want some coffee?"

Logan nodded. "I'll take some. You know how I like it."

His words came out so sexually charged that Jessa wasn't sure he was even talking about the coffee anymore. And since Valerie giggled, apparently she was correct about that.

"I'll take some," Max said. "Black, please."

Valerie gazed at Jessa. "What about you, Jess? Coffee?"

Jessa shook her head. "No, thank you. I'll need to get going soon."

"I can put it in a to-go cup for you."

"Okay. Well, in that case, I'd love some. With cream and sugar, if you don't mind."

Max and Logan grabbed four chairs from the surrounding tables and scooted them over next to Sam and Leah. Everyone took a seat and waited for Valerie to join them. She did so a minute later, carrying a tray with three mugs and one to-go cup of coffee.

"I brought the cream and sugar over since I wasn't sure how much you wanted, Jess."

"Thanks," she said, reaching for one at a time and adding both to her cup.

Max lifted his steaming mug of black coffee to his lips and sipped carefully as he watched her prepare her coffee. With as much cream and sugar as she added, it could probably be classified as more of a dessert. But that's how she liked it.

Although he never said a word, she occasionally caught him eyeing her light-colored coffee. A fit guy like him probably accounted for every calorie he'd ever consumed so he could work it off in the gym. Well, hell if she was going to go to that extreme. She had better things to do.

"How's the food truck business going?" Leah asked. "You seem to stay pretty busy over there at lunchtime."

"It's been going really well," Jessa told her. "And look who's talking. Every morning when I ride my bicycle past here on the way to the kitchen, you have a line out the door of your bakery. Seems you stay pretty busy as well."

Leah nodded. "We're slammed in the mornings when everyone is coming in to get bagels, doughnuts, and coffee, but it usually winds down around eleven. That's why we sometimes meet for coffee around this time. I'm just too busy in the mornings to sit still for long."

"I hear you. This is actually my busiest time, but since I have Lisa and Mary working, I was able to leave. I won't be able to do it all the time, but it's nice to take a short break." She glanced at her watch. "Speaking of which, I probably should be getting back just in case the girls need any help." She rose from her chair. "Sorry I can't stay longer."

"Well, what are you doing tonight?" Valerie asked. "We're all going to hang out at Bottoms Up and have a few drinks. Why don't you come over and sit with us after you get off work?"

Jessa shifted her eyes to Max. "Are you okay with that?"

"Why wouldn't I be?" He brought his coffee mug to his lips.

"Well, other people would see us out together, and then they'll know I'm dating the health inspector."

Max immediately began choking on his coffee, coughing violently as his eyes darted around to his friends, as if he wanted one of them to save him. But Jessa was the closest one to him, so she patted him on the back, hoping it would help.

Leah handed Max a napkin as she tilted her head toward Jessa. "You're dating the health inspector?"

Jessa nodded but squinted at her. What an odd question for Leah to ask. Hadn't she been paying attention a few minutes ago? Because she was pretty damn sure they'd already made it perfectly clear that she and Max were indeed dating. "Yes, that's what he just told you guys."

Valerie looked as lost as Leah did. "Who told us that?"

"Max just did," Jessa said, motioning to him. His coughing finally seemed to be subsiding, but his eyes darted to Logan and they exchanged a strange look. "Are you okay?"

"I'm, um...fine," he said, his voice sounding a bit strained.

"Wait, so who are you dating again?" Sam asked her. "I think we're all confused as to what's going on here."

Jessa sighed. It wasn't all that hard to understand, so she wasn't sure why she would need to explain it...again. "I'm dating Max."

"And the inspector?" Leah asked, her brows furrowing in confusion.

"Well, yes. I mean that is what Max—"

"Don't you have to get going?" Logan asked, cutting her words off. "You said you were running late."

"Oh, crap. Yeah, I do need to go. I've been gone for quite a while. But I would love to join you guys tonight. Any certain time I should be there?"

Valerie still looked confused as ever but shrugged. "Just come on over when you get off work. We'll already be there by then. Leah goes to bed early. Bakery hours," she explained.

"Okay, sounds good." She leaned over and kissed Max quickly on the cheek. "I'm hoping I can convince the inspector to give me a ride home afterward."

Everyone's eyes widened.

Sam shook his head at Max. "Dude, I thought you said you didn't share? Looks like you're sharing whether you want to or not."

Now it was Jessa's turn to be confused. "Huh? Why is everyone looking at me like you guys don't understand what I'm saying?" Had they all been hitting the sauce a little early or what?

Logan cleared his throat. "It's okay, Jess. I think they're just a little dense today. Don't worry. I'll explain everything," he said, his attention directing back to Max. "In the meantime, you should probably walk her out so she can get back to work."

"Good idea," Max said, practically leaping out of his chair and dragging Jessa toward the door of the bakery.

"Um, okay," Jessa said, heading out the door with a wave. "I'll see you all tonight."

Because after this weird conversation, she definitely needed a stiff drink. Maybe even several.

* * *

The moment she vacated the bakery, Max had sighed with relief. After spending a moment chatting with Jessa outside, he'd finally kissed her and sent her on her way, considering he still had to return inside to face the music.

He hated knowing he would have to explain to his friends why he'd been pretending to be the health inspector. Besides Logan, none of them had any idea about it. And no way were any of them going to let him off the hook. But after he'd narrowly avoided Jessa finding out the truth in just the few minutes she'd spent with them all, he didn't have much of a choice.

Tonight, they'd be hanging out in a group for probably several hours, and there was no way he would be able to avoid the subject all night long. He just couldn't take the chance. He had to tell them the truth or risk getting found out... which was something he didn't want to do. But maybe by confessing to his friends, it would make it easier for him to figure out a way to tell Jessa the truth once and for all.

And hopefully keep her from hating his guts. Because the longer this went on, the more likely it would be that he wasn't going to come out on the better side of any of this.

Max headed back inside the bakery and watched as each of his friends glared at him as he stepped back into the room. Apparently, Logan had talked fast and told them everything.

"Damn it, Max," Valerie said. "I can't believe what you're doing to that poor girl. What kind of sick game are you playing with her?"

"It's not a game, Val. It was more of an accidental thing that got out of hand. I never meant to take it this far. I'm trying to figure out a way to fix it."

"Well, that's easy enough. You have to tell her," Leah

said. "You're only making things worse for yourself the longer you let this go on."

He sighed. *No shit.* Time was running out, and his choice was a tough one. He could tell Jessa the truth about his lies and risk losing her forever. Or he could wait for her to figure it all out on her own and risk losing her forever anyway.

"I know. And I'm going to tell her the truth...tomorrow."

Valerie cut her eyes over to him. "Max."

"No, I'm serious." He held his hands up in surrender. "I need one more night with Jess before I tell her the whole truth about me. I have a bad feeling that when I do, she's not going to have anything else to do with me. So I'm taking one more night before that happens."

"That isn't fair to Jessa," Sam said, shaking his head. "And what the hell, Max? It's not like you at all to put your own needs before a woman. Stop being selfish and think of her."

"Screw you, Sam. That's easy to say when you're married to the woman you care about. You know Leah's not about to walk away from you. Unfortunately, I don't have that luxury."

"So you're just going to get your jollies once more before you let her go, is that it?" Logan asked. "Because if so, I just lost a hell of a lot more respect for you."

"Of course not. It has nothing to do with sex. I want to remind her how good we are together before I tell her something that is going to skew that perception. With any luck, she'll try to understand why I did it and stay with me. It's my only chance."

Sam sighed. "That's a desperate move on your part, buddy. You can't hang on to her like that."

"Maybe not. But don't act like you got to the place you're at with Leah without any mishaps on your part. I remember the look on Leah's face when you dissed her on the dance floor the night you met her. I also recall what she said to you the night you found her in the bar. You hurt her...both times."

Leah winced, which had Sam rising to his feet. He shoved Max. "You sonofabitch. Since when did whatever happened between Leah and me become any of your damn business?"

"The moment you started butting your nose into my relationship with Jessa. You aren't perfect, so you might want to be a little more careful about who the hell you're passing judgment on. My relationship with Jess is none of your—"

"What relationship?" Sam snarled. "Jessa doesn't even know who she's dating. Jesus, Max. She thinks you're somebody you're not."

Max grasped Sam's shirt with two hands and got into his face, nose to nose. "She may not know what I do for a living, but she knows me. Damn it, she knows what kind of man I am."

"One who lies?"

Max tightened his grip on Sam's shirt, but before he could say anything else, Logan spoke up. "All right, that's enough," he said, leaning back in his chair. "I hate to say it, but Max is right, Sam. You and I both made our own fair share of mistakes in our relationships. It isn't right to judge Max for screwing up too."

Max turned Sam loose and turned away from him. "At least someone fucking gets it."

Logan nodded. "I do get it. But that's why I'm going to make this real simple for you, Max." He waited for Max to turn around and face him before continuing. "You have until tomorrow night to tell Jessa the truth. If you don't do it by then, I'm going to. Trust me, it would be better coming from you."

Thank God. "That's all I wanted," he said, relieved that he had one more night to show Jessa who he really was. At least on the inside. "I swear I'll tell her tomorrow. You may not like me all that much, Logan, but there's one thing you should know. I'm a man of my word."

Well, he would be if he could stop lying to the woman he had fallen in love with.

Chapter Seventeen

Jessa arrived at the bar a little later than she'd planned.

She would've been here much earlier if it hadn't been for the unfortunate incident she had while cleaning out the food truck after hours. That one little accident had left her covered in oil from head to toe, leaving her no choice but to ride her bicycle home to change out of her grease-stained shirt and to take a quick shower. It was her own fault though. That was what she got for not keeping her apron on while cleaning out the food truck.

Oh well. Stuff happens. It didn't matter anymore now that she was finally at Bottoms Up. And she really wasn't all that late. Just by an hour or so. Actually, it was only nine o'clock, which—as far as bar standards went—was still pretty early for her to arrive.

From the look of things, there was a pretty good crowd already inside, but the place wasn't so packed that she couldn't move around freely. But give it another hour or two and the bar would probably be standing room only.

She'd never actually been inside the bar while it was open at night. Only during the day when the place was closed and there was no one else there except for Valerie or Logan. But they'd told her how much effort they'd put into keeping their regular customers happy and how busy their bar usually was.

Jessa was glad to hear it. She wanted Logan and Valerie's business to continue to do well. They clearly both worked very hard together and deserved every bit of success they achieved.

Gazing around the room, she didn't see Max anywhere. But while looking for him, she spotted Leah and Valerie sitting together at the end of the bar. They must've been there for a while since both women had an empty shot glass in front of them and had nearly finished their bright blue, fruity-looking cocktails. Whatever those were.

Jessa headed directly for them, hoping one of the girls would know whether Max had arrived yet. But as she approached from behind them, she overheard Valerie say, "Were you as surprised as I was about Max and Jessa? I mean, about them being a couple."

Jessa froze in place, not sure if she wanted to hear whatever they were talking about. It didn't sound good.

Leah nodded. "God, yes. She's not at all the type of woman Max usually goes for."

Yep, just like I thought, definitely not good.

"I know. I was thinking the same thing," Valerie agreed. "She's beautiful though and such a sweet girl. I can totally see why he's smitten with her."

"Same here. I think she's adorable."

Jessa's brows furrowed at that, and she cleared her throat. Once both women spun around looking at her with surprise lighting their eyes, Jessa crossed her arms. "Okay, what the hell? If you both like me and think I'm beautiful and sweet and adorable, then why wouldn't I be Max's type?"

Valerie winced. "I'm so sorry, Jess. I hope you didn't think we were talking bad about you. We weren't, I swear."

Leah nodded in agreement. "We were just surprised about you and Max being together. That's what we were talking about."

"I gathered that much already. And just for the record, I wasn't intentionally eavesdropping on your conversation. I was coming over to say hi. But I still don't understand why you two think Max wouldn't go for someone like me. What type of woman does he usually go for?"

Leah's eyes shifted to Valerie, who was cringing. But finally she said, "The last thing I want to do is offend you, Jess, so please don't take this to mean anything toward you personally. It's just that . . . well, when it comes to women, Max has always preferred a certain . . . er, body type over others in the past."

Jessa wasn't an idiot. She knew exactly what Valerie way saying. "You mean he's only ever dated slender women."

Though it wasn't posed as a question, Leah answered it anyway. "Yes. That probably sounds odd to you since you're in a relationship with him, but we've just never seen him dating a woman who actually has meat on her bones before."

"And why's that?"

Valerie shrugged. "We don't know. Although, to be honest, I'm not sure what you could call whatever he does with those ladies dating. Max hasn't been in a serious relationship for as long as I've known him."

"Sam has been friends with him a lot longer than we have," Leah admitted. "Years actually. But even he says that Max only associates with women who are the size of a fashion runway model."

"But he associates with the two of you," Jessa said without thinking. Then she sucked in a breath and covered her mouth. "Oh, I'm sorry. I didn't mean that quite the way it came out. I think both of you are beautiful women. I just meant—"

Valerie laughed and held up her hand. "It's okay, Jess. We're not at all offended. I think I can speak for both of us when I say that Leah and I know we don't look like fashion models. At least not the skinny ones." She winked. "But I think what Leah meant was that Max is associating with those women in more of a romantic aspect."

"Oh. Yeah, I guess that makes sense."

"Not really," Leah said, shaking her head. "I mean, why would any guy date a woman based solely on what size she is? It's kind of stupid when you think about it. Yet, it happens all the time."

"True," Valerie said, nodding. "But there're also guys out there that don't judge a woman on her hip size. We both know that. Just look at Sam and Logan."

"And Max," Jessa said, feeling the need to defend him. "I mean, I get what you two are saying about the women he's dated in the past, but he's never once made me feel like my body was something to be ashamed of."

Leah smiled. "Good. I'm glad to hear that."

"Me too," Valerie agreed. "Especially since I'd always wondered about the first night I met him in Rusty's Bucket. I mean, he was good looking and all. I just wasn't interested in him because I was still hung up on Logan. But knowing that Max wasn't interested in me either, I couldn't help but always wonder if it had something to do with my weight."

"Did he ever say something to that effect?" Jessa asked.

"Oh no. Of course not," Val said, shaking her head. "Max would never purposely make any woman feel bad about herself. I know that much about him. He's a good guy. We just always thought he favored one body type over another. Guess we were wrong about that."

"Apparently," Jessa said with a grin.

Valerie nodded. "Well, it's not the first time I've been wrong about something, and I'm sure it won't be the last," she said, smiling back. "Okay, enough of this heavy stuff. We're supposed to be having fun. I'm going to refresh our drinks. Jess, what are you having?"

She plopped down in the seat next to Valerie's. "A martini, please."

Valerie rose and moved around the counter to the other side, grabbing a martini glass to make the drink. "Do you want it dirty?"

"It's the only way I like it," Jessa said with a quick wink.

Leah laughed. "I think we just figured out why Max is all over you."

Jessa giggled but shook her head. "He's not *all over me*."

Valerie continued making their drinks on the other side of the wooden counter but glanced up. "You're kidding, right? After that kiss he laid on you in the bakery this morning? Clearly, the guy is crazy about you. And he should be. You're absolutely gorgeous."

"Thanks," Jessa said, her cheeks heating. "I think you're both lovely ladies as well."

"Thanks. That means a lot," Leah said, a genuine smile lifting the corners of her mouth. "I have to say, it's refreshing to be in a group of women who are so kind and supportive of one another."

"Well, why wouldn't we be?"

Valerie slid a dirty martini toward Jessa. "Sadly, not all women are like that. There are some that are just downright catty and will judge another woman based on her size. Men do it too, but I think it sometimes hurts more coming from another female. Especially when they're related to you." Her eyes drifted to Leah.

Leah nodded. "I know that's true from my own personal experience." She glanced over at Jessa. "You probably don't know this about me, Jess, but I grew up with a mother who always had something negative to say about me, and her comments were usually centered around my weight."

"Oh, Leah, that's terrible. I'm so sorry to hear it."

She shrugged as Valerie handed her another blue cocktail in a tall, curvy glass. "It's okay. My mom finally realized how damaging and hurtful her words could be and she put a stop to it. Our relationship has actually never been better than it is right now."

"That's wonderful." Jessa reached for her hand and squeezed it. "I'm so glad for you. I was always really close to my mom, so I feel bad any time I hear someone say they have a strained relationship with theirs."

"Does your mom live close?"

A familiar pain stabbed Jessa in the heart, the same one that happened any time she was asked about her mother. "No. She...um, died from cancer a few years ago."

It was Leah's turn to squeeze Jessa's hand. "Oh. I'm sorry."

Before Jessa could respond, Valerie stepped up from behind her and rubbed her shoulder lightly. "Me too." She slid onto her stool between Jessa and Leah.

"Thanks," Jessa said, feeling the sharp prick of tears at the back of her eyes. Not wanting to sit there feeling sorry for the rest of the evening, she blinked them away, cleared her throat, and changed the subject. "So where are the guys? Are they not here yet?"

"They're here," Valerie said. "They were playing pool in the back of the room, but I'm not sure where they ran off to now. Maybe to Logan's office. Who knows? I'm sure they'll come find us soon."

Ten minutes later, the women were sharing funny stories and giggling over them when a warm sensation caressed the back of Jessa's neck. Slowly, she turned and looked around, her gaze falling on Max standing on the other side of the room. She'd felt him watching her. He hadn't touched her physically, but his eyes pierced into her with an intensity that stole her breath and made her knees wobble.

His eyes lowered, trailing over her cleavage as he licked his lips and probed her body with an invisible touch all the way down to her curling toes. The blatant, unchecked hunger in his eyes had her heart skipping a beat and her thighs quivering. She'd never been with a guy before who could do so many dirty things to her with just his eyes.

At least not until Max.

But after what Valerie and Leah had told her, it only made her wonder why he was even attracted to her. Not that she wasn't cute or anything. If you asked her, she was adorable and had a great personality. She was at peace with her size, content with the way she looked, and in general felt great about her curvy body. Always had.

Maybe she didn't have a gap between her thighs and her stomach was bigger than what society deemed acceptable, but that didn't make her any less of a woman. A gal like her with a thicker waistline could be just as fun, lovable, and as sexy as the rest of them.

And since Jessa liked to think of herself as all of those things, it clearly wasn't her overall attractiveness that was in question here. No matter what Leah and Valerie had told her, there was definitely a smoldering interest pulsing off of Max from across the room.

Maybe in the past he had only dated thin women. But Jessa had no doubt that he was indeed attracted to her fuller figure... if the way he was looking at her right now was any indication.

* * *

Max was an idiot.

He couldn't believe he'd pulled his friends into this whole mess. Not because they were still irritated that they were having to lie for him, even if it was just for one night. They would eventually get over that. But it was because he genuinely wanted everything to work out between him and Jessa in the end. And he didn't think it would.

That bit of knowledge sent a dull ache spiraling through his chest and had been detrimental to his mood all night long. Damn it. He had a strong feeling that the moment he told her the truth, he was going to lose her for good. Unfortunately, there wasn't a damn thing he could do to stop it from happening.

"You fellas ready for another round?" Logan asked.

"I'm good," Sam told him.

Max downed the one he had. "I'll take another."

"Okay," Logan said, nodding. "But that will be your third one in half an hour. Slow down or I'm going to have to cut you off."

Max rolled his eyes. "Whatever you say, Dad."

Sam gripped him by the shoulder. "Stop looking so glum about tomorrow. Just think of it like this. Once you tell Jessa the truth, it'll be over."

"Yeah, that's the problem."

"I didn't mean the two of you would be over," Sam said, correcting himself. "I just meant you wouldn't have to worry about it anymore. Either way, all this moping around you're doing isn't helping matters any."

Turmoil continued to swish inside his veins. "Maybe. But you try to come up with a way to tell Leah that you've been lying to her since you first met, and let's see how you feel about how well she might take the news. Then we'll talk."

Logan had just finished giving the waitress their order. "Max, you know this is all your own fault. If you hadn't lied to her to begin with, then there would be nothing for you to have to come clean about."

Max rolled his eyes, his hand fisting tightly around his beer. "Thanks for pointing out the obvious," he growled, his low, rough tone scraping against his vocal cords. "You think I haven't thought of that already?"

"Hey, chill out, buddy." Sam pointed his beer bottle at Max. "We're here to have a good time tonight, and you're starting to drag me down with you. Just relax already."

"Sorry. I'm just wound up extra tight tonight and being overly dramatic."

Sam nodded. "No kidding. But look, I'm sure when you finally tell Jessa the truth tomorrow, she's not going to be very impressed with you lying to her. And chances are good that she'll be upset. But I know you, Max. If you want the girl, you'll get her. You just might have to prove yourself trustworthy before you get back into her good graces. That'll take time, but you can do it."

Sam was right about one thing. It would take him time to get back on her good side after lying to her from the beginning. But thankfully, it wasn't like there was another guy in the picture. He'd have time to win her over, wouldn't he?

Max glanced across the room where Jessa was sitting with the other women, and his eyes snagged on a young guy standing next to her. "What the hell?"

The big man had his hand on her back and was smirking while leaning over her, as if he were going to whisper something in her ear. And she looked to be leaning back as if she couldn't get far enough away from him. The bastard. Even though he didn't seem to be doing anything other than talking to her, it didn't matter. Either way, Max's assessment of the situation wasn't good. Because no matter what happened tomorrow, Jessa was *his* and he didn't like this guy—or any guy, really—hitting on his woman.

Call him territorial or insanely jealous or whatever the hell else you'd like, but he wasn't going to let some guy move in on her when he was about to tell her something that was going to stall their relationship, if not send it in reverse altogether. He couldn't lose her, and he wasn't just going to stand by and let it happen.

Without warning, Max leaped out of his chair and headed across the room with Logan and Sam scrambling after him. It was entirely possible that she didn't need saving from this random guy, but Max was going to make damn sure of it.

The moment he showed up at her side, Jessa's eyes fell on him. "Oh. Uh, there you are," she said, smiling at him before cutting her eyes to the big man standing beside her. "I've been looking everywhere for you, *honey.*"

The fact that she felt the need to cut her eyes at the dude standing next to her and then made sure to call Max a term of endearment she'd never used with him before said a whole lot about this guy's questionable motives and her comfort level.

"Well, I'm here now." His voice lowered. "Who's your friend?" Max made sure his tone was just sour enough to give the guy a hint that he wasn't welcome. An obvious one.

"Um, this is Eric. We just met so we're not really friends yet. More like acquaintances," Jessa said politely, as if she were trying to minimize their association.

"I don't mind if you consider me your friend," Eric said to her with a wink.

Maybe it was the alcohol talking or the pissed-off male inside of Max that was claiming what was rightfully his, but he wedged himself between her and the clown vying for her attention and puffed out his chest. "Well, I mind."

"Max," Sam said from behind him. "Be cool."

Eric lifted one brow. "You got a problem with me, buddy?"

"Yeah, I do."

The big guy shook his head. "Might want to watch yourself."

"Or what?"

"Don't make me knock you on your ass in front of your woman. It won't end well for you."

Max snorted. Hell, he had always been the type to go to the extremes. Besides, he wanted the guy to hit him. Someone needed to knock some fucking sense into him. "I'd like to see you try it, dickhead."

Without hesitation, the guy reared back and punched Max in the right eye, knocking him back against the bar. Pain exploded in his face, but almost instantly, Max lunged back up and launched himself at the man. Unfortunately, he didn't succeed in grabbing him before Logan interfered by blocking his path with his body.

Max shoved him. "Move."

Logan stumbled back a little but corrected himself quickly. "No. That's the end of it. Fight's over."

"The hell it is. It's just getting started."

Logan continued to stand in the way, acting as the buffer. "No, like I said, it's over."

"Why? Because you say so?"

"No. It's because you know damn well that you deserved that punch as much as you were asking for it. I only regret that I didn't throw it myself."

Seemingly unimpressed with his overabundance of testosterone, Jessa said, "Max, let's just go. I'll drive you home."

It was a smart idea, considering that he was losing his ever-loving mind over the thought of this being his last night with her. "Fine," he said, turning toward the exit.

Jessa started to move, but Logan held up one hand. "Jess, if you don't feel comfortable leaving with him, I'll take him home or call him a taxi. I don't want you to put yourself in a situation you don't want to be in by—"

"Logan," Sam interrupted evenly, "Max wouldn't do anything to hurt a woman. *Any* woman. I'd bet my life on that."

"I wasn't saying that," Logan replied. "I was just making sure she was okay with leaving with him. He's a bit of a loose cannon right now, and you know it."

Jessa shook her head at Logan. "It's fine, Logan. Thank you for your concern, but I'm perfectly okay with leaving with him. Max would never hurt me." She turned away to grab her keys from the counter.

Logan snorted and mumbled under his breath, "Yeah, right. Don't be too certain of that." Thankfully, Jessa hadn't heard him.

But Max sure did. If anyone deserved to be punched in the face right now, then that person was Logan. But instead of throwing that punch, Max decided to seek refuge from all the madness surrounding him at the moment. "Let's go, Jess," he said, heading toward the door.

She managed to follow him through the crowd without Logan trying to stop her from leaving. Otherwise, there would've been a fight all right. And there was enough tension flowing between Logan and Max right now that it would've been a good one.

Unfortunately, it wouldn't change the one thing that was bothering Max the most. He had fallen hard and fast for Jessa over the past few weeks, and he only had tonight to convince her how good they were together.

Otherwise, come tomorrow, he was screwed.

Chapter Eighteen

Jessa was so confused.

After loading her bicycle into the back of his truck, Max had handed her the keys to his truck because he was in no condition to drive. Whether that meant the alcohol or his currently angry state, she had no idea. But he hadn't said a single word the entire drive back to her home.

She didn't know what the hell had come over Max at the bar, but she wanted to find out. So once they made it to her house and walked inside, she set her purse down on an end table and said, "Are you okay?"

Max paced the floor like a caged tiger but stopped and glared at her with his one good eye, since the other was almost completely swollen shut. "Yeah," he growled. "Just peachy."

Okay, he was still clearly in a mood. She walked into the kitchen and grabbed an ice pack from the freezer, wrapping it in a dish cloth before handing it to him. "Put this over your eye. It will help with the swelling."

He was still very much on edge, his agitation prevalent in every move, but as he accepted the ice pack from her, he placed his trembling hand on hers. "I'm sorry I'm acting like this."

"Okay. I appreciate the apology. But *why* are you acting like this? What happened tonight?"

His brows collapsed over his eyes. "I...don't want to talk about it right now."

Figures. "Okay, then you just let me know when it's convenient for you," she said with sarcasm as she pulled her hand out of his and moved toward the bedroom.

A frustrated sound came from behind her, but she made it all the way into her room before a large hand grasped her, gently stopping her motion. "Jessa?"

"What?" Her tone wasn't friendly.

"Please, don't. I'm struggling here."

She gazed up at him. "I can see that. My problem is that I don't know what exactly you're struggling with. Why don't you fill me in?"

"I will...tomorrow. I promise. But tonight? I just want to lie with you and hold you in my arms. Can we do that? Please."

Jessa wanted to demand an explanation, but something in the way his voice had trembled when he said please kept her from pushing him. "Okay, fine. Let me just change out of these clothes first."

Max released her arm, and she went straight to her drawers to pull out something to sleep in. Slipping out of her tunic top and bra, she pulled a white tank top over her head and pulled it down to cover her breasts. Then she unbuttoned her jeans and shoved them down her legs until she could kick them from her feet, along with her slip-on sandals.

He must've been doing basically the same thing behind her because, as she turned around, she spotted him climbing into the bed with his black boxer-briefs still on. Huh. Weird since he didn't usually wear anything at all when he was sleeping in her bed. Yep, he was definitely acting strange tonight.

The moment she crawled onto her side of the bed, Max reached for her, pulling her to him and tucking her into his side and then sliding the covers over both of them. He held her tight against him, his warmth infiltrating her skin. Then he turned his head toward her and brushed a chaste, gentle kiss over her lips. "Good night, sweetheart."

Good night? "Okay, where's Max and what have you done with him?"

The dimly lit room only held the soft glow of moonlight, but she could see him blinking at her. "What do you mean?"

She pulled her head up to gaze directly at him. "We're not having sex?"

He settled her back into his arms. "No."

Was he kidding right now? She lifted her head from his shoulder. "What do you mean no?"

"Not tonight, baby. We're both tired, and we have a long day ahead of us tomorrow."

"When has that ever stopped you before?"

"It hasn't. But tonight's different. I just want to hold you while you sleep in my arms."

With all the odd tension emanating from him, it only

made her wonder if Leah and Valerie had been right all along. If they were correct that Max only wanted to be with thinner women, then maybe he hadn't fallen head over heels for her like she thought. Like she'd fallen for him.

As sad as it was, she felt the need to prove to herself once again that Max was attracted to her. That he wanted her as much as she wanted him. To have that physical connection to him to assure herself that she wasn't crazy.

Her hand reached out to him and touched the rough stubble along his jaw. "But I want you, Max."

Still, he shook his head and refused. "I can't, baby. Not tonight. I'm…just not in the right mind-set right now."

She leaned forward and brushed her lips gently over his anyway. "I need you, Max. Tonight. Right here, right now." She ran her tongue over his bottom lip. "Please."

A desperate groan tore from his chest as he flipped her onto her back and covered her body with his. "Stop. You don't know what you're asking me to do."

Her breath caught in her throat as his erection pressed against her panties. She released a slow breath. "Oh, I'm pretty certain I know exactly what I'm asking you to do." She spread her legs wider so the evidence of his arousal pushed more solidly into her. A moan sounded from her lips.

His glassy eyes glittered in the darkness, and his overwhelming response was immediate. Strong, gentle hands drew her forward as he took her mouth by force, thrusting his tongue past her lips and diving deep. Her stomach fluttered, and her nipples tightened with anticipation. He must've felt them stabbing into his chest because, within seconds, he yanked her tank top up over her breasts and suctioned his mouth over one hardened bud.

Her back arched at the strength of his mouth on her as she tingled from head to toe. Max was normally gentle, slow, and sure in his movements. Leisure strokes. Lazy exploring. But this was...well, not like that at all. His hands moved over her with a frantic pace, his fingers desperately groping wherever they landed.

He kissed her hungrily as one hand slid into her panties, and he inserted two rough fingers inside of her. Gasping, she squirmed against him, but he held her in place as he thrust into her tight wetness and ground his palm against her mound. She moaned loudly, her body straining against his as her fingernails scraped long and hard across his back. Grasping with want. Clawing with need.

There were no gentle caresses. No tender touches or kind words. This was all about immediate gratification. Primal. Raw. Plain and simple, she needed him, and he needed her. And if Jessa had it her way, both of them were going to get just that.

She started to slide her panties down, but Max immediately stilled her hands. Then with one firm tug, he tore the sheer scrap of fabric from her body and freed himself from his own underwear. Okay, apparently *he* was going to make sure they both got what they needed.

A strong arm snaked around her waist, and a firm hand grasped her hip. With a quick shift of his own, he yanked her onto his hard length. He groaned as her body closed around him, and even though the fullness was almost too much to bear, she surged upward to meet his thrust head-on anyway.

Oh God.

Wetness emanated from her sex, lubricating her sheath for the glide of his cock. Running his calloused hands under her, he palmed her derrière, giving it a squeeze. Then he pressed on her clit with his thumb, applying just the right amount of pressure, as he thrust into her over and over again.

She was so deeply engrossed in the way he was screwing her senseless that, within seconds, she came full-on in a screaming orgasm, one that snuck up on her fast and obliterated her into a thousand pieces. Breasts heaving and her breath panting, her body went limp while Max took his own pleasure.

It didn't take long, thank goodness. The man was so hard and long inside of her that it was starting to get a little uncomfortable. So relief swept through her when he finally buried his face into her neck and flew over the edge as well.

He collapsed on top of her, though he kept most of his weight on his forearms to keep from crushing her. But as they lay there together in the moonlit room for a long while, panting out rapid-fire breaths, Jessa reached a conclusion.

She had no doubt that Max was definitely into her. No one could fake that kind of sexual attraction. Ever. The man had come fast and hard, yet he was already starting to move inside of her again. If that didn't tell her that he wanted her, then nothing would.

Max rocked into her gently, easing himself in and out with a slow rhythm. His eyes closed, and a pained expression took over his face. "I'm sorry," he whispered.

Sorry? For what? Giving her a mind-numbing orgasm?

* * *

Max couldn't put it off any longer.

He'd been leaning against this tree in the park while trying to gather the courage to do what needed to finally be done. The moment Jessa stepped off the truck and closed down the outside window, he knew he needed to go to her. Before she drove away and he had to have this conversation at the kitchen in front of Mario. Or even worse, in front of Logan and Valerie.

He'd spent the entire day trying to figure out what he was going to say and how he was going to explain it all so he didn't come out looking like a jackass. Yeah, that hadn't happened. No matter how he put it, it looked bad, and she was going to be mad. So pissed, in fact, that he wouldn't blame her if she tried to kick him in the nuts.

It wasn't like he didn't deserve it after last night anyway.

He should've just come clean with her and told her what was bothering him. But instead of telling her the truth, he spent the whole night locked together with her in one long lovemaking session that hadn't ended until the wee hours of the morning. Actually, what they had done couldn't even be considered making love. He'd taken her out of desperation, claiming her body and marking her as his.

It wasn't a bad way to spend his night, but that sexual rendezvous had severely deviated from the plan he'd outlined in his head. He'd only meant to hold her all night, reminding her how good they felt together and showing her that they should be together. He'd hoped that would help all the stars align, and it would be the one memory that she'd hang on to while deciding their fate.

Damn that fate and stars shit.

Max sighed and headed for the truck. He could hear her putting things away inside and knew he didn't have much time left. He rapped on the door with his knuckles and then stepped back and waited for her to open it. Within seconds, she did just that with a huge smile on her face. The same one she was wearing this morning when he'd kissed her good-bye.

"Hey," she said. "I didn't know you were going to stop by this evening. I thought I'd see you at my place later tonight."

"Yeah, about that..." He ran his hand through his hair. "I think we need to talk first."

She gazed at him curiously but shoved the door open wider. "Okay, come inside then while I'm finishing up the last few things."

He stepped past her and waited for her to close the door behind them. Then she walked over to him and gave him a friendly kiss. "I missed you today."

Max cringed inwardly. God, he hoped she'd understand and forgive him. "I missed you too."

"So what's on your mind? What did you want to talk about?"

"Well, I...I guess first I want to apologize again for last night. I didn't hurt you, did I?"

She leaned into him, wrapping her hands around his neck. "Oh, you did," she said with a smile. "I'm deliciously sore today. Every time I move, I remember last night."

"I'm sorry," he said, lowering his head.

Jessa squinted at him. "For what? If my multi-orgasms didn't clue you in, I'm pretty sure I enjoyed everything we did. You didn't? Because I know you had several yourself."

"Of course I enjoyed it," he said, then shook his head. "It's not that. I just feel bad because I shouldn't have…" His words trailed off.

"Shouldn't have what? Been so rough with me? Is that what you're worried about?"

"Well, yeah, that's part of it. I'm not normally that…demanding."

Jessa laughed. Loudly. "I have news for you, Max Hager. You're always that demanding in bed. You just normally do it in such an unhurried manner that it doesn't come across as demanding. Most of the time anyway. But I've slept with you enough times to know better. You're usually slow and steady, whereas last night you were fast and insistent. Trust me, I love both."

He scowled. "Maybe, but I don't like making you feel like I'm a rutting bull trying to get my rocks off on the first female I come across. You know I'm not like that with you. You're different."

She cocked her head. "So you're saying you've been that way with other women?"

Of course she picked up on that right away. He cringed. "Yeah, I guess. I mean, it wasn't like I treated them poorly. The whole act just didn't mean as much with them. It was all about the sex. That was pretty much it. There were no feelings involved with those women. At least nothing more than a mutual attraction."

"In other words, they were one-night stands?"

Max nodded. God, why was he telling her all of this? It only made him sound worse. *Not the smartest thing to lead with, dipshit.*

Her hands moved onto his chest. "Max, I know you have had other women. It's not like I thought you were a virgin when I met you."

"I know, but—"

Jessa placed one finger over his lips. "Listen. We both have had past sexual experiences. I'm not going to hold that over your head anymore than I would want you to hold mine against me."

He pulled his head back so he could talk. "We're getting off track. The reason I'm here doesn't have anything to do with that. I need to tell you—" The words stalled on his lips as she unzipped his pants. He swallowed hard. "Jessa?"

She knelt down in front of him and licked her lips. "Mmm-hmm?"

"What the hell are you doing?"

"Don't worry. I locked the door," she said, grinning. "I've been wanting to do this to you since almost the first day we met." She opened his jeans, freeing his rapidly hardening member.

Holy hell.

Her hands glided over him, and his legs damn near gave out from under him. Lord help him. He would almost swear the woman was ambidextrous. Probably from all the stuff she does in the kitchen that requires the use of both hands. Normally, he didn't mind benefiting from it, but right now... Well, this wasn't what he was supposed to be doing. "Jess, wait."

But it was too late. The moment he got the words out, her warm mouth surrounded him and caressed up and down his shaft. He grunted, and his hips thrust forward involuntarily as he braced himself against the counter. Something hot moved swiftly through him as need coiled into a tight ball in the pit of his stomach.

Christ. What the hell just happened? He marveled at the mystic power she had over him. One minute he was trying to tell her the truth no matter what, and the next, the woman had her mouth on him and his body so twisted up that his brain had malfunctioned. His hand had even reached out to stop her, but instead ended up knotting into her hair and pulling her mouth farther onto his length.

Her greedy mouth obliged him, sucking him hard, and then licking softly around his shaft before curling her tongue over his engorged head. "You're so hard," she said, taking him into her mouth once more.

He groaned. "I won't be much longer if you keep doing that... and we'll probably have a mess to clean up."

She didn't seem to care. She increased the suction, and flames of hellfire rose up inside him. Sweet Jesus. Just watching her mouth form over the shape of his cock had him already about to come, and she had barely even started on him. What was it about this woman that made his entire system go crazy with desire?

A knock sounded on the door, and he cursed under his breath. Damn it, he was so fucking close. "Ignore it," he whispered.

Unfortunately, she didn't listen. She stopped and rose

to her feet. "I can't. If it's one of the girls, they have a key to that door. The last thing I want is for one of them to walk in on us like this."

Damn it. He tucked himself back inside his jeans, which was one hell of a feat since he was still as hard as a rock. As she started to move away, he grabbed her and pulled her back to him for a kiss. "Hurry back then."

Jessa headed for the door but waited for Max to right his clothing completely before opening it. When she finally swung the door open, an older gentleman with salt-and-pepper hair stood a few feet away but smiled politely up at her.

Impeccable fucking timing, dickhead.

"Oh, hi there. Can I help you?" she asked.

"Are you the owner of this food truck, ma'am?"

She nodded. "Yes, I'm Jessa Gibson. But I'm sorry. We're closed right now. If you want to come back tomorrow between—"

"Oh no," the man said with a chuckle. "I'm not here to eat. Although I will say I've heard how delicious your food is, and I can't wait to try it for myself."

"Um, okay," Jessa said, confusion filling her voice. "So what is it that I can do for you, Mr....uh..."

"Halloway. Jerry Halloway, to be exact. Feel free to call me Jerry."

"All right. Well, Jerry, what can I help you with?"

"I was just on my way home and happened to be passing by when I spotted your truck still parked over here, so I thought I'd stop in and introduce myself." He smiled wide. "I'm the new city health inspector."

Max's head snapped up. *Oh fuck.*

Chapter Nineteen

Jessa blinked rapidly at the older gentleman in front of her.

At first, she thought she'd misunderstood what the man had said. But when she turned around and saw the horrified look on Max's face, she had a feeling she'd heard him correctly.

She searched Max's eyes for answers but unfortunately found none. "Max?"

The uncertainty of her voice seemed to cut right through him because he suddenly cringed and said, "Jess, I can explain."

"Then maybe you should," she stated firmly. "Because right now I don't have a clue as to what the hell's going on."

And she clearly wasn't the only one. The man in the doorway claiming to be the new health inspector looked just as confused as she probably did. But he at least seemed to understand there was something happening. Something that this guy apparently wanted no part of. "Ms. Gibson, I can see that you're, ah...busy. Why don't I set up a time to speak with you at a later date? I have my appointment book in my car if you'd like to walk me out so we can arrange something for later in the week."

"I, uh...yes, I think that would be best." She ran a shaky hand through her hair. "Okay, let's do that."

Max stayed inside the truck as she stepped out with the inspector. That was probably a good thing because she needed a minute to register what was truly going on here and didn't want to say any more until this guy left. She followed Mr. Halloway across the parking lot to a white Buick and waited as he reached inside.

When the man straightened he held a leather-bound scheduling pad, and clipped on the side was an official badge that identified him as the city inspector. Jessa swayed in place as nausea bombarded her stomach. God, it was true then? Jerry Halloway was the new city health inspector. And if so, who the hell was Max and why in the hell had he lied to her all this time? It'd been a couple of weeks since she first met him.

Mr. Halloway named a couple of different dates and times for the following week and asked her which one she preferred. Numbly, she told him any of them would be fine although she never actually paid attention to what he said. Her overwhelmed mind and pounding heart were both still racing over the shocking news that Max wasn't the health inspector.

But the man didn't seem to notice her total indifference to what he was saying. Or maybe he did but

understood that she was very upset at the moment by
something going on and was just playing along, hoping
she'd actually remember to show up at her scheduled
time. Because the moment she agreed to whatever date
he'd mentioned, the man said his farewell to her and got
the heck out of Dodge.

Jessa walked back to the food truck, her gaze directly
on Max's somber face. He watched in silence as she
stepped back inside the truck and shut the door behind
her. When she turned to face him, the deep regret in his
eyes said everything she needed to know. "You're not a
health inspector." It wasn't posed as a question. Just a
plain, glaring fact.

"No. I'm not." Max hung his head. "But it's not what
you think."

A stony silence lingered between them as she played
back the last few weeks in her mind and put together the
sequence of events that had led to this very moment. She
didn't understand anything about what he'd done or why,
but enough of the puzzle pieces clicked into place that
she could see the bigger picture. Max was a liar. "You
conniving prick!"

He winced. "Baby, please. I—"

"No." Jessa crossed her arms, closing herself off to
him. She'd warned herself not to get involved with him,
but apparently she didn't know how to listen to good advice. Max had been lying to her from the first day they'd
met. And she couldn't think of anything else to say except for, "Why? Why would you do this to me?"

He closed his eyes and expelled a hard breath. "That
first day when I came over here to talk to you, I pretended to be the health inspector because you were

parked across the street from my buddy's restaurant. He was losing business, and I was trying to help him by forcing you into leaving."

Unbelievable. She shook her head. "So you manipulated me into believing that you wanted me just so that you could ruin *my* business and run me out of town? You're a...a...shameless asshole."

"No, you don't understand, Jess. That's not what happened. In the beginning, I only meant to harass you a little. Actually, I didn't even know *you* owned the truck. And of course I never dreamed we would actually wind up in bed together. None of that had ever been planned out. You have to believe that at least."

"That's where you're wrong, Max. I don't have to believe a damn word you say. You think just because you hang a curtain of excuses over a dirty window that the dirt isn't still there? Whether it was intentional or not, you slept with me, damn it. And you did so while knowing you were lying through your teeth. Do you even have an actual job?"

Max sighed. "Yes. I'm an electrician. I run my own business, but my larger jobs usually involve working for Sam's construction company. That's why I was able to make my own hours and come by here so often."

If she thought that it couldn't have gotten any worse, he'd just proved her wrong. Fury lit through her faster than a hot fuse on a firecracker. "So Sam and your other friends knew that you were lying to me all along?"

"No, not the whole time. They found out when you kissed me in the bakery. That's why I was acting so weird. I was afraid one of them was about to accidentally rat me out so I told them after you left."

"Well, that's just great. Well, I hope you all had a great laugh at my expense."

He reached for her, but she moved out of his grasp so he let his hand drop to his side. "Honey, no one was laughing at you. They were all pissed as hell that I was lying to you and have done nothing but encourage me to tell you the truth ever since. This isn't on them. It's all *my* fault. They had nothing to do with it, I swear."

"And that's supposed to make me feel any better?"

"No, I'm sure it doesn't. I'm sorry, Jess. If I could go back in time and take all the lies back, I would. I never meant to cause you any pain. You have to believe that. I would never do anything to hurt you."

"Yeah, well you did." Tears burned behind her eyelids, but she blinked rapidly to keep them at bay. The last thing she wanted to do was cry in front of him. "I don't want to talk about this anymore. Please leave."

"Sweetheart, just listen to me…" He reached for her arm again.

She shrugged him off and moved away. "Don't touch me ever again. I mean it. You may have fooled me once. I'll give you credit for that. But trust me when I say it won't happen a second time."

"Damn it, Jess. It wasn't like that. I never meant to—"

"Shut up. I don't want to hear anything that comes out of your lying mouth. Not anymore. You had every chance to tell me the truth and chose not to. Maybe you're smooth enough to fool all the other women in this town, but if you think for one second I'm going to believe another word you say, you're delusional." She shoved him toward the door. "Now get out of my truck."

He stepped outside but stayed on the pavement just outside the door. Apparently, he wasn't giving up that easily. "Don't do this," he pleaded, motioning to the two of them. "Don't throw this thing between us away over something stupid that doesn't mean anything."

Jessa blinked. "Doesn't mean any—" She couldn't believe the nerve of this man. Her gaze locked with his. "You know what, Max? Maybe to you this doesn't change anything, because you weren't the one being lied to. But to me, it changes everything."

"What are you saying?"

"You wanted my absence, right? Fine. You've got it." She stepped out of the truck and slammed the back door closed before heading around to the driver's side of the vehicle.

He caught up with her as she opened the front door, his eyes wide. "You can't leave like this. What about us?"

Although her heart shriveled in her chest under his pleading eyes, she climbed confidently into the cab of the truck and gave him a look filled with disgust. "There is no us anymore. Good-bye, Max." With that, she slammed the door to the truck closed and locked it for good measure.

"Jessa, come on. Open the door. Don't leave it like this." When she started the truck and turned on the headlights, his pleading became more urgent. "Baby, I'll do anything to make this right. Please. I don't want to lose you. I need you."

His last words hurt so much that she knew she needed to drive away or she would end up opening the door and falling back into his arms. So she put the truck into gear and pulled away from the curb.

* * *

Hours later, Max beat on her front door for the umpteenth time.

He had no doubt Jessa was inside and just ignoring his persistent banging, but if he kept doing it much longer, someone was going to call the cops. The neighborhood dogs were already barking like crazy, and her neighbors' lights had recently flickered on.

"Jess, I know you're in there. Just let me in to talk. Five minutes, okay? That's all I ask."

"No," she said from the other side of the door.

Okay, that was progress. She hadn't answered him for the last half hour. Maybe he was wearing her down a little. "Baby, please. Five minutes. After that, if you want me to leave, I'll go and won't bother you anymore tonight."

"Yeah, like I can believe anything you say. You're a liar!"

He sighed. "I know I lied," he told her, his face pressed against the cool painted wood of her front door. "But I'm not going to do it again, I promise. I never meant to do it in the first place."

"No, I mean you're lying right now. If I give you five minutes, you aren't going to leave when those five minutes are up."

He flattened his palm against the door. "I swear I will. If that's what you want."

There was a long enough pause that Max didn't think

he'd gotten through to her, but the front door finally creaked open to reveal Jessa standing there in a white robe.

For some strange reason, he'd expected her to have a bright red face, filled with anger, as well as surly eyes and an expression that mimicked a shark right before they took a bite out of you. But instead, her face was drawn, and her cheeks were stained with dried-up tears. But it was the deep sadness he saw in her eyes that gutted him completely. He'd done that to her, damn him.

At first they stood there, regarding each other cautiously. Then she said, "You get five minutes. After that, if you don't leave, I'll call the cops on you myself." It was said in such a civil tone that it was hard to even fathom that it was a threat.

"I promised you I would. I wasn't lying when I said it. I plan on keeping every promise I ever make to you from now on."

"I don't want any promises from you. In fact, I don't want anything from you. I clearly can't trust you to tell me the truth." With that, she pushed the door open to allow him access and backed away as he passed by her, as if she couldn't stand the thought of him accidentally touching her.

Once they were both in the living room, Jessa pulled her robe around her and tightened the knot. The sore spot he'd created with her had only been festering for about two hours, but seeing her gut-wrenching reactions to him only made Max acutely aware of how much she was trying to protect herself and keep her distance.

He tried to take her hand, but she took a step back. "Don't touch me."

"Okay," he said, releasing a heavy sigh and backing away to allow her some breathing room. He shoved his hands in his pockets to keep from reaching for her again. "First off, I want you to know how sorry I am. I know apologizing doesn't fix this, but I need you to know how sincere I'm being right now. I never meant to hurt you, Jess."

"Yet, you still did."

He nodded. "You're right. I did. But you have to know it wasn't intentional. When I first met you, I didn't know you were the owner of that truck. You know that, Jess. You were there."

"I do know that. But once you found out who I was, you could've told me the truth. You didn't have to keep lying to my face."

He shook his head. "You're right, I didn't. But I was trying to help out my friend. He's an old man, and his only source of income is the café across the street from you. He was losing all of his business, and he was going under."

"Don't try to guilt trip me with that. It wasn't like I was intentionally poaching his customers. I had no idea. Why didn't you just walk over and tell me that to begin with? I would've moved my truck voluntarily. I wasn't trying to harm anyone else's business...unlike you."

"Jessa."

"No, I've listened to you. Now it's your turn to listen to me. What I did to your friend was harmless and unintentional. Hell, I didn't even know I was doing anything wrong. But what you did to me was despicable and disgusting. All of those ordinances you spouted off. Those were fake, right?"

He cringed. "Yes. I made them up on the spot. It was stupid and rash, which is why none of them made any sense. I didn't even think you would buy any of it to begin with."

"Yet I just took what you told me at face value and never once questioned it. I guess that makes me the trusting dummy, doesn't it?"

"That's not what I meant, Jess. Yes, you're trusting, but that's one of the things I love about you. I don't want what I did to change that about you."

"Well, you're too late on that one. I told you from almost the beginning that I don't like being made a fool of. But you couldn't help yourself, could you?"

He shook his head. "You're not the fool here, Jess. I am. This was all on me."

"You're right, it is."

"Look, I didn't mean to hurt you. I care about you, Jess. But when I first started all of this, I didn't even know you. And once I had already lied, it was too late to back out of it. I was stuck in a bad position and didn't know how to turn things around. But I didn't want to lose you. You have to believe that, Jess."

She shook her head. "I don't know what to believe anymore. I get wanting to help a friend, even if your methods were questionable. But what I can't wrap my brain around is why you would continue lying when you knew you would be hurting me. You had to realize I would find out the truth eventually."

"I did, but I didn't have a choice. I owed it to Pops. After everything that man has done for me..."

Jessa shook her head adamantly. "What could your friend have possibly done for you that would require you to pay him back by screwing over someone you claim to care for?"

Max stared at her in silence. He wasn't comfortable talking about his issues with food and didn't want to explain how Pops made him a special every day so that he could stay on track with his health and fitness goals. So finally, he said, "He's just been a good friend to me."

She gazed at him curiously, her interest clearly piqued. "Why do I get the feeling that there's more to that than what you're telling me?"

"Like what?"

"I don't know. But I'm betting you do."

Damn it. He didn't want to lie to her again by denying it, but he wasn't ready or willing to share that part of himself with anyone. "I told you—"

"Yeah, I know what you told me. And I'm not buying it. As sad as it is, you still can't be completely honest with me, Max. But that's okay because I now have the common sense not to listen to you anymore. Nothing else you have to say to me matters. I think it's time you leave."

"Jessa, wait."

"No. Your five minutes are up. You promised you would go. I expect you to keep your word. I don't want to lose any more respect for you than I already have, so you need to leave."

Max felt a heavy weight sink inside of him, but he moved toward the door in silence. She followed him, and when he stepped outside, she started to close the door behind him.

He put his hand against the door long enough to say, "I'm sorry, baby. I know you might not believe me, but I am. And I'm not giving up on us, Jess. I'm leaving now only because I promised you I would, but don't you think for one second that I'm not coming back for you. I will always come back for you. You can count on it."

"Don't bother," she said, her voice trembling. "I won't be here much longer anyway. I'm packing up and leaving town."

Chapter Twenty

Jessa sank to the floor on the other side of the door and cried until her eyes were raw and swollen. She hated to think she was going to have to leave the one place where she felt close to her mom, but she didn't know what else to do. She couldn't possibly stay here now knowing that she would run into Max at every turn.

It was bad enough that she was going to have to face Logan and Valerie at least once more to turn in her keys and tell them she was leaving. The mere idea that all of his friends knew about Max's lies filled her with embarrassment all over again. Not that she thought any of them would've laughed about his deceit. None of them seemed like the kind of people who got their kicks by enjoying someone else's misery.

Well, except for Max.

He was a guy who liked to push other people's buttons. Maybe it had something to do with his overinflated ego, or he was overcompensating for some strange masculine insecurities, but he got off on riling others up.

But that wasn't how she was. Jessa was easygoing and laid back. She liked to live in the moment and have peace and harmony around her at all times. Staying in a town where Max Hager lived and would be coming around would be the exact opposite of peace and harmony.

She had told Max that she was leaving only to hurt him, which was a rotten thing to do. But now that she'd said it, the idea was sounding better by the second. It was the only way she would be able to move on and not think about Max. Besides, the last thing she wanted to do was stay in a town where he would eventually be dating other women and flaunting them in her face.

Not that he would probably do that, but it would still feel that way to her.

The good thing was that she hadn't been in town long enough to put down any real roots, like buying a house or opening a restaurant here. Sure, she'd fallen in love with... damn it. She hadn't realized it until just now, but she'd fallen completely in love with that bastard. Just great.

Now she had no choice but to leave.

But God, she loved this small town so much. If only her mother hadn't mentioned Granite to her in the first place, then Jessa would've never met Max. *Thanks a lot, Mom. You should've warned me off this place instead.*

Her eyes filled with tears as she remembered the travel journals her mother had left behind. She had told Max that she hadn't read the one about Granite because she was afraid that the town would lose some of its magic. But now, she was hoping she was right.

Because something needed to push her away from this place.

She had no family ties here beyond her mother. Sure, she had made plenty of friends, but it wasn't like she couldn't keep in contact with them while living somewhere else. That would be better than facing Max every day or running into him every time she turned a corner.

So Jessa lifted herself up from the floor and did the one thing she'd never thought she would do. She fetched her mother's travel journal for Granite, Texas, and nestled herself into the recliner to read it. But as she opened the pages, a handwritten note fell out.

My dearest Jessa,

I'm writing this for you because my time is almost at an end. Though there are many things I want to tell you, one thing stands out above the rest. I know it will be hard to hear the news after I'm gone, but I didn't have the strength to tell you before now. I never meant to leave you alone in this world. So to make sure that doesn't happen, I wrote this journal for you. I hope you'll read it with an open heart and an understanding mind. Be strong, my darling. I miss you already.

Love, Mom

She wasn't sure what her mother had written for her inside the pages, but she had no choice but to trust her late mother to guide her next move. So with tears in her eyes, Jessa read the journal from front to back. By the time she was finished, her life had unexpectedly changed its course. If she had ever believed in fate and the alignment of the stars, it was right now.

*   *   *

Jessa reined in her nerves and knocked on the door.

She smoothed her trembling hand over her hair and waited patiently as the sound of heavy footsteps neared. The door flung open, and Logan stood on the threshold, looking as tall and handsome as ever.

"Hi, Logan. Can I...can I talk to you for a minute? It's important."

Concern filled his eyes, and he pushed the door open wider. "Of course. Come on in."

She stepped inside the spacious living room and instantly spotted Valerie standing in a kitchen doorway. "Hey, Jess. We were just sitting down for lunch. Would you like to join us?"

"No, that's okay. Thank you. I don't think I can eat right now." Her hands were shaking beyond all control. "I need to talk to Logan."

Valerie came closer as she exchanged a glance with Logan. "Everything okay, honey? You look a little pale. Do you need to sit down?"

"It's fine. I mean, I'm fine. I just...uh...came here to tell Logan something that I thought he should know."

Logan placed one hand on her shoulder and led her to the couch. "Please sit down. You look so jittery that I'm afraid you're going to fall over. What happened?"

"Nothing happened. I just needed to tell you—"

An older woman with short, light brown hair stepped out of the kitchen. "Logan, I made your favorite...Oh."

The woman froze in place when she noticed that there was a guest in the room.

Logan spoke up. "Mom, this is Jessa Gibson. She's the one renting the kitchen at the bar for her food truck business, the Gypsy Cantina. Jessa, this is my mother, Julie Mathis."

"Hello," Jessa said, her voice barely a whisper. God, she couldn't do this. Especially in front of his mother. This had been a bad idea. The urge to run out of there was strong, but she tried to do it with as much grace as possible. "I...really shouldn't have come. Please just forget that I said anything. I'm sorry." Jessa stood and moved quickly toward the door.

She had barely placed her hand on the knob when a soft voice behind her said, "You look just like your mother."

Jessa stopped dead in her tracks, hesitated, and then turned back around. "How do you..."

Logan's mother smiled sincerely, her hands clasped in front of her. "I recognized your last name. You're Mariah's daughter."

She blinked. "You...uh, knew my mother?"

"Not well, but I met her once. She passed through here almost...my goodness, thirty years ago, I believe. Such a lovely woman with a bright, warm personality. Unfortunately, I didn't meet her under the best of circumstances. Had things been different between us, I just know we would've been good friends though."

Jessa's eyes widened. "So...you know?"

Ms. Mathis nodded, and her eyes watered. "About the past? Yes, dear. I know." Her gaze trailed over Jessa's face, and she gave her another polite smile. "But I didn't know about you. Not until this very moment."

Logan shook his head. "I don't get it, Mom. What the heck's going on?"

Ms. Mathis smiled. "Would you like to tell him, Jessa?"

Not knowing what she would even say, Jessa shook her head. She had a hard time believing it herself. She didn't think she could say the words out loud and have them make any sense to him.

"Okay, then I'll be happy to do the honors." Ms. Mathis walked over and took Jessa's hand, bringing her closer to her son. "Logan, Jessa is your sister."

Eyes wide, Logan exchanged glances with Valerie, and then his gaze landed on his mother before shifting onto Jessa. "Is this some kind of joke? Because if so, it isn't at all funny."

Jessa shook her head. "No, it's true, Logan. I just found out myself, but I'm related to you. We're half siblings."

"How is that even possible?"

She faltered, unable to tell him the events of the past. "I...uh..."

Ms. Mathis rushed to her rescue again. "Would you like me to explain it, dear? You seem a little shaky still."

"Please. I mean, if you don't mind," Jessa whispered. "It would probably be better coming from you anyway. I was dreading having to tell him that part."

Ms. Mathis nodded and took her son's hand. "Logan, back when you were about three years old, your father didn't come home one night. So I asked a neighbor to look after you and went looking for him at the local bar, where he would usually end up if he wasn't at a casino. But he wasn't there either. When I asked about him, I was told by one of the waitresses that he left with a slender redhead. I drove to every motel in Granite before I finally found his old beat-up truck parked in front of one of the rooms. I went inside and asked who the room was registered to. Back then, they weren't as careful about giving out a room occupant's information as they are nowadays," she explained. "I found out the room was registered to a lady by the name of Mariah Gibson. She was the redhead your father left the bar with that night."

The look on Logan's face was murderous, and Jessa's eyes instantly filled with tears. "I know this is probably hard to hear. I'm so sorry."

Ms. Mathis was as calm as ever and shook her head. "Don't be, dear. You have nothing to apologize for."

Logan nodded. "I agree. It's not you, Jessa. It's that godforsaken man. He spent the past thirty years hurting my mother, and she stayed with—"

"Logan," Valerie said, her eyes widening.

Ms. Mathis touched his arm. "No, no, it's okay. You can say it, son. I stayed with your father all of those years." She patted him, trying to comfort him. "Just not in a true marital sense."

Logan ran his hand roughly through his hair. "What are you talking about, Mom? You only recently had your divorced finalized."

"Yes, but I never let that man put his hands on me ever again. I had always wanted you to have a brother or sister, but I couldn't let him touch me. Never again. Not in that way." She turned toward Jessa. "And I'm not say-

ing anything negative toward Mariah. I just couldn't trust
that he wasn't sleeping with other women too."

Jessa didn't know what to say. To think that this
woman had been married to a husband, one who had lied
and cheated on her, even in name only, for over thirty
years boggled her mind. Especially since she'd dumped
Max because he'd lied only once. And it wasn't even for
anything near as bad as what this man had done.

"Did you confront him?" Logan asked his mother, his
voice still filled with anger.

His mother sighed. "I'd planned to. But I had gone inside to ask who the room was registered to, and by the
time I came out, he was already gone."

"Of course he was. That chickenshit bastard. He probably saw you pull up. I should kill that sonofabitch."

Valerie put her hand on Logan's shoulder. "Please calm
down. I know this is all so tough to hear and probably
comes as quite a shock, but I'm sure it's very hard for your
mother to tell this story to you too. Just let her finish."

Logan nodded, and his mother continued. "Your father was gone already, but the woman wasn't. The light
was on and someone was pacing in front of the curtain.
So I knocked on the door, planning to give this stranger
a piece of my mind about taking home a married man.
But when she answered it and saw me standing there, she
burst into tears. She knew exactly who I was and why I
was there."

Jessa gasped. "Oh my God. My mother knew he was
a married man and slept with him anyway?"

"No, dear," Ms. Mathis said. "Please don't think that.
Your mother had only found out he was married and had
a child *after* they'd slept together. A picture of the three

of us had fallen out of his wallet, and since he'd already gotten what he had wanted from her, he admitted to all of it. You mother had thrown him out of her motel room, which was why he was gone by the time I got back from the front desk."

Logan breathed out a heavy sigh. "You don't know this about him, but he's a real jerk, Jess. Trust me when I say that you don't want anything to do with him."

His mother hushed him. "That's not for you to decide, Logan. Jessa has to make that call all on her own."

Jessa shook her head. "Between my mother and the things I've heard just now, I can tell you now that I want nothing to do with this man. Any person who would treat a woman like that doesn't deserve me in his life."

"It amazes me how much you sound just like your mother," Ms. Mathis told her. "She was such a strong, proud woman and had so much life in her. She'd apologized profusely, though I told her over and over that it wasn't necessary. She hadn't known. That was all on him. But she'd hated that she couldn't make it right. We ended up chatting over coffee until dawn about our lives, her travels, my son, and even the cheating man who had brought us together briefly. She was so genuine and honest. I really liked her a lot."

A tear fell on Jessa's cheek. "I'm so sorry about what happened to you. But I'm glad you were able to see my mother as I see her. I was afraid..."

"That we would think less of her? Not at all." Ms. Mathis offered her a sincere smile. "I wish I could say we kept in touch, but we didn't. I tried to look her up years ago, but she moved so much that I was never able to find her. And I'm not sure she would've wanted to hear from me anyway. I think maybe that would've been too awkward for her after what happened. But I would love to know how your mother is doing now, Jessa."

"Actually, she…passed away a few years ago from liver cancer."

Ms. Mathis immediately wrapped her arms around Jessa and hugged her close. "Oh, I'm sorry. I didn't know. May Mariah's soul rest in peace."

"Thank you," Jess said, sniffling a little.

When the woman released her, she took a step back and paused. "Wait a minute. You said you just found out about all of this. So if you didn't learn of any of it from your mother, then who told you?"

"Well, my mother did. She always talked about how much she loved Granite and how wonderful the people were here. Now that I've met you, I can only assume she meant you in particular. But she'd also kept travel journals that she wrote in at every new location she went to. There was a lot of them, but right after her death, I'd boxed them up. It was too painful for me to read them at the time. But last night I, uh…well, I sort of needed to be close to her, so I opened them back up and started reading through the one she wrote where she passed through Granite."

"I'm curious. Did she tell you the whole story?"

"Most of it. But not in quite so much detail. The thing that mattered most to me was that she mentioned that I had an older brother. As shocking as that bit of news was, you can imagine my surprise when I read the name Logan Mathis. I couldn't stop shaking. Apparently she'd seen his name on the back of the photo or maybe you mentioned it to her and she remembered it. But the moment she found out she was pregnant with me, she added a note to her journal with his name."

Jessa realized how quiet Logan had gotten and glanced over at him. "I'm sorry if all of this has caught you off guard. But I want you to know that I don't expect anything from you. Nothing has to change between us just because you found out you have a half sister. I'm not trying to cause any—"

Without warning, Logan pulled her into his strong arms and squeezed hard. "You're my sister, Jessa. There's no such thing as a half in my world."

Tears pricked her eyes, and she hugged him back fiercely. "Thank you. I feel the same way. I actually always wanted an older brother."

Valerie stood off to the side with moisture in her own eyes, but she giggled. "You're *so* going to regret saying that. I know this from experience."

They all laughed, but Jessa gazed at Logan and shook her head. "Never."

Ms. Mathis touched her shoulder. "Jessa, I hope you will also consider me as part of your family too. I know you had a wonderful mother, and I would never try to take her place. But I would be honored if you would let me get to know you better and come to me if you ever need anything. Sort of like an honorary godmother."

Jessa gave her a watery smile. She was no longer alone in this world. She had family. People who cared enough to want her in their lives. "Thank you, Ms. Mathis. I'd love to have you as my honorary godmother. You were very kind to my mom, given the circumstances, and I'll never forget that. I know she didn't either."

Valerie waited for her turn and then reached out to hug

Jessa as well. "Guess this means we'll be sisters soon."

Jessa squeezed her tight. "I always wanted one of those too. Thank you all for welcoming me with open arms. It's nice to know that I'm not alone anymore."

Logan put his arm around her and pulled her into his side. "Jessa, I know this is probably going to sound crazy, but since the day you arrived, you weren't alone. I swear I could feel this strong connection with you. I don't know how, but it was there from the first time I saw you standing in that grocery store. I thought I was crazy for thinking it."

"It's true," Valerie agreed. "We talked about it several times. He said it was like he felt responsible for you or something." Then she grinned. "Your brother's really lucky I trust him and that I'm not an insecure person, or he'd have been missing some of his favorite parts of his anatomy by now."

They all laughed again, and the sound was pure joy to Jessa's ears. And Jessa had her own funny story to share. "I had something similar happen to me. I'd casually mentioned that I thought it was fate that I met Logan, and Max didn't—"

"That sonofabitch!" Logan yelled, startling all three of them as he headed straight for the door.

"Logan, what in the world? Where are you going?" Valerie asked, uncertainty in her voice.

"To find Max," he ground out. "Before, I stayed out of it because I didn't have any right to interfere in Jessa's life. But now that we know we're related, I'm going to kill that bastard for messing around with my little sister."

"Oh crap," Jessa said, running after him.

Her and her big mouth.

Chapter Twenty-one

Max stared out the front windows of the Empty Plate Café to the empty lot across the street. Windsor Park had been deserted for the past two days. No people. No food truck. And no Jessa.

He'd been sitting in the same place every day, hoping to catch a glimpse of her. But the woman had completely vanished... and it was all his fault.

God, what had he done?

He'd blown it, damn it. That's what.

And now he'd lost her forever.

Not only was the food truck gone, but Pops' customers hadn't come back either. Max was alone in the vacant restaurant, except for Pops who had just come out of the kitchen with a sign in his hands. "It's time," Pops said, his low voice wrought with emotion. "I've put it off for as long as I could."

Max eyed the For Sale sign. "Jesus, Pops. Can't you hang on a little longer?"

"That's what I was doing in hopes that a miracle would come along. But I can't keep lying to myself. I can't afford to update the restaurant, much less compete with the innovative menu items that your young woman was offering to my customers. Times have changed, and unfortunately I'm not able to change with them anymore. I'm too old to even want to change with them."

Max had come clean to Pops about his relationship with Jessa, and the old man had gotten a good laugh out of it. It wasn't exactly the reaction that Max thought he'd get, but he was glad that the old man hadn't started hating him too. "God, I'm sorry, Pops. I was really hoping something would work out for you."

"I know, son." The old man squeezed Max's shoulder as he passed by him. "But don't you worry about it. You'll find another place to eat your lunch every day."

"Jesus. That's what you think I'm worried about? After losing Jessa and watching your business go down the drain, I don't have the stomach to eat ever again. I'm just worried about what you're going to do now." *And where the hell she is.*

"Well, I thought it over plenty the last few weeks, and I kind of liked having all this extra time on my hands. So I think I'm going to use the money I get from the sale of the restaurant to retire on. I've put in my years, and it's about time I slowed down anyway. I've got some more fishing to do."

"But what about cooking? Aren't you going to miss it?"

"Sure I will. But I'm betting I know a young man who

would be willing to stop by my house for lunch on occasion," he said with a chuckle.

Max grinned. "Anytime you want company, you let me know and I'll be there. I'd never pass up one of your meals."

Pops nodded. "That's pretty much what I thought."

The door chimed, and Sam waltzed in. "Hey, fellas."

Pops greeted him with a wave. "You here for lunch, Sam?"

"Sure. Why not? I'll have the special."

"All out," the old man replied.

Sam sighed. "Figures."

Max smiled. Damn, he was going to miss that. He loved it when Pops rattled Sam's chains. "Give him a cheeseburger and fries, Pops."

"Coming right up," he said, heading to the kitchen.

Sam pulled out a chair and took a seat across from Max. "Ya know, I've been calling you for the past two days."

"I know, but I didn't feel like talking. I told you that already on the voice mail I left for you the other night. I said I wasn't coming in for a few days. I had some personal things to attend to."

"Any of those personal things happen to involve Jessa?"

Max leaned back in his chair. "Like I said, I don't want to talk about it."

"She found out that you lied to her before you had a chance to tell her, didn't she?"

Anger swirled through him. "Do you not understand the meaning of 'don't want to talk about it'?"

Sam grinned. "Yeah, I understand it. But since you

didn't listen to me when I said the same thing to you about Leah, then that's just too damn bad."

God, had I really been so annoying about it at the time? "Look, it's over. She's gone, and she's never coming back. There's nothing left to say."

"That's what you think," Sam said vaguely.

Don't do it, Max. Don't take a bite out of that bait. "Okay, so you obviously know something. What do you mean?"

Sam chuckled. "Thought you didn't want to talk about it?"

"You asshole. You better start talking, or Leah's going to wonder where you got that black eye from."

"What black eye?"

"The one I'm about to give you. Now spill it."

Sam laughed but held his hands up in surrender. The dickhead was enjoying this way too much. "Okay, okay. So from what I hear, the reason Jessa left the park and hasn't come back is because she *can't* come back."

"What do you mean she can't come back? Why the hell not? Who's stopping her?"

"The city health inspector. Ya know, the real one." He grinned again. "Apparently, there's a city ordinance that won't allow a food truck to park within a certain distance from a free-standing restaurant. Though she didn't know it at the time, Jessa had been violating a code—a real one—the whole damn time."

"Christ. Did she get a fine?"

"Nope. The new inspector seems to be a pretty fair guy. He actually let her off with a warning and asked her not to park across the street from the Empty Plate Café anymore."

"How in the hell do you know all of this? Have you been talking to the inspector or something? Who told you that?"

"Jessa did."

Max sat in stunned silence for a moment before rolling his eyes. "You're full of it, buddy. She left town. I went by her place this morning and looked through the windows. Her things have been cleared out. The house is completely empty."

"Yep, it is. Logan and I helped her load all of her stuff. It's now sitting at the bakery. Well, above it, technically. Since Valerie moved in with Logan, Leah offered the apartment to Jessa. She moved in yesterday."

What? He'd expected her to get as far away from him as humanly possible. "Sam, if you're bullshitting me..."

"I'm not, I swear. If you don't believe me, you can go by the bakery and see for yourself. The other night, after the two of you had it out, Valerie found her in the bar's kitchen, washing dishes while she was crying her eyes out. She was talking about leaving town, but Leah and Valerie rallied around her and wouldn't allow it."

Max ran a hand over his face. "Thank God for that," he said, letting out a huge sigh of relief. "I was afraid I'd never see her again."

"Well, I wouldn't get too comfortable with the idea of seeing her quite yet. From my understanding, she's still pretty pissed about the whole health inspector thing. You really messed with that girl's head."

"Up yours, Sam. I didn't mess with anyone's head." *Except maybe my own.* "Yeah, I lied to her about being the health inspector, and that's on me. But everything else between us is real."

"Oh yeah?" One curious eyebrow lifted. "So what ex-actly *is* between the two of you?"

"That's none of your damn business. Why don't you quit pestering me and find something better to do? Don't you have a wife at home waiting on you at the door naked with a chocolate soufflé or something?"

Sam chuckled. "Damn, I wish."

Pops came out of the back, carrying a plate with Sam's burger and fries. He set them down in front of him, along with a glass of iced sweet tea. "Need anything else?"

Sam shook his head. "Nah. Thanks, Pops. It looks great."

Once Pops returned to the kitchen, Sam pointed a French fry at Max. "So what do you plan to do now?"

"I've got to go find her and try to win her back."

"Or maybe you've done enough damage and should just leave the poor girl alone."

"What? You're kidding, right? I can't just let her go."

Sam shrugged. "Why not?"

Damn him. He just wants me to say it out loud. Well, that was fine by Max. Because he planned to shout it from the rooftops when he finally found Jessa anyway. "I'm in love with her, you moron."

Sam gave him a shit-eating grin. "Yeah, I know. But it's about damn time you caught on to what the rest of us have known for a while. Now why don't you quit sitting here pouting like a baby, man up, and go get your woman back?"

Max laughed. "Yeah, I think I will. But I...well, I have something else I need to do first." He knew what he needed to do. And after he did it, the first person he was going to see was Jessa.

Confusion took over Sam's face. "I thought you just said you were in love with her. What in the hell could be more important right now than winning your woman back?"

Max glanced at the For Sale sign in the window and then gazed back at Sam. "Winning back her trust. Because without that, I don't have a leg to stand on with Jessa. I'm in love with a woman who doesn't even know who I really am. For once, I'm going to put it all on the line and show her that she can trust me."

His buddy nodded his approval. "Smart move."

"Yeah, I thought so too. Of course, I'll still have to convince Jessa of that." Max slid his chair out and stood.

Without a word, Sam continued eating his lunch.

Max started for the kitchen but only made it halfway before he paused mid-step. He had been so lost in his thoughts that he almost hadn't caught the mysterious gleam in Sam's eye.

God, I'm an idiot. "You sonofabitch. You know where her truck is parked right now, don't you?"

Sam grinned again. "Maybe. But before I tell you where you can find her, you might want to know who's looking for you."

"Jessa's looking for me?"

"No, but her brother is."

Max shook his head. "I think you're confused. Jess doesn't have a brother. She's an only child."

"That's what she thought too...until she found out differently. Apparently, all those years ago when her mother passed through town, she slept with a married man who already had a child. A boy. Jessa's brother."

"Oh man, she must've read her mother's journal. Is she okay with it? I mean, finding out something like that had to be upsetting."

Sam grinned. "Oh no. She's happy as shit about it. Her brother is too. They already knew each other. He welcomed her to his family, and now he's looking for you. You're probably lucky you've been holed up here and he hasn't found you yet."

"So let me get this straight. She knew her brother the whole time she's been in town? And now he wants to kick my ass?"

"Yep." Sam chuckled.

"For what?"

"What do all older brothers want to kick someone's ass for? For messing with their little sister and breaking her heart."

Max sighed. "Okay, fine. Who's her older brother?"

* * *

The last person Jessa wanted to see strolling across the parking lot to her food truck was Max Hager... *if* that was even his real name. Actually, she knew it was since she'd already asked Valerie and Leah that question, but she wasn't feeling the least bit charitable toward him at the moment. She'd heard enough of his lies to last her a lifetime.

Jessa had figured he would eventually find the Gypsy Cantina parked on Sam's construction site. How could he not? Max was a freelance electrician who did a lot of work for Sam. Not only that, but they were also best friends. So of course he would locate her and show up to grovel his way back into her life once again. But that didn't mean she was going to make it easy on him.

She reached over and locked the truck's door, which made Lisa and Mary both giggle. At least that would keep him at a bit of a distance for the time being. The last two times she'd had it out with him, he reached for her. She couldn't handle him trying to touch her right now. Not after being away from him for several days. And judging by the determined look on his handsome face, that was probably exactly what he would try to do.

But she was surprised when he didn't come to the door at all. Instead, he did something even more irritating. He got in line and waited his turn.

Damn him.

Max was taller than most of the men in line, so he had a perfect shot of her. And since the food truck's platform wasn't exactly on ground level, she had a clear view of him too. Though he watched her calmly from the back of the line, the way he stared at her was so intense, so fierce, that it threw Jessa into a tailspin.

Flustered and unable to concentrate, she turned away from the order window and grasped the steel counter with a white-knuckled grip. God. Why was he doing this to her? And why had she stopped Logan from going after him and killing him? The jerk deserved to be strangled in a choke hold right about now.

Lisa, who had been cooking on the grill, gazed outside at Max standing in line and then patted her shoulder. "Are you okay, honey?"

She nodded. "Of course. He's... an idiot."

Mary handed an order out the pick-up window and

nodded. "That he is, but maybe you should just go talk to him and get it over with."

"No, I'm just going to pretend that he isn't here. He'll eventually go away."

Jessa pulled herself together and got back to work. She could ignore him, couldn't she? Especially since they were so busy. It was lunchtime, and Sam had a huge construction crew that was relying on the women to feed them before they headed back to work. So that was exactly what she set out to do. Though every order she took and completed brought Max one step closer to her, making her heart pound harder in her chest.

And he looked good, damn it. He wore a blue plaid button-down over a white undershirt, but he hadn't bothered to button it up or tuck it in either. The tight pair of jeans stretched across his powerfully built thighs would probably show off his fine, muscular rear end nicely too. If she wasn't so pissed off at him right now, she would've gotten in line behind him just to admire the view.

When he finally reached the front of the line, he smiled wide, as if that sexy little grin of his was going to work magic on her. Okay, so maybe it did send butterflies fluttering in her stomach, but she could ignore her traitorous body just as well as him.

She didn't greet him. Didn't smile at him. Instead, she picked up a black permanent marker and a piece of paper and began writing.

Lisa started for the window. "I'll get this one, Jess."

"No, that's okay. Thank you, but I'm taking care of it."

Jessa put down the black marker, grabbed a piece of tape, and then headed back to the order window where she hung her new sign. It read, WE RESERVE THE RIGHT TO REFUSE SERVICE TO ANYONE. ESPECIALLY TO MAX BECAUSE HE'S A JACKASS.

He read the sign, and his face fell. "Jess, I just want to talk to you for a moment. I didn't come here to send you over the moon by pissing you off more."

"Well, too late. You've achieved liftoff."

"Just give me five more minutes of your time. If you don't like what I have to say, then I'll go away and leave you alone."

"Yeah right. You said that last time."

"True, but I also warned you before I left that I was coming back for you. Well guess what, baby? I'm here, and the time is now."

"I'm not the least bit interested." Now who was the liar?

He leaned against the order counter on the truck, one of his brows rising in challenge. "Then I guess I'll just have to stand here all day and wait for you to change your mind."

She glanced at all the hungry men standing behind him. Damn it. She didn't want to listen to his explanation as to why he was a big, stupid moron who told her a dumb lie and tricked her into believing he was something he wasn't. But it wasn't like she had much of a choice. He was holding up the line.

"Fine. You get three minutes of my time," she snapped, pulling her gloves off and throwing them into the trash. "And then you're leaving."

"Okay, but first you have to open the door and come outside. I don't want to do this through a window."

"Max, you're pushing your luck with me."

"Please, just come out here. I have something I want to give you."

She rolled her eyes. "What? Your penis? Because if so, then I can tell you where you can shove it."

Laughter sounded from the men behind Max, and he turned and glared at them until their chuckles died out. "No, it's not my dick. Because we both know it wouldn't fit in this," he said, holding up a large brown mailing envelope held closed by a metal clasp.

Okay, he had her there. It was a big envelope, but she doubted his penis would fit inside. "Well, whether it's your penis or something else, I don't want anything from you," she said. But she headed outside anyway. At least that would get him out of the order window area and allow Lisa and Mary to keep working. Not that it mattered since everyone in line was now more interested in watching them than ordering lunch.

She was probably going to lose money today all because of Max.

He stepped off to the side and waited for her to reach him. He looked uncomfortable, queasy even. Good. Maybe he should've thought about that before he started screwing with other people's heads. The liar.

As she neared him, she caught a glimpse of Sam standing nearby with a huge grin on his face. "Is this your doing, Sam?"

He shrugged lightly. "He would've eventually found out where you were camping out. Besides, I told you that I wouldn't keep it from him if I ran into him."

"That you did," she said with a nod. "But somehow I have a feeling you made sure you ran into him, you meddler."

Sam only grinned wider. She couldn't really be upset with him though. She knew he was friends with Max well before he'd ever met her. Of course he was going to take his buddy's side. But couldn't the guy give her a little warning?

She shook her head. Of course not. Because then she would've made sure to avoid the place to keep from setting eyes on Max. And Sam had already told her that he was rooting for his buddy to win her back. Sam was a jerk too, but a very sweet one.

Jessa stopped in front of Max and scowled at him. "Okay, what do you want?" she asked, crossing her arms.

"For starters, your trust. I know I hurt you, sweetheart, and I'm sorry about that. It won't ever happen again. I swear that to you on my life. I know I can't force you to forgive me and that it's going to take some time, but I want you to know that I only want the best for you." He opened the brown envelope and pulled out a small stack of papers. "I wanted to repair some of the damage I caused."

"And just how do you think you're going to do that?"

"Well, I know you have dreams of opening your own restaurant some day, and I want to help you make your dreams a reality."

"What are you talking about? Help me how?"

He handed her the stack of papers and waited in silence as she glanced them over.

Her eyes lifted to his. "This is a title of deed for the Empty Plate Café."

"I know. I just bought it…for you." He reached into the envelope and pulled out a set of shiny new keys. He pressed them into her hand, closing her fingers around them. "These are yours. I bought you a restaurant."

Jessa's head snapped up. "You did what?" Huh? Why would he help her after trying to get rid of her? Was the guilt too much for him to handle? Otherwise, it didn't make any sense.

"It was the one thing you'd always said you wanted, and I wanted to help you achieve your goal. I cashed in some old stocks and bonds I had and bought the Empty Plate Café for you. I know it's not much to look at right now and needs a lot of remodeling, but I've already hired Sam's crew to come out next week and go through it with you. Whatever you want changed or updated in the building will be taken care of immediately . . . at my expense. Either way, it's yours to do whatever you'd like with it."

Her mind was reeling from the shock of it all. He bought her a restaurant? She shook her head. "I . . . I don't know what to say."

"You don't have to say anything, Jess. Just please accept this gift as a sign of how sorry I am and how much I want you to stay in town. I never meant to hurt you, I swear."

His sincere words had moisture pooling in her eyes, but it wasn't happy tears clogging her lashes. "I don't want it."

Max blinked rapidly at her. "What do you mean you don't want it? You have to take it. I already bought it for you. It's yours."

She shook her head furiously. "No, it's yours."

"Is that what's bothering you—that I paid for it? I bought it for you, sweetheart. My name isn't the one going on the deed. Only yours. The restaurant is yours to do whatever you wish with it."

"No, that's not what I meant. I just thought—never

mind. It doesn't matter anymore." She turned away from him.

He reached for her. "Jess, please..."

Damn it, she knew that would happen if she got anywhere near him. She shrugged his hand off her shoulder. "No, you just don't get it. For a second, I thought you did...but you clearly don't."

"Okay, then tell me what it is that I don't get."

Although her dream of one day owning a restaurant was important to her, Max had completely missed what mattered most to her. Her hands fisted at her sides as she spun on him, anger washing over her like a volcanic wave. "Me, damn you. You don't get me. If you did, you would know that a restaurant isn't what I care about. I thought you..." Her words trailed off, and she shook her head, trying to push away the hurt bubbling up inside of her.

"Go on. Say it."

Her heart squeezed so tight in her chest that it was hard to breathe. She swiped at a stray tear trailing down her face and let out a heavy sigh. "I had hoped you were here to win *me* back."

Max grinned. "What makes you think I'm not?" Then he gestured to her hand that held the keys to the restaurant.

Jess opened her palm. She hadn't noticed it when he'd first handed the keys to her, but there was a sparkling solitaire diamond ring linked to the silver key ring. A very pretty one, at that. Her eyes blurred with more tears. "I...I don't know what to say."

"You already said that," he told her, his grin widening. "But let me do the talking right now." He took her hand in his, rubbing circles on her palm with his thumb. "I may have pretended to be something I'm not, but nothing about our relationship has ever been a lie, Jess. I never faked how I felt about you, how much you mean to me, or how much I loved having you in my life, my bed, and my heart."

Her teary gaze held his. "Oh, Max."

"I've fallen for you, Jess. I'm pretty sure I started my descent from the first moment I laid eyes on you. Now I have an important question for you, but I want you to know that this is in no way a stipulation. As I said before, the restaurant is yours. I believe in you and know you'll do amazing things with it. I just hope that you'll allow me to be at your side through it all."

"Max, wait a minute. I—"

But he didn't. He knelt down in front of her on one knee, his hand still holding hers. "I love you, Jessa Gibson. I want to spend the rest of my life showing you just how much. Will you marry me?"

Jessa expelled another tear as she squeezed her eyes shut tight. She shook her head firmly. "No. I'm sorry, Max, but I can't marry you."

Chapter Twenty-two

Max's entire body went numb.

He thought he'd misheard the answer to his question until the gasps and murmurs from the surrounding audience began. Then as quickly as that, the hurt slammed into him. A sharp pain, swift and hot, stabbed into his heart repeatedly like a deranged psychopath.

No? She'd told him no? He didn't understand. Not because he was so conceited that he thought all women in the world wanted him. It was just that...this one *did*. He felt it. Hell, he could see it in her teary eyes right now. She loved him, damn it. Why the hell wasn't she accepting his proposal? He thought for sure that, by helping her achieve her goals, she would forgive him and move past it all...with him.

Hot lava flowed in his veins, yet her rejection of him had caused an aching sensation deep down inside of him. As if anger and hurt waged war in his head. But Max pushed aside the hurt feelings because being pissed felt better. "You mean, you *won't* marry me. Because can't and won't are two very different things."

She sniffled and swiped at the steady tears trailing down both cheeks. "It's both. I'm sorry."

He stood, dusting off his knee. He'd been hurt a lot in his life, but none of it compared to the way she'd just torn his heart in two. "Is this your way of hurting me back, Jess? Because if so, let me tell you, it worked beautifully. I'm hurt."

She shook her head adamantly. "No, of course not. I don't want to hurt you, Max."

"Yet, like you said to me . . . it didn't stop you from doing just that."

"This wasn't payback. Please don't think that, Max."

"What the hell else am I supposed to think?" The woman he loved was standing right in front of him, and he couldn't have her. It was fucking killing him. "Tell me why you refuse to marry me."

"Because you still don't get it."

What the fuck was he supposed to get? "Baby, how do I know what it is you want from me if you don't tell me?"

She breathed out a hard, stuttered breath. "You. That's all I want. I don't need the restaurant or the pretty ring. What I need is you."

Max rubbed at his face. "You're right. Then I just don't get it. Because I just offered myself on a platter, and you snubbed your nose at it."

"No. What you offered was a diluted version of yourself and expected me to jump at the chance to have only a part of you. But I won't settle, Max. If you only want to show the side of you that you think people will like, then that's fine. But with me, it's either all or nothing. There is no in between." Another tear fell.

Christ. Only then did he know what he needed to do. This was something he planned to share with her later once he got her alone, but it was clearly what she needed now. God, he hated being vulnerable. Especially with so many prying eyes on him. But he wasn't going to risk losing her just to save his pride. He leaned down and picked up the brown envelope off the ground. He hadn't even remembered dropping it, but he must've done so when she'd surprised him with her answer to his proposal.

He held the envelope out to her. "The other day when I was standing inside your house begging your forgiveness, you asked me to sacrifice something that I wasn't ready to give up. I planned to do this in private later anyway, but if this is what you need from me, then now's just as good a time as any."

"What is it?" she asked, taking the envelope from him warily.

"A part of me. A big part."

She opened the large envelope and slid out a blown-up photo of Max as a teenager. A very heavy, overweight teenager with severe acne, crooked teeth, and a mullet hairdo.

"That's what I looked like fifteen years ago when I was a teenager. I was the chubby kid who got picked on relentlessly all throughout my early school years. In high school, it only got worse."

"I'm sorry. Kids can be so cruel sometimes."

"I thought the same thing. And then I got out of high

school and found that it didn't get any better. Adults can be the same way. So I got a haircut, visited a dermatologist, got some braces, and then began a strict diet regimen and exercise plan that took off the extra weight."

"You didn't have to do that for...those people. Who cares what they think?"

"You're right. The reason I lost weight was because I had a history of being bullied. But honestly, once I became more fit, I discovered I actually liked being in shape and didn't want to go back to how I was before. Women gave me the time of day. Other men didn't kick sand in my eyes. No one made fun of me." He glanced over to Sam and grinned. "Well, except for that bastard, but he doesn't count."

Several people chuckled, including Sam. "Someone has to keep that ego of yours in check, buddy."

Max grinned and glanced back to Jessa. "Here's the thing though. I thought I had adopted a healthier lifestyle all those years ago, but I was wrong. I mean, I did physically. I ate right and exercised regularly, which changed the way I looked on the outside. But mentally, I still had my guard up and kept others at a distance. I told people what they wanted to hear rather than the truth about me.

"Even the attention I received from women only led to a string of unhealthy sexual relationships that were never fully satisfying. Not because of whichever woman I was with at the time. It was all on me. I'm not proud of it, but I charmed women into my bed. But in the end, I was the one who was unsatisfied because I couldn't seem to let down my guard completely with them."

"Why?" Jessa asked.

"Because none of them ever challenged me to. And

I needed that. Because I never risked anyone liking the real me. Hell, I think even I was starting to believe my own bullshit."

"After what you went through, I think we can all understand that," Jessa said, sympathizing with him.

"Maybe. But I never truly let go of the past. I may have changed the way I looked on the outside, but deep down inside of me, I'm still him."

Her eyes watered. "Oh, Max. That's not true."

"It is," he said, pointing to the photo. "I've always been that chubby kid who got into trouble because he was trying to keep others at a distance. The same one who hid himself away because he didn't think people would like who he was. The kid who didn't know how to handle himself when he was in an uncomfortable situation so he overate as a form of self-medication. But I learned something about myself. I am still him, but I'm also a better version. I *can* control myself."

She nodded. "Of course you can. You're the strongest man I know, Max. You can do anything you put your mind to. But you don't have anything to prove to anyone."

"That's where you're wrong, Jess." He reached for her, threading his fingers into her hair around the base of her neck. He gazed lovingly into her eyes, wanting her to see the truth there. "I need to prove to you that I'm the man for you. The one who will love you forever and never let you go."

Her eyes welled up with tears again. "You've already proven that to me. It took a lot of bravery to show me this and face your past in front of a crowd of people."

His forehead lowered to hers, and he breathed out a

sigh. "I don't see anyone here but you and me...and that's just how I want it. You and me. Forever. Please, baby, say you'll marry me. I want you to be mine."

She swallowed hard. "Being with you is all I've wanted since I met you. I'm yours, Max."

"That's a yes?" he asked, his heart swelling with hope.

She wrapped her arms around his neck. "Yes!"

"Thank God." Max caught her around the waist and lifted her, swinging her in a circle as everyone cheered and applauded his victory. "I love you, sweetheart."

"I love you too," she said, laughing.

He set her back down and closed the gap between them, covering her mouth with his. Almost instantly, several wolf-whistles came from the crowd, along with a couple of men telling them to get a room. Which Max planned to do as soon as he could talk Jessa into taking the day off.

His woman. Forever.

Damn, he loved the sound of that.

Epilogue

Max gazed around the renovated dining room with pride. The old café looked like a completely different place now that Jess had transformed it into her dream restaurant. The whole room exhibited an abundance of textures and patterns like the interior of some kind of romantic gypsy caravan.

A huge chandelier hung in the center of the room surrounded by a canopy of bold red fabrics draped from the ceiling. Large gold medallions accented the walls between each arched window. Colorful glass lanterns trimmed with cascading jewels lit every table while throw pillows of rich hues and mixed prints decorated each chair. There was even a vintage dessert cart featuring pastries by Leah's bakery.

Jessa had finally done it. She'd thrown this new gourmet restaurant together quicker than anything he'd ever seen before, and it was absolutely beautiful.

Two arms wrapped around his waist from behind. "Why are you not helping the others?" a sultry feminine voice said. "Are you trying to conserve your energy?"

He pulled Jessa around in front of him and nuzzled his face into her sweet-smelling neck. "You know it. I need all of it for later tonight after closing time. I have something for you, and I can tell you right now, it isn't going to fit inside an envelope…even a big one." He rubbed the hardening bulge in his pants nonchalantly up against her abdomen.

She laughed and gave him a quick kiss. "It better be a penis."

He lifted his head and then his eyebrow. "A penis?"

"Okay, *your* penis, if we're getting specific."

"You're my wife, Jess. You better damn well be specific when you're talking about penises."

She grinned. "I still can't believe we had such a shotgun wedding. I don't think two people have ever married so fast."

"Well, that's because your stupid brother wanted to do a double wedding ceremony."

"Max."

"What? Logan is stupid. He keeps threatening to hit me. I think he has anger management issues."

"Well, if you would stop instigating when it comes to him, then I'm betting he would leave you alone."

Max laughed. "Hell, where's the fun in that?"

"Well, just for the record, the double wedding wasn't Logan's idea. Valerie and I were the ones who came up with it. You said you wanted to get married right away, and they were the ones who already had a wedding mostly planned out. Seemed like a good idea at the time.

Especially with us spending so much to open the restaurant."

"Speaking of which, it looks great, babe. You did an outstanding job."

Leah passed by them and gazed out the nearest window. "Wow! The line out there is halfway down the block. You're about to get slammed, Jess."

Max gazed at his wife. "You sure you don't want to be in the kitchen cooking tonight?"

Jessa shook her head. "No, Mary and Lisa know what they're doing back there and can handle it. Tonight I'm going to be out here greeting my customers and making sure everything is running smoothly. Besides, I want to make sure everyone is enjoying the new menu items. But I've already told Lisa and Mary to let me know if they need me though. I doubt there will be any problems. Those ladies are terrific."

Sam passed by carrying some extra chairs toward the dining room. "Val is about to open the doors. Might want to prepare yourself for a stampede."

Max and Jessa laughed. Who stampeded into a gourmet restaurant?

Moments later, Valerie opened the doors, and a flood of hungry patrons filled the dining room. Jessa had hired a lot of new staff for her restaurant, but they were all experienced and knew what they were expected to do. Everything was under control and looking great. She totally had this.

As she and Max watched the crowd entering, a couple waved at Jessa and the woman rushed over to give her a quick hug. "Hi, how are you?"

"Hey, Cindy. I'm great. How are you?"

"Wonderful. You remember Kevin?"

"Of course," Jessa said, nodding at him. "Have you guys met my husband, Max?"

Max shook both of their hands. "Nice to meet you two."

"So you're Max," the woman said, giggling as she elbowed her husband who was grinning from ear to ear.

"I am. I take it Jessa mentioned my name?"

"Repeatedly," the woman said, which made Jessa grin.

After a moment, Kevin finally shuffled Cindy off to their table, and Max turned to Jessa. "Okay, what did I miss? Who the hell were those people?"

"My old neighbors."

Max chuckled. "Oh shit."

"Yep, exactly what you're thinking. They never met you in person, but they were very familiar with your name. Heard it plenty of times. Even said they felt like they almost knew you."

He rubbed a hand over his face. "Christ. That does it. We're buying a house in the middle of nowhere."

Jessa laughed. "Oh, don't act like you don't love that you can make me scream loud enough that my neighbors hear every word."

He winked at her.

They turned and looked out over the dining room together. It was a packed house, and everyone seemed to be enjoying themselves so far. Jessa's new dishes on the menu were going to blow these people away. And not only that, but she'd even made sure to come up with a few low-calorie entrées that were just as delicious as everything else she made.

The rest of the gang crossed the room and joined the two of them.

Leah smiled at Jessa. "Congratulations, Jess. You did it. You have officially opened your first restaurant."

Jessa shook her head. "No, *we* did it. All of us," she said, glancing around at their closest friends. "Thank you all for your help. I don't know what I would've done without your support. It means the world to me."

"That's what we're here for," Valerie replied, hugging her.

Sam nodded in agreement. "Exactly what friends are for."

Logan slung his arm around Max's shoulders. "I think the six of us make a pretty good team."

Max smirked at the kind gesture by his new brother-in-law. He guessed eventually they'd learn to love each other. "Yep. I guess you could say we're all a perfect fit."

Thanks to her bangin' curves, Valerie Carmichael has always turned heads—with the exception of seriously sexy Logan Mathis. Just Valerie's luck that the object of her lust-filled affection is also best friends with her over-protective brother.

An excerpt from
On the Plus Side
follows.

Chapter One

Valerie Carmichael needed a drink. A strong one. Because it was the only way she envisioned herself getting through the night.

Then again, maybe if she drank enough, the alcohol would sour her stomach and give her a good excuse to bail out and take the first cab home. Sadly, that option sounded the most appealing.

An elbow nudged into her side, bringing her thoughts back to the crowded bar. "I can't see anything through all of these people," Brett said, scanning the room with his eyes. "Come on, let's go to the other side so I can get a better view."

Sighing, Valerie trudged behind him without a word.

When Brett had asked her to attend the grand opening of Bottoms Up, a new bar in their hometown of Granite, Texas, she'd hesitated to say yes. Sure, she was curious what the inside of the recently remodeled bar looked like and had no doubt the place would be jam-packed with handsome, available men. But it was still the last place on earth she wanted to be.

She knew better than to hang out in bars with her older and only—*thank God*—brother. Every time she'd done so in the past, the nights had always ended the same way. Brett would spend the entire evening hovering over her like a rabid pit bull, daring any single guy with a glint in his eye to look her way. And eventually, one of them would.

At least one brave soul, brimming with liquid courage, would be dumb enough—or drunk enough— to risk approaching her while Brett stood guard. Then the potentially suicidal man would quickly find out what a hot-tempered asshole her brother could be. It was in-evitable.

Because Valerie turned heads. She always had.

Oh, she wasn't silly enough to believe she looked like some gorgeous supermodel with a lean, trim figure or anything. She definitely didn't. But she had a pretty face, banging plus-size curves, and a lively personality. And that was good enough for her. Valerie was just... Valerie. And damn proud of it.

Unfortunately, that noteworthy self-confidence of hers was akin to a powerful magnet, drawing unassuming male moths to her female flame. Which meant, as with any heat source, there was always a chance someone would get burned. And with Brett around, odds were in her favor that it wasn't going to be her.

As they made their way across the room, Brett's mus-cular frame easily parted the sea of people, giving her plenty of space to walk behind him without bumping into anyone. But even then, she only made it ten feet before a masculine arm circled her waist and pulled her back against a hard body. "Hey, baby. Wanna dance?"

Valerie winced. *Another guy with a death wish. Lovely.*

No, wait. She recognized that voice, didn't she?

Glancing over her right shoulder, she stared directly into Max's playful eyes just as Brett whipped around and shoved Max away from her. "Get your hands off my sister, jackass."

Max released her and held his hands up in surrender. "Whoa! I was just playing around with her. No need to get pissy about it, buddy."

"I'm not your goddamn buddy," Brett sneered, fire flashing in his eyes as he stepped toward Max.

Valerie scrambled into her brother's path to keep him at bay. "Stop it! He's just a friend of mine, Brett. You don't have to go all caveman on him."

"Then tell your *friend* to keep his damn hands off you." Her brother shot Max one of his blue-eyed Taser glares, which usually sent most men retreating.

But Max wasn't like most men and continued to stand there, as if he was throwing down a challenge of his own. One Brett was clearly willing to accept, since he started for Max.

Jesus. Here we go again. Valerie readjusted her position and placed her hands on Brett's chest to stop him. "Knock it off right now. Damn it, you promised to behave yourself tonight. If you can't control yourself, then I'm going home." She almost hoped Brett would throw a punch just so she had a reason to leave. *Sorry, Max.*

"Me?" Brett asked innocently, his eyes widening. "I

didn't do anything... *yet*." He zapped another threatening look in Max's direction for good measure.

Valerie shook her head, annoyed with the whole situation. "Why don't you just go ahead without me, and I'll catch up to you in a little bit?"

Her brother didn't move.

God, why did I come out tonight? Me and my bright ideas. "Damn it, Brett. Just go already. I'll be fine. I want to talk to Max." Her brother planted his feet, as if he planned to wait for her, so she added, "Without my bodyguard present, if you don't mind."

Brett gritted his teeth and set his jaw but eventually stalked away. Once Valerie was sure he wasn't coming back, she turned her attention to Max and sighed. "Sorry about that. My brother's a little... intense."

"Who, that guy? Nah." Max's sardonic tone wasn't lost on her, but then he shrugged. "No big deal, Val. You warned me that your brother was an asshole. If I had known he was with you tonight, I wouldn't have grabbed you like that."

She grinned. "You're such a liar."

The corner of his mouth lifted in a tiny smirk. "I know."

Though they'd met only six months before at Rusty's Bucket—a seedy local dive bar that made this place look like some kind of upscale cocktail lounge—she'd had Max's number from the beginning. And she wasn't referring to his telephone digits... though she had those too.

Upon meeting Max, Valerie had quickly figured out two things about him. One, he was a decent guy, even though he was a bit of a troublemaker at times. Two, he hadn't been remotely attracted to her. Which was fine with her, since she hadn't been interested in him either.

She hadn't lied when she told Brett that Max was just a friend. Nothing romantic had ever evolved between them and never would. At the time, they had each unknowingly used the opportunity to set up their best friends, Leah and Sam, by feigning interest in each other.

And it had worked! The lucky couple were now engaged and living together in Sam's apartment while his construction crew built their new house not far from Leah's bakery, Sweets n' Treats. Within three weeks, Leah would have her intimate beach wedding and be moving into her glorious new home with the man of her dreams.

And Valerie couldn't be happier for them.

Especially since the one-bedroom apartment over the bakery was now available for Valerie to rent, thus making Leah not only her best friend and employer but also her landlord.

"I'm surprised to see you here tonight," Max said, steering Valerie toward a surprisingly vacant seat at the small side bar in the corner. "Leah said you weren't coming."

"I didn't plan to," she said, noting how strange it was that there were plenty of seats in the area around them while the rest of the bar harbored wall-to-wall people. She slid onto the black, vinyl-covered stool as Max stationed himself next to her. "I know it's hard to believe I'd miss it though."

"No kidding. Since when do you not enjoy the bar scene, party girl?"

Okay, so maybe I'm not the only one who's got some-one's number.

Grinning, she ignored his question and glanced around the room. "So where are Leah and Sam? I thought they'd be here by now."

"They're here," he confirmed. "They headed over to the main bar to get a drink. The bartenders over there are much faster than this one is," Max said, gesturing to the young man fumbling with a glass behind the bar. "If you want something to drink, you better tell me quick. If he has to make more than one drink at a time, you'll die of thirst before I can save you."

Normally, Valerie would have ordered a beer, but the shiny metallic bandage dress she wore showed off her feminine side and wasn't really the kind of outfit a lady would drink a beer in. *Hmm. Something colorful and fruity perhaps?* Besides, the hard liquor would probably help ease some of the tension she'd felt creeping up her spine since she'd entered the building. "Um, how about an appletini?"

"A what?"

She grinned. "An apple martini."

Max nodded. "You got it. Coming right...er, scratch that. You might get it soon, if you're lucky." He grinned and then leaned over the bar and repeated the order to the young bartender.

The barkeep nodded in acknowledgment but seemed a bit unsure of what to do. When he finally made the deci-sion to reach for a glass, it took him three tries before he found the one used for martinis. Even as he chilled the glass with ice, he moved so slowly and deliberately that Valerie wondered if he was pacing himself so he didn't pull a muscle in his hand. If he didn't learn to speed up, the thirsty bar-goers would eat him for breakfast. Because, chances were, it would take him until morning to finish making one drink. *Jeez.*

While they waited for her drink, Max and Valerie lingered at the bar counter chatting about their friends' pending nuptials. Since they were the best man and maid-of-honor, Max and Valerie would soon be walking down the aisle together. Of course, she wouldn't dare word it that way to her brother or he'd jump to conclusions and blow a gasket.

After a few minutes, Sam and Leah emerged from the dense crowd, with a beer bottle for him and a glass of water for her. Apparently, Leah was still on that damn diet and counting calories so she would fit into her wedding dress. Though why she didn't just buy the dress in a larger size was beyond Valerie.

Leah blinked at the sight of her sitting with Max. "Val? What are you doing here? You said you weren't coming."

Valerie shrugged. "I changed my mind."

"Are you feeling okay?"

"Yeah, sure. Why?"

"When you said you didn't want to go out, I assumed you were sick. You *never* turn down a night out. Actually, you're the one who's always asking me to go." Leah placed her palm lightly against Valerie's forehead. "You sure you don't have the flu or something?"

Valerie laughed and pushed her friend's hand away. "Oh, stop it. I just didn't feel like getting dressed up. I'm getting tired of the whole bar scene."

Leah squinted with disbelief. "Since when?"

Since three weeks ago when I found out this place was opening. Valerie gazed expectantly at the bartender, who was using a jigger to carefully measure out the vodka for her cocktail. Damn, she could really use that drink about now. She sighed inwardly. "I'm fine," she told Leah. "I was tired, but the mood passed."

"Good," Sam said cheerfully, clasping a hand on his buddy's shoulder. "Then maybe you can help us keep Max out of trouble for one evening. Lord knows he needs all the help he can get."

Max just grinned.

"Already on top of it," Valerie replied. "A few minutes ago, he met my brother."

Leah's eyes widened. "Oh no. Brett's here? I can only imagine how well that went over."

"Yep, exactly what you're thinking. It didn't. But I managed to send Brett away for the time being. I'm sure he's still watching me from some dark corner though." She leaned over to Max and loudly mock-whispered, "If you want to keep your arms attached to your body, I wouldn't make any sudden movements in my direction."

They all laughed, probably because a truer statement had never been spoken. As the chuckling died down, the young bartender finally slid a green-tinted apple martini on the counter in front of Valerie. *Thank goodness.*

Max reached for his wallet and nodded across the room in the direction Brett had wandered off in. "Think I can get away with paying for your drink, smart-ass? Or should I consult your brother first?"

She smiled up at him, her eyes twinkling with mirth. "Oh no. You don't have to ask his permission for that."

Then her gaze followed the same trail Max's had. "Always feel free to pay for my—"

Valerie's heart stopped, along with her lips. *Oh God.*

Across the room, Brett stood there talking to a tall, dark-haired man who had one thumb hooked in the front pocket of his jeans while he leaned comfortably against the wall with his right shoulder. She couldn't see the other guy's face, but she didn't need to. Valerie recognized all six feet, two inches of him.

Jesus. I don't think I can do this.

"Can't do what?" Leah asked, puzzlement filling her voice.

Shit. Had she said that out loud?

Valerie winced. Her friends probably thought Brett's ridiculous brotherly behavior had been the motivation for her wanting to stay home tonight…and that was partly true. But she hadn't told them the real reason—a bigger reason—for wanting to avoid stepping into the hottest new bar in town. And that reason not only had a name, but he was the owner. Logan Mathis.

"Val?" Leah placed her hand on Valerie's shoulder, pulling her out of her thoughts and right back into her noisy surroundings.

She immediately lifted her drink and downed the martini in one gulp, then rubbed a flat hand across her queasy stomach. "I *can* do this," she whispered in encouragement to herself.

Sam and Max were no longer paying attention and were busy having a heated football discussion, but Leah raised one suspicious brow. "What the hell are you talking about?" she asked before her gaze fell on the empty martini glass. "How many of those have you had?"

Valerie glanced across the room again at the man who had her insides tied up in knots and sighed heavily. "Not nearly enough."

Leah's gaze immediately followed the invisible trail of bread crumbs Valerie had left behind. She grinned and pointed across the bar. "Hey, isn't that—"

"Logan Mathis," Valerie groaned, not bothering to hide the contempt in her voice.

"Yeah, that's the one. He was your brother's—"

"Best friend."

She nodded. "Yep, but didn't he move away like—"

"Eight years ago."

Leah pursed her mouth in annoyance. "Okay, how about you actually let me ask the question before you answer it?"

Despite the way her stomach was churning, Valerie couldn't help but grin. "Sorry. Go ahead."

"Isn't he the guy you had that huge crush on back then?"

Valerie blinked rapidly. "Wait. H-how did you..."

"Oh, come on," Leah said, rolling her eyes. "You didn't really think you fooled me, did ya? You mooned over the Mathis boy every chance you got. And the way you always wanted to tag along with the two of them, though Brett frustrated the hell out of you most days. It was obvious."

Great. Just great. Valerie closed her eyes and rubbed at her temples before looking back at Logan. He had shifted his position and was now leaning with his back against the brick wall, which gave her a clear view of his face. Her mouth went dry. *Good Lord. Could he possibly get any hotter?*

He had the same brooding brown eyes from before, but his muscled frame had filled out and taken on a more rugged appearance. A five-o'clock shadow now graced his chiseled jaw but gave his face more depth and dimension.

His clothes, however, were a bit misleading from the Logan she remembered. The neutral-toned flannel shirt permitted him an almost respectable, approachable look that was probably good for his business. But then she noticed that he'd only slightly tucked in the front of the shirt, enough to showcase the noticeable bulge beneath his belt buckle. As if he were putting his manhood on display.

There's the Logan she remembered. *That damn subtle arrogance of his.*

Leah eyed her warily. "So that's why you're acting so weird tonight? You still have a thing for Logan?"

"No, I don't," Valerie answered quickly.

"Oh my God. You do! You're practically sweating right now," Leah accused, grinning her ass off. She peeked over at him again. "Hmm. Well, he does look good."

"Really? I haven't noticed," Valerie said, keeping herself from taking another peek.

Leah looked more confused than ever. "But haven't you seen him since he got back into town?"

"No. I've been … busy. I had all that unpacking to do, ya know? And I'm pretty sure that opening a new bar required a lot of his attention."

"Val, you moved into my old apartment a month ago, and I helped you unpack everything the first week you were …" Leah paused. "Hold on. Did you say he opened a new bar? As in *this* bar?"

"Um, yeah. It's his place."

"I didn't know that. I guess all this wedding planning has kept me distracted and out of the loop. I'm surprised you didn't mention it thou…" Leah paused, then threw back her head and cackled. "Oh, I get it! So that's why you didn't want to come out tonight. You're avoiding him."

When Valerie bit her lip, Leah grinned wider, apparently enjoying the role reversal they had going on. Then she eyed Logan from across the room once more. "I never thought I'd say this to you, Valerie, but payback is a real bitch."

Before Valerie could stop her, Leah waved her hand in the air, snaring Brett's attention. He immediately recognized his sister's best friend and nodded to her before leaning toward Logan. Brett's mouth moved with inaudible words that had Logan's head spinning in the girls' direction.

Valerie leaned back quickly so that Max's body blocked her from view as Logan glanced over. "Leah, what the hell?" She peeked around Max's shoulder in time to see Brett start in their direction…with Logan on his heels. "Oh God! Why the hell did you do that?"

"Because I'm your friend. There's no point in avoiding him. It's like ripping off a bandage. Just get it over with already."

"Damn it, Leah…"

"Don't be mad. Besides, Granite isn't that big of a town, and you were bound to run into him sooner or later anyway."

"I was good with later."

Leah giggled and then tapped Sam on the shoulder,

interrupting his conversation with Max. "Why don't the three of us go grab another round of drinks from across the room? Brett's coming over here, and I'm pretty sure Valerie is going to need a refill...or possibly ten."

"What?" Valerie blinked at her. "Now you're leaving me all by myself? Gee, thanks. Some friend you are."

"I'm doing you a favor. You'll thank me for it later. Besides, you wouldn't want me standing here grinning like a fool when he walks up," Leah said with a wink. "Let me know what happens though. I'm dying to hear how all this plays out." Then she flitted away, taking Sam and Max with her.

Traitor. She'll be lucky if I tell her anything at all.

Brett and Logan wove their way through the crush of people invading the bar, and with every step they took in her direction, Valerie could feel the room growing considerably smaller. Unwilling to make eye contact, she turned her body to the bar and stared straight ahead. Adrenaline raced through her veins, and her nerves surged with anxiety. *Yep, definitely going to throw up.*

The moment the air pressure surrounding her changed, she knew Logan—and his overbearing male presence—was standing behind her. It was as if she could feel the tension rolling off him in waves.

Unfortunately, she couldn't put it off any longer. Straightening her posture, she sucked in a calming breath and crossed her legs, allowing her short skirt to ride up her thighs a little more than was polite. She planted a big smile on her face, spun around on her bar stool, and looked directly at Logan's unsmiling face. He had always towered over her much shorter frame, but somehow she'd forgotten how impossibly small he could make her feel with just one simple look.

Logan's eyes met hers head-on, and his lips curved. "Well, well. If it isn't Princess Valerie."

ABOUT THE AUTHOR

Alison Bliss grew up in Small Town, Texas, but currently resides in the Midwest with her husband and two sons. With so much testosterone in her home, it's no wonder she writes "girl books." She believes the best way to know if someone is your soul mate is by canoeing with them because if you both make it back alive, it's obviously meant to be. Alison pens the type of books she loves to read most: fun, steamy love stories with heart, heat, laughter, and usually a cowboy or two. As she calls it, "Romance…with a sense of humor."

To learn more, visit her at:
http://authoralisonbliss.com
Facebook/AuthorAlisonBliss
Twitter @AlisonBliss2

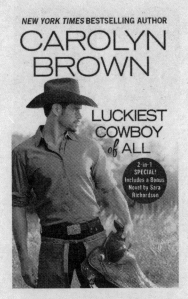

NEW YORK TIMES BESTSELLING AUTHOR
CAROLYN BROWN

LUCKIEST COWBOY *of* ALL

2-in-1 SPECIAL! Includes a Bonus Novel by Sara Richardson

LUCKIEST COWBOY OF ALL
By Carolyn Brown

This special 2-in-1 edition features an all-new book from *USA Today* bestseller Carolyn Brown plus *Hometown Cowboy* by Sara Richardson! Carlene Varner's homecoming isn't going to plan. Within days of her arrival, her house burns down and she and her daughter have no choice but to move in with Jace Dawson, the father Tilly has never known. Jace is so not ready to be a dad...Yet the more time he spends with Carlene and little Tilly, the harder it is to imagine life without them...

Fall in Love with Forever Romance

MORE TO LOVE
By Alison Bliss

Max Hager isn't exactly who he says he is. Pretending to be a health inspector is (mostly) an innocent mistake. A mistake made way worse by Max's immediate, electrifying attraction to a sexy, redheaded chef. Throw in a whole lot of lust, and things in Jessa's little kitchen are about to really start heating up. But can Max find a way to come clean with Jessa before his little deception turns into a big, beautiful recipe for disaster?

Fall in Love with Forever Romance

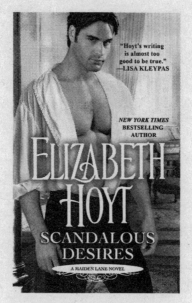

"Hoyt's writing is almost too good to be true."
—LISA KLEYPAS

NEW YORK TIMES BESTSELLING AUTHOR

ELIZABETH HOYT

SCANDALOUS DESIRES

A MAIDEN LANE NOVEL

SCANDALOUS DESIRES
By Elizabeth Hoyt

Rediscover the Maiden Lane Series by *New York Times* bestselling author Elizabeth Hoyt in this beautiful reissue with an all-new cover! River pirate "Charming" Mickey O'Connor gets anything he wants—with one exception. Silence Hollingbrook has finally found peace when Mickey comes storming back into her life with an offer she can't refuse. But when Mickey's past comes back to torment him, the two must face mounting danger, and both will have to surrender to something even more terrifying...true love.